Desiree Adler does not want a girlfriend. Why would she? She has a demanding career as a photographer and content creator, an eccentric but supportive family, and a huge responsibility as a foster parent to a teenager named Hope.

Desi's life is just fine the way it is. Why risk another heartbreak?

However, Desi's sister is annoyingly persistent and when she arranges a blind date for Desi, it's less trouble to agree, get it over with, and return to normal life. The blind date is every bit as terrible as predicted. So why can't Desi stop thinking about Soledad Reyes?

If Desi has any hope of finding balance in life, she must help Hope confront the ghosts of her past, while confronting her own assumptions about race, power, and identity in the present.

NURTURING
HOPE

KARA RIPLEY

A NineStar Press Publication

www.ninestarpress.com

Nurturing Hope

First Edition, August 2022

ISBN: 978-1-64890-533-9

Also available in eBook, ISBN: 978-1-64890-532-2

CONTENT WARNING:
This book contains sexually explicit content, which may only be suitable for mature readers. Depictions of drug/alcohol use/addiction, guns, incarceration, past trauma, racism, racial violence, torture (mention of), war

For Steph, who made me believe in the kind of love found in books.

Author's Note

I spent more than two and a half years researching, writing, and editing this book and so, dear reader, please know that it was close to completion before the bush fires once again ravaged my Australian home. Before COVID-19. Before George Floyd. Before Australia had its own Black Lives Matter protests. How quickly the world changes. And how much the world, sadly, stays the same.

Though this is a novel, a work of fiction, the story takes place in a world with a very real context. As such there are some things you need to know about me, the writer of this novel.

I am, like my character, a foster carer.

I do, like my character, have endometriosis.

However,

I am white.

I am middle-class.

I am not an American.

I have never been personally hurt by the truly insidious horrors of racism.

I have been complicit in upholding white supremacist systems.

I want to do better.

I know I will make mistakes.

Writing this book has sent me deeper into myself, my white privilege, my white exceptionalism, and my white silence than I ever could have predicted. When I started, I knew that diverse characters were integral to interrupting white centrism in popular culture. I knew that I wanted to do the best I could by my readers, but also by the communities and people who have inspired both my reflective journey, and the writing of this story. But I had no idea how much I didn't know. That I could never know. I didn't realize how many mistakes I had made and how far I had to go, and will always have to go.

Some of my early readers, including those who work in publishing, suggested that I re-write half of this book from the point of view of Soledad. They told me that she, a Latinx police officer, was such a fantastic character with such an amazing life experience that readers would be frustrated not to hear from her more directly. While I was ecstatic to hear such positive feedback about a character that I had tried so hard to build into an authentic and rich personality, I am sorry to tell those readers that I chose not to do this.

Soledad Reyes, a woman of colour, a member of a police force deeply entrenched in systemic racism, who is also a lesbian, is the daughter of trauma survivors. She is a force for change and a complex woman of such strength that I could only hope to one day be even ten per cent as resilient as she and her family would have had to have been. As my friend, Claudia, who shares a few of these experiences and who helped me so much with this book, has been.

Though sensitivity readers have told me that it is not unacceptable for white writers to work from the point of view of a person of colour, as long as they have thoroughly and suitably researched real-world experiences for that group and sought the assistance of professional sensitivity readers, it didn't feel right. There are mixed opinions and experiences in this area and, in danger of being a coward, I took the 'safer road'. And so, this story remains firmly set in the voice of Desiree, who, like me, will never stop learning how to disrupt the white supremacy she has benefited from her entire life. Instead, I will seek out and read more fiction and art created by people of colour rather than trying to write it through eyes I can never understand. I hope you will do so, as well.

You may be wondering why a fictional novel, a book that is ultimately a lesbian romance, includes a bibliography. It is important to thank and acknowledge the writers, producers, journalists, historians, and commentators who have contributed to the growth of this book, and my own internal reflections. Many of these people have been subjected to unacceptable racism, both overt and aggressive, as well as the more sinister modernized forms of racism, such as microaggressions and institutionalized white privilege. The fact they have risked so much to share, to teach, is not only admirable, it has been dangerous for them, and as a benefactor of their work, it must be acknowledged.

Lastly, I want you all to know that I intend to take responsibility for any mistakes I have made in this story and in my life. Though I have tried hard to research, to learn, and to refine this book as a result of what I have learned, I know that interrupting racism and becoming a genuine ally is lifelong work. Diverse characters are important. Breaking white silence and white centrism is important. It must be done, and it is up to every person who benefits from racist systems to do so. But I own my mistakes. Please, though I do not expect the emotional labour of people of colour to correct what I have misunderstood or misrepresented, I appreciate and accept any criticism that may come my way. Those mistakes are my own. Lay them at my feet if you will. I want to do better. I need to do better. I will work to do better.

CHAPTER ONE

CALIFORNIA
2019

THERE ARE A lot of things I love about living in Sacramento. For a start, there's enough distance from Silicon Valley that I can actually afford rent. Having grown up in one of the less-appealing suburbs of San Francisco, being able to get a place with a bathroom built for actual human beings and a little yard space is a nice change from the sardine box I'd shared with my parents and sisters.

Then there's the aesthetics of the city. Driving beyond the stoic government buildings and office spaces, citrus trees line the streets like scented sigils and neat, paved driveways stretch up to meet welcoming houses. The whole place has a real sense of home about it, the kind of comfort and connection that can only come from a well-organized city with a steady rhythm of activity.

I've got routines, things I do to provide structure to my life. Early on Sundays, before I dig into my work for the day, I take my teenage foster daughter to the Farmer's Market and we wander through stalls that sell the best fresh food California has to offer. Strawberries. Beets. Eggs. All of it delectable. Hope says she hates our weekend excursions, but I think I'm gradually wearing her down, convincing her that maybe she isn't allergic to peaches, tomatoes, and fresh air after all.

Given the nature of my work, with most of my time spent in an office chair staring at a computer screen, getting outside, whether to the market, to the gym, or, like today, to an off-site job, was normally a real joy.

I grimaced as I scanned yet another useless street sign. I normally love driving around Sacramento. But I *don't* love being lost when I'm meant to be at a job site taking photographs.

"Where the heck is this damned street?" I yelled at my steering wheel, which obstinately refused to help. Surely cars should be advanced enough to get me where I need to go. I mean, it's the twenty-first century and that's a basic part of the job description for a vehicle: taking me from one place to another.

"Turn left here." The assertive New Yorker who voiced my GPS had never annoyed me more.

"There is no left!" I waved toward the sidewalk to prove my point. I was already fifteen minutes late and the car's navigation system wasn't doing me any favors by insisting I drive straight into some poor family's front lawn.

I'm not always this irritable, honest. Most of the time, I'm fairly calm. But today was not my day.

"Does this place even exist?" I drummed my fingers against the gear shift. "This is *your* fault. Why can't you find Morts Road? What am I even paying you for?" I shook my head. "Meet Desiree Adler folks, the woman who drives around yelling at nobody."

The fact I was arguing with a piece of software didn't deter me from swearing at her repeated instruction. It felt like whatever could go wrong that morning, had gone wrong.

My water heater, after weeks of whining and moaning every time someone took a shower, made a valiant last stand before finally dying in a cacophony of hoots and whistles. Of course, this happened before I needed to rinse the conditioner from my hair.

Let's not even talk about what our ten-month-old Labrador did to my new jeans while I finished off my ice-cold shower. I'd planned to wear those jeans to the blind date my sister Clara had lined up for that night. It took about sixty minutes of throwing clothes about my bedroom to finally decide on a suitable replacement outfit, and even then, I settled for something that looked kind of ordinary because I was sick of trying things on.

Ginger Snaps—I let my boss's son name the dog—may be freaking adorable, but she's also a menace.

So, given the first two hours of my day had already been pretty crappy, when the police lights flashed red and blue in my rear-view mirror, you can imagine the whole new level of obscenities that escaped my mouth. But, if you can't, it was something like this: "For fucking fuck's sake. Just fuck right off, fucking fucker." The Monty Python team would have been proud.

Shaking my head, I flicked on my turn signal and pulled over. I sighed as I tapped at the steering wheel. I wasn't sure what I had done but between arguing with the GPS and rolling my eyes at non-existent roads, I certainly hadn't noticed myself speeding or going through a red light. Maybe the cop needed to meet some quota for random breath tests. I just hoped he was quick about it. My boss was not exactly going to get happier the later I was.

I glanced in my rear-view mirror and nearly spat out the gum I'd been chewing. The cop wasn't a he. It was a she, and I started to wonder if she'd gotten lost on the way to the audition for a blockbuster film.

There's no way a police officer, on an average day at work, should be allowed to be that attractive. As she sauntered toward me, I watched her move in line with my side-view mirror. The officer had a dark beige complexion and long, black hair pulled into a tight and high ponytail. Intelligent brown eyes rested between slightly arched eyebrows and an aquiline nose that complimented the delicious seriousness of her face. It wasn't normal for a real-life human being to be so beautiful.

I couldn't be sure if I hated her for being stunning, or if I wanted her to show me how her handcuffs worked. A confusing thought, given the way my palms always turned clammy whenever cops were around.

Knock knock.

I started. I hadn't realized she was directly next to my car now; I'd been too busy salivating like a teenager and momentarily switched off from reality.

I grinned awkwardly as I held the button to lower the window. As the tinted divider between us retracted, I cleared my throat. "Is there an officer, problem?"

She looked at me quizzically. "Excuse me?" Her voice was rich and velvety, like someone who narrated nature documentaries. Look out, Richard Attenborough. Or was it David Attenborough? I always mixed up the *Jurassic Park* guy with the nature guy. When I failed to respond, she asked for my license and registration and, fumbling with the glove compartment, I retrieved the documents.

Focus, Desi. You're about to be fined or arrested or something. Don't act like you're unstable.

I held my hand to my chest and coughed, though I had no real need to, then tried again after she'd checked my license. "What have I done wrong?" The question sounded more abrasive than I'd meant it to, and the narrowing of the police officer's eyes was a clear sign she hadn't appreciated my tone. Still, it was the best I could manage. A police stop from years ago, albeit very different to this one, had left me forever unsure about where a simple interaction with a cop might lead.

The officer pulled a set of aviator sunglasses from her shirt pocket and slid them on as though preparing herself. Then, she retrieved a hand-held device from a pouch on her belt and started tapping, looking at the screen as she spoke again. "You were traveling thirty miles per hour in a twenty-five zone and changed lanes without signaling."

The steering wheel squeaked a little, drawing the woman's eyes to my white-knuckled fingers.

"Are you sure?" I asked through gritted teeth. A couple

stared as they strolled hand-in-hand along the sidewalk, obviously slowing down to try to work out why I'd attracted the
attention of a cop.

It truly was turning out to be an increasingly shitty day.

The officer used the tip of her index finger to drag her
sunglasses down her nose, like something out of a Michael
Jackson music video. She considered me over the top rim as
she spoke in a highly professional tone. "Are you suggesting
I've invented a traffic infringement, ma'am?"

Ouch. The way she'd said *ma'am* was not what I'd had
in mind when I'd considered the handcuffs earlier. I wanted
to get away. It had been a long time since I'd had any interactions with a police officer, and though this was unlikely to
end as badly as the last incident had, my nerve-endings tingled with suppressed concern.

I dropped my head as I let out an exasperated sigh. "No,
Officer. I would never suggest such a thing. Can you please
issue my ticket so I can get to work?"

She planted a hand against the window frame and
leaned forward, enough that I could see most of my face in
her sunglasses. I realized then my hair was disheveled and
I'd left the house without a scrap of make-up on. I looked
like I'd gotten into the car immediately after falling out of
bed, without so much as a glance at a reflective surface.

"I can imagine your job must be important." The playful
curl of her mouth made it clear she was mocking me a little,
though she somehow managed to do it whilst maintaining a
degree of stoicism.

The officer's perfume reminded me of cherries, but that
didn't diminish the heat of frustration creeping up my neck.
I needed to get moving; real estate photos didn't take

themselves and the owners wouldn't be happy about being asked to stay away for even longer. My stomach fluttered as I eyed the clock in my dashboard.

"I'm sorry." I dropped my gaze to my lap and tried to check my attitude, the one that had been simmering all morning and wasn't this woman's fault. "I know I'm not exactly saving lives or anything. I know that, but I would appreciate being able to make my appointment. I fully accept that I've done the wrong thing."

The police officer stood straight, her muscled arm falling to her side. "Name, please?"

Hadn't she noted that from my license? Was her memory worse than mine? "Desiree Adler."

An inexplicable sort of recognition flashed in her eyes, but it disappeared so quickly that I questioned if she'd reacted at all. Without speaking again, the police officer walked to the rear of my car and took note of the plate number, though I could have sworn she'd already done that before even leaving her own car. I know my understanding of police procedures is based more on trashy television than reality, but something seemed off.

When she returned, the clock in front of me ticked over again.

"Can I go?" I regretted the acerbic question as soon as I'd said it, having failed my self-imposed test of restraint. I promise I'm not always this much of a grump, but I hated being late, and police officers aren't exactly my favorite people after what happened to Jason.

She sighed, her thumb hooking around her belt. Her fingernails were short, but well-groomed, unlike my horrible chewed-on stubs.

I tried to silently retract my curt question, but I suspect the actual expression looked more like a grimace. On top of my anxiety about being over half an hour late for work, I was also suddenly worrying that the boots I'd picked out for that night's blind date made me look like a wannabe Spice Girl. A fine time to indulge in such inane thoughts.

"Again, I apologize," I said. "It's been one of those mornings."

She pushed her sunglasses to the top of her nose and, without a word, slipped her tablet into its pouch. I couldn't blame her for ignoring the apology. Even I wasn't all that convinced, though I *was* sorry. This woman was doing her job, preventing accidents by enforcing the law, but even though the logical part of my brain knew that, the childish part of my brain that hated to lose an argument wanted to keep baiting her, to have the final word.

I realized I was still chewing gum, which probably added to my whole aura of contempt. I needed to get rid of it so I didn't look like quite as big an asshole. Trying to be subtle, I held my hand over my mouth and yawned softly, palming the gum so she didn't see me spit it out and take that as some sort of insult.

If I'd been using my brain at that point, I would have swallowed the gum, but it turned out my ability to think had gone down the drain with the last of my hot water.

"I won't take up any more of your time," she said.

Oh, shit. Had I genuinely struck a nerve or upset her? I had just yawned, after all. "No, wait, I didn't —"

She held up a hand. "It's fine, ma'am." She offered a slip of paper, probably my fine or some sort of incident number, but I didn't look, only shoved it into the center console.

"Drive safely and stick to the speed limit."

With that, she returned to her car. I watched her slide into her seat and remove her sunglasses. She massaged her temples for a moment before putting them back on. Was that the hint of a grin on her face?

I shook my head, trying to dispel the whole awkward experience, as well as the fact I'd cost myself a couple hundred dollars and my spotless driving record. I forced myself to stop staring at her in the mirror and looked out through the windshield. I couldn't help but laugh when I saw that, about fifty feet ahead, was the entrance to Morts Road.

CHAPTER TWO

JUDGING BY THE narrowing of her eyes and the hand at her hip, Gina's morning had been about as relaxing as mine.

Gina Montgomery was something of a whirlwind. At thirty-eight years old, she'd already established her own successful business. Hers was a small agency with only three employees and a couple of contractors like myself, but after four years, it was holding its own despite stiff competition from larger real estate corporations.

At six feet tall, with dark skin, intelligent eyes, and a sharp sense of humor, Gina was a formidable woman. Most of the time, I thoroughly enjoyed spending time with her. That said, when Gina was pissed off, I'd be the first to run for an exit. A leaking thermos in my handbag. A stubbed toe. A chipped tooth. Any excuse would do when she'd reached the end of her tether. There was no point trying to be an immovable object in front of an unstoppable force, after all. You couldn't help but admire someone with that kind of tenacity.

"Nice of you to turn up." Gina's foot tapped against the porch of the sprawling ranch house, and I wondered if there might be a way to smooth things over or if I needed to simply accept the lecture that would ensue.

"I know! I'm sorry. Really. Let me get my stuff and I can explain." I rummaged in the backseat of my car, racing to retrieve the equipment I'd need to highlight the best features of the house. My palms were a little sweaty and my fingers shook as I sorted through the camera, lenses, and flashes. The skin of my face and neck ran hot and the seconds dragged. Now I'd finally gotten to where I needed to be, the morning's general chaos had caught up with me, and I was on edge.

"Desi, are you okay?" I hadn't heard Gina come up behind me, and I knocked my head against the ceiling of the car. My skull throbbed instantly.

"Oh crap, sorry! I didn't mean to scare you. You looked so damned stressed, honey." The tone of Gina's voice softened, and she stepped away to give me room to back out of the car's doorway. She'd called me "honey"—a good sign that maybe I'd stay out of the line of fire for today.

"It's not your fault." I turned to face her and she dragged me in for a hug. I had to brace my legs to avoid falling over, but once I'd regained my balance, I returned the hug and savored the warmth. "Geez, Gina, are *you* okay? This is way too much physical affection. I'm concerned."

She let go and tugged at her dress to smooth it out. "Yep.

I'm fine." Gina used her thumb to dismiss a curl that had fallen across her eye. "I shouldn't have been harsh. I know you wouldn't be late without good reason. Were you having endo pain? Is everything all right with Hope?"

I slung my camera bag over my shoulder, patting it to reassure myself the DSLR was still inside. Real estate photography requires a considerable investment, and now that I had found the right camera for both interior and exterior shots, I'd become precious about always knowing where it was.

"Oh sure, Hope is okay," I said, working hard to lighten the tone of my voice. "She's been moody lately, but she's sixteen in a few months, so no surprises there. I think she's having some drama at school."

Gina shook her head sympathetically and my pulse slowed at last. I'd overestimated how mad she was going to be. I'd been projecting, since it was me who'd been generally impatient with the universe lately.

"I still have no idea how you manage to look after other people's kids. And you're only thirty-three, for Christ's sake. So damn young to be looking after teenagers. I can barely stand my own kid half the time, and he's not even school age." She smirked, knowing full well her four-year-old son was nothing short of an angel.

Seriously, I sometimes wondered if that boy was even human. I once caught Daxton saying "shit" when he dropped a handful of coins he'd been counting. The poor kid burst into tears because he was so upset he'd said a bad word. I only made it worse when I laughed. I couldn't help it! There's something adorable about someone that age swearing, and it was even more adorable he'd admonished himself. Daxton is a cutie-pie; that's for sure.

It's probably a good thing I won't be having any biolog-ical children, even though the choice was taken out of my hands. I don't think anyone under ten would be able to deal with me. Best stick to caring for adolescents.

"Hmm." I cocked my head as I thought about my foster daughter, who was not quite as reserved as Dax. "Someone's gotta do these things." I exhaled loudly, thoughts of the other teens I'd looked after floating through my head. I shook them off, not having time to linger on my past mis-takes in the middle of a working day. "Is the client able to give me time here?" I indicated the house with my chin.

Gina waggled the keys at me. I couldn't help but stare at her perfectly manicured gel fingernails, painted a luscious pink, so much longer and more colorful than the police of-ficer's. *What a weird thing to think about when you're about to start a shoot–that cop's quietly graceful hands.* "I called them just before you got here. They're happy to stay out for a while."

"Okay." I exhaled, settling into work mode. "At least something has gone right today."

"Sounds like you have a story to tell." She held out her arm, offering to help me carry in the equipment. "Give me the Cliffs Notes?"

I passed her my other bag. "First off, I should avoid any more entanglements with local law enforcement. I also need a new water heater, and there's the fact I have no idea what to wear to my first date in over a year because the dog ate my favorite pair of jeans."

She quirked an eyebrow. "Good story. I know interac-tions with your police aren't exactly your favorite thing in the world." Gina's mouth curled. "So, it sounds like taking a few pictures should be a breeze, even with the weirdly narrow living room."

I laughed and, as I did, my whole body suddenly seemed lighter, as if a pressure valve had been triggered. I could always rely on Gina to make light of a situation—well, as long as it wasn't a work-related situation. As abrupt and short-tempered as she could be, Gina was still one of the most vivacious and considerate people I'd ever met. If it hadn't been for her, who knows how I would be making a living?

Some days my pain levels made it difficult to function. With a job like this one, I could do a large part of the work from home and make a living despite the gremlins that seemed to live in my lower back and pelvis. Gina had given me a chance in a field I'd previously had no professional experience in, and I'd be forever grateful.

It took about two hours to photograph the house, but the real magic would happen on my computer.

I checked the time as I began to pack away my gear. *Shit!* I needed to get my ass across town fast if I was going to pick up Hope. Most days, she'd happily take the bus home, but she'd begged me to give her a ride today. She had a date of her own, and it would save her thirty minutes if she didn't have to catch the bus. We'd no doubt be fighting each other for shower time and asking about our outfits over and over, so it was worth the frantic rush across town to add a few more minutes to our preparation time.

As I slid into the driver's seat, I urged myself to calm down, to drive carefully. If I was a couple of minutes late to collect Hope, she'd forgive me. The last thing I needed was another ticket.

HOPE WAS LESS than impressed when I told her I'd forgotten to call a plumber about the water heater, but she had no choice but to deal with it.

"Come on, your hair looks great," I told her. She frowned, one hand hanging by her side, the other resting on her hip. "I mean it. This date of yours is going to go wild when they see you."

Hope crossed her arms over her chest. "This"—she indicated her hair with a dramatic gesture—"looks like crap. Cold water destroyed it. There isn't enough gel in the world to fix this mess."

About three weeks ago, Hope had taken a pair of clippers to her long red hair, leaving behind uneven patches that we did our best to repair—her own personal *moment*. It had come on the back of an especially challenging supervised visit with her mother.

I think she'd expected me to yell at her, to punish her in some way. I'd passed over all the products I'd used back when my hair was a purposely messy collection of light-brown spikes and taken her to a hairdresser to even it all out.

"The gel might be the problem. I think you put too much product in it. Why don't you try wiping some out with a damp towel? I'm sure it'll stand up straighter if you do."

She sighed in that way only teenagers can, her eyes rolling as though drawn by magnets. Without another word, she slipped back into the bathroom and resumed applying makeup, so I headed to my room to do the same. Though, why I was putting in so much effort for someone I'd never even met was baffling. Sure, you only get one chance at a first impression, but I had no delusions about this woman. I was sure she was lovely, or Clara wouldn't have made such a fuss about setting us up, yet doubts festered within me, as they always did. After a decade of on-again-off-again episodes of dating, I'd learned not to get my hopes up.

"It's a guy by the way," Hope called out.

"Huh? Sorry?" My voice traveled across the hall to the vanity.

"My date. I caught that gender-neutral pronoun." Her words echoed off the bathroom tiles.

"Oh, right. Well, male, female, trans, enby, pan, bi, demi, ace, aro...whatever makes you happy and hopeful."

"Argh. Good thing there's no one else here. You're embarrassing."

I could practically hear her grin. She always protested when I gave her the *whatever makes you happy and hopeful* line. I was certain she secretly loved it though. I've always believed that it's the little things that hold people together and define relationships. A teasing line. A shared irony. A common memory. It was important as a foster carer to build as many of those things as possible.

Music blared from inside the bathroom, a not-so-subtle hint our bantering was over for now and she wanted to concentrate. I couldn't tell you the name of the band, the song, or even identify a genre to be honest. Nothing makes me feel old like having no freaking idea what my kid is listening to.

Hope has been in my care for over a year and a half now, and it's finally starting to feel like she isn't walking on eggshells all the time. It must be so damned hard to constantly feel like a visitor in the place that's meant to be your home, as though you're a stranger with your proxy family.

When she had first arrived at the age of almost fourteen, she'd already had to change placements nine times since she was eight.

Fast forward to the present, and Hope doesn't ask me if she's allowed to have a glass of juice, if it's okay to use the telephone, or get awkward whenever she needs tampons. They may sound like small victories, but after being a foster carer for eight years, I'm convinced those things are important.

I twirled in front of the mirror on my bedroom door. The crimson dress I wore managed to make my breasts look even smaller, despite the push-up bra. The jeans Ginger Snaps had eaten would have looked so much better. They went so damned well with my black blouse.

I examined myself again and sighed. The flare dress didn't sit quite right. Rose had once told me she loved this outfit on me. I wasn't sure if that had been the reason I'd kept it for the last few years, or the reason that this was the first time I'd put it on since she left. More than two years on and I still wasn't entirely clear on all of the reasons Rose had broken up with me. Two years and I could still catch myself questioning how much that wound had truly healed. *Stop that. It's just a dress.*

I slipped my hand down the front of my body and readjusted my breasts, trying to find the best position to leave them, then stood to full height and took stock one last time. At least my hair didn't look too bad.

"Hey, Hope?" I called out. When she didn't reply, I made my way to the bathroom and knocked until the volume of the music lowered. It didn't take as long as I'd expected given how loud she'd had it.

Looking annoyed at first, her features softened as soon as she'd opened the door all the way and taken me in.

"Wow," she said.

I pressed my hands to my belly. "Do you think this looks all right?"

She looked me up and down again, then stroked her chin as though she were sizing up a used car. I gave her a *stop-picking-on-me* glare. "More than all right, Desi. This woman isn't going to keep her hands off you."

I blushed and gently smacked her arm. "Hey! Don't make it awkward. As long as I'm presentable."

Hope cleared her throat like she'd walked in on two people making out. "You look presentable. Your hair's nice."

Without thinking, I teased the tips of my short, choppy hair with my fingers. "That's a first."

She rolled her eyes gently. "You know you look hot with the shorter haircut. It's a shame you never go anywhere to let people see it." I fixed her with a withering glare, but it seemed to have no effect. "It's true! This is the first time you've gone out with anyone since I moved in. Even old people need to date, don't they?"

I blinked at her, slowly. "There's more to life than dating, you know."

"Such as?"

"Family. Art. Social harmony. Fighting for a cause like Black Lives Matter or the Me Too movement. Plenty of things."

She nodded, agreeing but also dismissive. "Okay, okay. You have a point. But I think you're allowed to have a family, make art, and care about equality at the same time as experiencing sweet lady kisses. Now go have your date-that-apparently-won't-go-anywhere. Have fun, k-thanks-bye." She'd closed the door before I could properly respond, and I shook my head and smiled. Though her mood had darkened a little in recent days, there were still plenty of nice moments that reminded me how well we got along. That said, she had definitely been spending too much time with Clara, and I made a note to tell my sister to stop teaching her phrases like "sweet lady kisses."

I returned to my room to find some shoes that wouldn't leave me hobbling by the end of the night. Three pairs later, I settled on a set of strappy sandals. As I leaned over to fasten the clip, my lower back twitched. An indolent ache clinched the bottom of my spine. Closing my eyes, I bit into my lip and counted backward from twenty-five. By the time I had reached zero, the sensation had dissipated. With any luck, the endometriosis pain would let me have the night off.

I exhaled unevenly as I indulged in one last glance at the mirror. Why the heck had I let my sister talk me into this? Blind dates felt like an anachronism, not the kind of thing people *still* did. The sad thing was, despite myself, I was also beginning to look forward to it.

CHAPTER THREE

CLARA HAD BOOKED a table for my date and me at Lucca, a Mediterranean place downtown. My sister, being her usual insistent self, had not only organized the finer details, but wouldn't even tell me how she and this woman knew one each other.

Clara had returned from an Australian vacation all loved-up, having had a great time with this cowgirl she'd met on a cattle drive. My mother always joked that she had a matching set. There was me, the lesbian and the oldest of the three. Then Clara, who was two years younger and bi-sexual, with our considerably youngest sister, Brenna, as our heterosexual representative.

"Tell me the woman's name for frak's sake," I'd said to Clara over the phone the day before.

"Nope."

"Why are you such a pain? It's just a name."

"You're such a control freak, Desi. I'm not giving you any details that could somehow lead to you canceling yet another potential date. Let yourself experience a bit of mystery for once."

"Wow," I had replied. "That Aussie did a real number on you."

"Ha! I suppose so. On that note, I have a Skype date with Evie, so no more arguing. Turn up, give them my name at the door, and you might be led to the love of your life."

I'd huffed at that, hooking my thumb into my pants pocket. "You're incorrigible!"

"You know you love me."

"Maybe."

That was the usual way our calls ended, with truth masquerading as sarcasm. It's how we show affection.

I wanted to keep my options open, so I took an Uber to the restaurant. And by options, I'm talking about alcohol, in case that wasn't clear.

I'd never eaten at Lucca before, but I had to admit Clara had chosen well. The ambiance was great. A sophisticated, classy kind of restaurant, it was still comfortable, with soft lighting and walls of warm brick. The place was full of chatter, cheery voices rising and falling, glasses clinking, creating a real sociable symphony.

A portly woman with sleek black hair greeted me. "Good evening and welcome! Do you have a reservation tonight?"

Her perfectly white teeth were distracting, and I realized, after an awkward moment had passed, that I'd been staring. "Sorry. Yeah, I'm meeting someone. The table is listed under Clara Adler."

The host zigzagged between the tables, leading me to a spot near the crackling fire. Candles lined the top shelf above the fireplace, and a beautiful circular mirror clutched the wall. It surprised me that my sister, sometimes too intelligent and cynical for her own good, had chosen somewhere this picturesque.

I'd been so enamored by the interior of the restaurant that I hadn't noticed the person sitting at the table I'd been led to. When I finally looked at the woman smiling up at me, I blurted out, "Holy shit."

The police officer. It was her. *She* was my blind date. What the actual heck, universe?

"Desiree Adler." She said my name as though she were trying to taste it, swishing it around in her mouth like a previously untested wine.

I slumped down in the chair opposite, gaping at her like some sort of maniac. My mouth was open so wide it was a miracle I didn't catch flies.

"Can I get you anything to drink?" A waiter, a blond young man with rather long ears, held his hands behind his back, smiling at me expectantly.

"I...ahh...yes." I scrambled to look at the drinks list, but my eyes wouldn't focus. I could sense the officer's amused, lingering stare washing over me, and I couldn't think.

"Wine?" my date said.

"Huh? Sorry, I mean, pardon?" I looked up at her.

"How about I order a bottle of wine?" She smiled cordially, and a few fine lines appeared around the outer edges of her eyes. "White or red?"

"I...yes. Wine, I do like wine."

"Okay." The police officer elongated the word like elastic. She offered her hand, and I passed over the menu so she could choose for us. "Let's have some sangria and hope for the best, then." In contrast to the cool professionalism she'd manifested this morning, her voice was smooth and delicious, like warmed honey.

I, on the other hand, seemed to be speaking with all of the allure of a rusty gate.

"Thanks. Well, this is awkward," I said, my tone weary.

"Yes. I hadn't imagined the flustered woman I pulled over this morning could have transformed into this." She moved her hand up and down, indicating my entire body. "You look amazing, by the way."

My cheeks flushed.

"Not that you weren't adorable when you were being fined too," she added, as though she'd read my mind.

I tilted my head questioningly and, blushing, she redirected her attention elsewhere. Was she embarrassed? Did I *want* her to be embarrassed?

"Thanks" was all I managed to say. "You look good too."

Way to go, Desi. Such a stellar accolade.

Now I'd commented, though, I took her in properly for the first time. Her glossy hair, straight and dark, had been released, flowing down past her shoulders. She wore a fitted, sleeveless top with three open buttons at her neck, her firm biceps and smooth forearms visible, as well as a tasteful hint of cleavage. She wasn't what I'd consider butch, but she had a sporty look about her, a transparent toughness that made her an appealing mix of the feminine and the masculine.

I sighed inwardly though, because she was still the police officer that I'd had such an awkward interaction with earlier. She was still a police officer—full stop.

"You haven't asked my name." Her statement towed my focus back to her cognac brown eyes.

She was right. I'd been so busy examining her and re-playing our run-in this morning, I'd forgotten I didn't even know who she was.

"Sorry. I think I'm still surprised to see you here." More surprised than she seemed to be, at least. I rolled one shoulder, fighting against the knot forming in the muscle at the base of my neck. "What *is* your name?"

She held her arm out. "Soledad Reyes. Good to meet you, properly."

I shook her hand gently. Her fingers were lithe, palms slightly rough, though the reverse of her hand was soft. As we broke apart, the waiter reappeared with our sangria and poured out two glasses before setting the carafe between us. A mixture of red wine and fruit, the concoction looked deli-cious. I'd barely let the waiter walk away before I was taking my first, curative sip. I hadn't realized how dry my throat was until that moment.

"Good?" Soledad asked.

"Absolutely." I put my glass down and dropped my hands to my lap to smooth out my dress, which was ridicu-lous because she couldn't even see the fabric under the table.

She took a sip of her beverage, a pensive expression passing over her face. "Not bad," she said decidedly. "Not as nice as the borgoña my mother makes, though." I looked up as Soledad spoke. She had a raised eyebrow. "You don't have to stay, you know."

I love women who can raise one eyebrow. Clara and I have often lamented our inability to pull off the gesture ourselves—my sister shares my inappropriate attraction to single-brow-raisers, as we call them.

"I get it," she continued. "I pulled you over and gave you a ticket. It's not a fantastic first impression, though I admit I find it a little funny now that we're here. It doesn't mean you need to have dinner with me. I'm sure Clara won't mind if we call it a night."

At the mention of my sister, I huffed gently. "Clara. She's got a funny sense of humor; that's for sure."

"How so?" She lifted her glass.

I couldn't help but watch as her enticing lips gently enveloped the rim, inviting the liquid into her mouth. I was even confusing myself now. Was I attracted to this woman, or still associating her with my annoyance with the whole world from this morning?

I shook my head. "It's nothing."

My heart rate jumped. She was one of those people who smiled with her whole face, her cheeks lifting, her eyes stretching wide, and her chin rising. Absolutely beautiful.

"Come on, tell me," she urged. "What about this makes Clara funny? She couldn't have known about this morning when she set us up."

"True," I replied. "But I'm surprised she set me up with you at all."

Her face dropped. "Why? You don't like Chileans?"

I reached out, my hand finding hers on the table. "No, no! Nothing like that. I can't say I've known many people from Chile, but it's not that."

She grinned and dropped her chin.

I fell against my seat. She was messing with me. "You're teasing me."

"Maybe." She tapped her fingers against the side of the menu she'd been holding, gazing at me suggestively. "But there's really only one way to find out."

And there went that heart of mine again. Blood pumped furiously throughout my chest, a maddening drum that seemed to beat at Soledad's mercy. At this rate, I was going to burn more calories on a date with this woman than I had in spin class.

Like a switch, Soledad laid the menu down and adopted a more benign expression. "But in all seriousness, why wouldn't you expect Clara to set us up?"

"I guess... well...because you're a cop."

"Seriously? I thought you were just having a crappy morning, not that you genuinely have a problem with police officers." Her mouth pulled into a frown, and her hands searched for something to do before finally falling in her lap. She seemed disappointed, as though she'd had someone reject her because of her job in the past.

"No, of course I don't. It's...well, it's more because of my position on certain things."

"Such as?"

"Police brutality, mostly," I replied without hesitation or pause. I did not want to offend Soledad, but when it came to issues like this one, I had no filter.

"Black Lives Matter. Is that what you mean?"

As though he knew I needed a moment of respite, the waiter reappeared.

Soledad didn't take her eyes off me as I ordered us some appetizers. I could tell from her expression she wasn't going to let me change the subject.

"I hope you like zucchini chips and roasted asparagus,"

I chirped.

"I do," she replied. "Now tell me why something to do with my job means Clara wouldn't have thought to set us up. She's been telling me about you for months."

I reached for my glass and, realizing it was empty, redirected my hand toward the carafe. After filling my glass and taking the slowest sip of sangria I could force myself to take, I set the glass aside.

She was still looking at me, her eyes penetrating and uncompromising. No wonder she'd become an officer; no way could any criminal not crack under that kind of pressure. I certainly was. I could feel a sense of urgency to explain myself, my nerves tingling.

"There have been so many awful things happening in this country, in this state, involving police officers and victims from minority groups. The Black Lives Matter movement is important. And you're a cop. It all adds up to a compatibility problem, I think." I shuddered internally as I imagined a weapon nestled inside Soledad's handbag, or strapped to her ankle, or wherever it was off-duty officers might conceal a weapon. Or, more specifically, what it could be used for.

Soledad blinked a few times, like she was flicking her way through thoughts, deciding which to ignore and which to pursue. "I carry a gun. I practice shooting at least once a week to make sure I use it as effectively and safely as possible if I need to use it in the line of duty. But I've never killed anyone, if that's what you're thinking. And I sincerely believe I've never targeted someone for an arrest because of their skin color."

"But...you *could*," I replied. Thoughts rushed about my

head faster than I could properly process, and it became a struggle to filter my words before they were released into the world. "You have the power to kill someone and, let's face it, there have been a lot of times when police have pulled the trigger on people for all the wrong reasons. Even if you haven't, the fact you spend so much time...with people who've used them for..." I paused, searching for the right words. "It's not something I'm comfortable with."

"I suppose that makes us even, because I'm not very comfortable with assumptions about what I do with my service weapon, nor assumptions about the colleagues I associate with." I almost expected her to call me *ma'am* again, her tone was so icy. "I know that some cops out there have done awful things. Horrific things. But we aren't all the same. There are a lot of reasons I do this job. Besides, I'm not only a cop. I'm also a sister, a daughter, a friend, an indoor rock-climber, a mentor...and yeah, a cop, too."

I knew she was right of course; I was being unfair toward her, even if she had encouraged me to explain myself. I still couldn't shake my discomfort about the fact she was attached to a force that, for plenty of people, symbolized oppression just as much as—if not more so than—protection. I didn't understand why American police were so quick to draw their weapons. Plenty of defensive organizations in other parts of the world managed to serve and protect without wounding or killing so many people, so why couldn't ours? The combination of systemic racism and readily available weapons had brought about countless tragedies, and it was a system that, no matter how you sliced it, Soledad was part of.

"I can understand that," I said. "I *can't* understand how

so many police officers keep targeting, assaulting, or even killing people of color and getting away with it. You're part of a system that's...that's broken."

I could practically hear my grandmother's voice coming from my mouth. She'd always been extremely passionate about addressing racism head-on, ever since she first started to see the world for what it was during the civil rights movement. Silence and complacency, she'd told my sisters and me, especially from white people, was tantamount to supporting the system that left people of color perpetually oppressed. It was a message she'd learned from her African American friends, people she'd admired and been inspired by, and it was a message she'd shared with anyone she met. Anyone she could have those difficult conversations with.

"I don't understand it either," Soledad murmured, more to herself than to me. Her volume increased as she spoke again. "But I do appreciate your feelings here. Given the track record of this city's police department, I do understand."

"There's so much state-sanctioned violence and anti-Black racism in California though, don't you think? But most of those incidents happen with beat cops, don't they?" I replied, searching for a reprieve from the tension, a poor attempt to retreat from any personal offense I'd caused. I knew, deep down, I was clutching at straws. I wasn't explaining myself very well because I was trying too hard not to completely alienate her, feeling myself lost in a vortex of thoughts and reactions. "I mean, did you ever consider becoming a detective—don't they draw their weapons on people of color, on anyone, less often? That's what I've heard."

Just stop, idiot!

Politics is a dangerous topic for any first date, let alone one with a police officer. I puffed my cheeks, searching the ceiling for the words continuing to allude me. The silence stretched taut.

A few moments later, I returned my attention to Soledad. "I don't have a problem with you as a person. I mean, I don't know you. But I'd find it hard to date someone, to be genuinely connected and let myself care about someone, who is part of an institution with such a bad human rights record. Innocent people get hurt or lose someone they love because it's assumed that they're dangerous. People whose only 'crime' is being Black. People are lost to the authorities that are supposedly meant to protect them." My cheeks burned and the heat spread down my neck whilst I spoke.

I should have told her about Jason. Sweet, nerdy Jason, who had been unfairly targeted when we were kids, whose face I always imagined whenever I saw a person of color approached by a cop. But that was not a story I told to just anyone. It hurt too much. "I'm sorry, Soledad. I'm not sure what part of the system I'm most mad at, but it's not you; it's the system your job has come to represent. Trigger-happy police officers have been socially engineered by systemic structures to assume a Black kid in a hoodie is up to no good. Then legislators who water-down changes to bills like AB 392."

Soledad remained quiet as I tossed more thoughts about, trying to articulate my converging views.

"I don't know. I don't know how to explain everything I think and feel about these issues. I just know I wish there were less guns in general and that, when they *are* used, it's only ever as the absolute last resort and only ever by responsible cops."

The waiter cut the space between Soledad and me, setting two plates of delectable-looking food on the table and resting an empty plate in front of each of us. I nibbled at my top lip for a second as embarrassment washed over me in a torrid wave. I barely knew this woman, and here I was letting loose my inner frustrations at the state of a really controversial issue, one much closer to home for her than for me.

"Have you decided what you'd like for your entrees?" The waiter beamed.

I looked to Soledad. Her eyes seemed glassy and she didn't answer. After my uncontrolled tirade, I suspected she didn't want to commit to a long meal.

"I think we'll wait on that," I said. "Thank you."

He pulled his lips into a thin line. I think he was getting frustrated at our indecision. I couldn't blame him; the restaurant was busy, and I wasn't making it easy by expecting him to keep coming back.

"I'm guessing you've heard of Stephon Clark?" she asked, her tone as unreadable as her expression, her face a little grim.

I nodded once, my head heavy. "Yes." I didn't tell her my sisters and I had been at a protest outside of the Sacramento Police Department in the days after it had been announced that the people who had murdered him were not to be prosecuted. The reality of that case still made so angry. And so very, very sad.

"Those were Sacramento cops that killed him," Soledad said, stating a fact more than framing any kind of argument. I wondered if she knew the men responsible. If she'd worked with them. How would that have impacted upon her? Especially when they'd returned to work. "I do understand why you'd feel so strongly about police brutality, and why you'd connect that to anyone who is part of the police."

I straightened my spine. "You do?"

She gave a light shrug. "Their defense. That Clark was apparently standing in a shooting posture. It's not good enough. I believe that there are too many guns in this country, but they shouldn't be using that as a justification for something so extreme."

"Yeah," I said meekly. "I don't hate all guns, or all people who use them, or anything like that. But the culture they're intertwined with, a culture where a twenty-two-year-old kid jumping the fence into his own grandmother's yard is assumed to be holding a weapon rather than a cell phone. They shot him so many times."

"I know," she said, her voice weary and framed by sadness. She rubbed at the bridge of her nose, her eyes slowly closing. She had more about this to say than she was letting on; that much was clear. How had I fallen into one of the most intense conversations I'd had in a long time with such a new acquaintance? Was it a sign we were completely mismatched, or that we had an intrinsic sense we could be honest?

"I'm sorry. I didn't mean to offend you," I said, quieter now. "But you asked, and I didn't want to lie. I'm not good at explaining myself sometimes, but Clara knows what I'm like. I have worse verbal vomit than Cady Heron."

The quizzical look on Soledad's face coupled with a few moments of quiet, changed the mood, and I knew my inarticulate exposition was over, and I wanted it to be. Gina had told me once that she could become exhausted by talking to people about race, wanting one day of her life where she wasn't reminded how deeply the tentacles of racism go in society. I was tired from only this one discussion, and I had the privilege of only having such conversations every so often. I can't imagine what it must be like to live those realities every day, then wind up talking about those realities on a regular basis because you either have to or are expected to.

After a time, she tilted her head as though she'd realized something and had become confused. "Who's Cady Heron?" Soledad's question snapped me into the present.

"Cady Heron," I repeated. "You know, from *Mean Girls*?"

She shrugged, though her features were less strained than a few moments earlier.

Yep. If she couldn't quote Regina George and Janis Ian with me, this was not going to work. One of my favorite drinking games with my sisters was taking a shot every time someone said "gruel" or "fetch." It was always hilarious, but I suspected Officer Reyes wouldn't enjoy the pastime. She seemed somehow too serious, too thoughtful for that kind of thing. Not that I'd let the poor woman get much of a word in. Why was I acting like this? I didn't normally pounce on people I'd just met with some of my deepest-held worldviews.

"Look, I am truly sorry. I do respect what you do. I struggle sometimes, trying to understand all the things that go on out there, and why they happen."

"You and me both." She spoke dryly, her gaze firmly fixed on the still-untouched food as she once again became serious.

I didn't like the melancholic expression on her face, and the fact I'd upset her gnawed at me. "Listen, I'll pay for this and leave you in peace, okay?" I said, planting my palms against the table-top, preparing to stand. "It looks delicious, so you should stay and eat."

"You're leaving?" She met my eyes with hers, and I couldn't tell if she was disappointed or relieved. Perhaps, like me, it was both.

"I think I should. This isn't the worst date I'm sure either of us have been on. But I've been here fifteen minutes and managed to offend the hell out of you. I don't even make much sense to myself sometimes. Thanks, though, for giving it a try. And for sitting through my...well, whatever that was."

Soledad glanced at her watch. "Brings a whole new meaning to the notion of speed dating." Her soft tone suggested the joke was meant to be sad, rather than funny.

I gave her a half-smile. "Who knows, maybe if you stay for a few minutes, someone worth having a date with will turn up. I mean, gorgeous, fit, and funny to boot. How are you even single?"

She leaned back, holding her wine glass in front of her chest, opposite hand draped across the crook of her elbow. "*Now* you start flirting?"

"Sure." I dipped my head slightly. "There's no pressure now. I've already tanked the whole thing."

"I see your point. No pressure is a good thing."

"Enjoy your dinner, Soledad Reyes."

"Thank you, Desiree Adler."

We said our goodbyes and I left, paying for the food on the way out. As I tapped the Uber app on my phone, disappointment bloomed in my chest. Why did I have to bring up something as serious as Black Lives Matter with a cop? On a first date, no less. *Not one of your best ideas, Desi.*

Though, it was better to voice my views on such big issues sooner rather than later. That sort of fundamental, philosophical difference was bound to cause problems at some point. It would have been far worse if we'd started to like each other before finding out we disagreed, before she realized how uncomfortable her job made me.

Soledad may have been a quixotic representation of all my sporty-girl-in-uniform fantasies, but she was also living in a world I didn't understand or know how to respond to.

With any luck, Hope was having a better time with her date than I'd had with mine.

CHAPTER FOUR

THE HOUSE WAS eerily quiet when I arrived home. I flicked on the lights and made my way down the hall, only to stop as I passed a full-length mirror on the outside of the bathroom door.

The dress didn't look too bad in the end, but my face was haggard, eyes circled by darkness thanks to the hours of sleep I lost to chronic pain. I'd cropped my long, lifeless brown hair recently, going for a Ruby Rose kind of look, but I wasn't convinced I pulled it off. I supposed I was still getting used to it.

I shook my head. Overanalyzing my reflection wouldn't help anything. What a pointless exercise: to wonder if a woman I'd consciously walked away from found me attractive.

For a moment, I considered starting up the computer to toy with the outdoor photographs I'd taken of Ginger Snaps and Hope last week. Creative editing to quiet my mind could be the ticket. But tiredness won out, and I made my way to the bedroom and flopped onto the bed, my ankles and feet dangling off the edge. I kicked off my shoes and buried my face in the pillow.

Then, the pain started.

As if it knew I was about to let relaxation take me, that monster living inside my torso stirred. Spreading like spilled fluid, the dull, heavy ache moved across my lower back, and I drew my legs into my stomach, curling into the smallest ball I could manage. Turning over, I reached for the bottle of anti-inflammatory pills that lived on my nightstand and dry-swallowed two of them.

My doctor told me I needed to stop taking so many painkillers, but he had no freaking idea how hard it was to function without them.

At one stage, Dr. Lynetti had prescribed me a once-a-day medication for inflammation he said would cause less damage in the long term, but it didn't even make a dent in the tenacious pain that took over my body so often. He'd sent me for physio, X-rays, and ultrasounds, all the while suspecting something was wrong with my spine.

Eventually, I'd managed to convince him the pain was connected to the fact I'd had a period that hadn't let up for ten months, so he'd also prescribed a range of different contraceptive pills, none of which fixed the bleeding or the pain.

When I worked a more traditional job, I'd spent all my time worrying about if the doubling up of a tampon with a maxi pad would be enough to keep my clothes protected until I had a chance to get to a bathroom. Sometimes, it didn't, so I started taking a spare set of pants with me everywhere I went.

People don't like to talk about these things, but it got to be the only thing I could ever think about.

The doctor still seemed unsure about the whole thing, since women with polycystic ovaries or endometriosis usually have aches in the front of their pelvis, not in their back, but both problems had developed at the same time, and I *knew* they were related. A trip to the emergency room with debilitating pain and a hemorrhage so bad I depleted most of my iron finally had helped change the direction of the conversations with my doctor.

It hurt so damned much every time and I had become so damned sick of it. Sometimes I thought my insides were tearing themselves apart. I had burned my skin with heat patches, desperate for relief. Piping-hot baths had stopped helping long ago. Nothing helped. I had spent hours wandering up and down my house, unable to sit still or lie down because, if I stopped moving, I would sink into the pain even further; it would envelop me.

The good news, though, was that a specialist Dr. Lynetti had referred me to recently had implanted a Mirena inside my uterus. Though having the thing inserted had been about as pleasant as a pap smear performed with a serving fork, it had finally stopped the bleeding, which had—to an extent— helped me reclaim my life.

Now, though, crying into my own arms as I'd done so many times, I wanted to scream. I wanted to scream at the people who'd taught sex ed and left out the part about a huge number of women that don't have "normal" cycles, as well as the part about how it was next to impossible to properly diagnose problems like endo without surgery. Surgeries that general practitioners were nervous to recommend and insurance companies were unlikely to approve.

Even after navigating the hellish web of medical jargon and second opinions, I still had months of waiting ahead of me to have a laparoscopy. To find out what exactly was going on inside my body.

When I was done with the PE teachers and doctors, I would scream at all the movies and books and TV shows that treated women's bodies like some kind of well-functioning machine always at factory settings, making people like me feel *wrong*.

Where were the ten percent with PCOS on TV, huh? Or the other ten percent with endo? And then the other ten percent with unexplained and undiagnosed issues related to their reproductive system? Normal, my ass. Who's normal, anyway?

I laughed. There I was again, hugging my own knees and ranting at popular culture and high school teachers in my head. Rolling over, I grabbed a bottle of water from the nightstand and forced a slow sip. Using measured exhalations, I concentrated on calming down.

A high-pitched whimper trumpeted through the wall. Ginger Snaps. *Damn.* I'd forgotten to let her in when I had come home. *Poor thing.* At ten months old, she was still very much a puppy and didn't like to be on her own for long.

I winced as I stood, but at least I *could* stand. The pills were beginning to work. They weren't exactly a miracle cure, but at least they made it possible to walk along the corridor.

As I reached for the knob on my back door, a gentle

buzzing noise in the kitchen caught my attention: my cell phone ringing atop the bench. Checking the caller ID, I accepted the call. "Hope? How's the date going?"

"D...Desi..." She spoke through tears so thick they almost streamed through the phone.

"Hope. What is it? What's happening?"

She sniffled and my chest tightened. I'd cared for kids more walled-off than Hope, but she still had a tendency to hide her emotions, which made it all the more terrifying to hear her like this. "I need you—" A husky cough cut the sentence off. "Can you pick me up?"

"Of course." I rummaged through the basket on the bench, madly trying to find a pen that worked. *Why the hell do I own so many ink-less pens!* "Where are you?" I clicked the end of a Parker I'd been given for my birthday and let out a relieved sigh when squiggly lines appeared on the magnetic notepad on my fridge.

A few moments of silence passed, though Hope's breathing came down the line in clear, heavy bursts. "The police station."

CHAPTER FIVE

BY THE TIME my car slumped into a parking space outside of the police station, I was so wound up my nerves were vibrating, competing with the gentle humming of the electric car's engine. Revving like a supercharged turbo, my nerves were the stronger of the two.

It had taken months to build even a basic relationship with Hope, and we were in a good place now. She'd told me about one or two of her friends, she'd sent me a few memes that I'd pretended were funny though I didn't understand, and there was generally less awkward silence about the house. I didn't want to mess all that up by handling this situation badly.

At the same time, I was pissed. She'd been picked up by the police! Not even sixteen and she'd already been a police car.

Apparently, they'd rounded her up with a fairly large group and weren't going to formally charge her. Yet, the situation was bad enough they wanted a parent to pick her up so an officer could discuss what had happened.

How on Earth did she go from being on a date with a guy she liked to calling me from a police station?

As I clicked off the ignition, I huffed. This would be the third time today I'd interacted with a representative of the law. At this rate, I might develop a reputation for legal improprieties. Or, at the very least, social improprieties.

Third time's a charm, right?

As I walked toward the building, a familiar craving burned in my throat and my chest. I hadn't smoked a cigarette in over seven years, but there were moments when even the oldest of habits wanted to reassert themselves. They were normally moments when I needed a distraction from reality. I balled my right hand into a fist as though crushing the instinct to reach for a smoke, then shook away the tension.

The automatic doors at the front of the building seemed to think I didn't exist, and I had to perform a special interpretive dance to set off the sensor and gain admittance to the station. Given how badly I didn't want to be there, the indignity only added to my frustration.

As I stepped inside, I sensed someone's attention on me. I looked around and found an older man with thin, graying hair and a yellow-stained horseshoe mustache grinning at me, amused. "Having trouble with the door there, ma'am? It can be temperamental, sometimes." His Southern accent leaned on the *r* sounds more than others I'd heard, his speech calmer than the loud, energetic Californian notes I was used to.

I willed myself to be civil, though my mood was anything but. "Yep. Had to work some magic to get it open."

"And what charming magic it was." He clicked his tongue, folding his hands across the round belly spilling over the top of his trousers. "Can I help you with anything?"

I readjusted the strap of my shoulder bag and approached the desk. My back still ached, and I had to take soft, short steps to avoid turning the dull heat into a sharp stab.

Given the late hour, only a few hushed voices and the click-clack of one person's shoes echoed through the large, tiled space. "I received a call from my foster daughter. I'm here to pick her up."

He rolled his chair closer to the desk and positioned his fingers over a keyboard, having assumed a more professional expression and tone than he'd had a few moments ago. "What's the name?"

"Hope Murphy."

He typed the name so fast that if I'd blinked, I would have missed it.

He clicked his tongue again as he waited for the computer to do its thing. "And..." He swiveled in his chair, still staring at the screen. After a couple of seconds, he looked at me. "She's up one floor. Ask for Officer Washington."

"Thank you," I said.

"My pleasure. Good luck with whatever it is that brought you here."

"Thanks. I appreciate that."

The phone by the computer rang loudly and he gave me

a polite nod as he reached for the receiver, and I moved away.

The next floor must've been where all the action was because when I stepped out of the elevator my senses were accosted. The strong scent of coffee blended with musky body odor saturated the air. My head reeled from the clamorous symphony of heavy boots crossing the hard floor, phones ringing all about, and rambunctious conversations coming from all directions.

As someone who thoroughly appreciated my alone time, the whole scene was enough to make me miss my near-silent office space at home.

There were desks with hutches lined up in sets of two, resting back-to-back perhaps to create a false sense of privacy for the people working there. I couldn't identify an obvious administration desk or clerk, so I stood around awkwardly for a minute or so until one of the officers moving about the floor noticed me.

The woman looked me up and down as though trying to work out if I were going to cause trouble. "Who are you after?" she asked. The brunette was in her early forties, considerably taller than me, and had the build of a runner, fit and lithe.

I blinked a few times to snap out of my small moment of inappropriate ogling. "Umm." I gulped. "Officer Washington, please."

She nodded, then turned and moved away. A few moments later, a man with short coal-colored curls and deep-brown skin approached me. Wearing a wide, contagious grin that struck me as out of place in this environment, he extended a hand and I shook it.

"I'm here for Hope Murphy."

"I thought as much," he replied.

Officer Washington's high cheekbones and broad shoulders added to the aura of strength projected by his intelligent eyes. "She said you were her foster parent, and you don't seem old enough to be the mom of one of the other kids I picked up."

Kids. I sighed, ignoring his thinly veiled comment about my age, though he was spot-on. "How many of them were there?"

He half turned his body toward the bullpen, holding his arm out to direct me. "Let's sit down."

"Where's Hope?"

"She's with one of our youth liaison officers; they're having a chat. My partner usually handles those sorts of discussions, but I'm on my own tonight, so I asked Officer Huynh to spare a few minutes."

Was Hope alone with one of the officers? Without any witnesses or protection? The concern firing in my chest must have flashed across my face because Washington raised his hands in a gesture of appeasement. "She's okay. Officer Huynh is great. She'll be talking to Hope about ways she can respond to difficult situations with her peers and letting her know about a few youth-at-risk projects we run in the city if she ever needs help. And there's always another person present for any of those discussions. Let's sit down and we can talk some more."

I nodded, not entirely convinced Hope wasn't in a compromised position, but I had no choice but to follow Officer Washington.

He ushered me to one of the neatest desks in the

bullpen and offered a chair situated to the side of the desk. There's something uncomfortable about sitting on an office chair that isn't behind a desk or bench. I wanted to get out of there as fast as possible though, so I sat where he asked and waited quietly while he rifled through a manila folder.

"How much trouble is Hope in?" I asked when the waiting became unbearable.

Washington set the papers down and interlaced his fingers. He considered me with bright, sympathetic eyes, his eyebrows reaching for his hairline as he spoke. "Not a great deal," he replied. "But she could have been."

I relaxed into the chair as I exhaled. *Thank goodness.* "She didn't tell me anything specific on the phone. She was supposed to be on a date."

Officer Washington picked up a pen and rolled it between his fingers. "Afraid not. We found her up at a rave after we had a few noise complaints from the neighbors."

I rubbed my neck then dropped my hand to my lap. "Were there drugs?"

"Yes," he replied in an emotionless tone.

I shook my head, not at him, but at the situation. "Did she take any?"

"That's the good news," he said. "I don't think she did. Which is part of the reason we aren't charging her. She didn't show any signs of being under the influence. She may have simply been in the wrong place at the wrong time. But she was found in possession of more than five hundred dollars. Hope has admitted to holding the money for a friend of hers who was selling the drugs to the other young adults at the rave. He was apparently worried about being robbed if he held on to it all himself, and she wanted to...well, she says she wanted to be a good friend."

My jaw tightened the more I imagined her in that situation. I pictured Hope following some adolescent criminal around a thumping, writhing, hormonal party, protecting his money—and adopting all of the risk that came along with it.

Holding cash for a teenage drug dealer? *Freaking hell, Hope.* Being picked up by the police was the best outcome, given the possibilities. So many things could have gone wrong.

"She lied to me," I muttered. "They were meant to be going bowling and eating junk food, or seeing a movie or something. Not popping pills. Not selling drugs."

Officer Washington remained silent. He could probably tell I was thinking aloud rather than initiating a conversation about Hope's deception.

Nearby, a woman began sobbing, arresting my attention. She was middle-aged, with deep-set eyes and brown skin. The distress etched across her face reminded me of Jason's mother. Though it had been so long ago, I could still remember the exact moment I saw her heart ripped in two, when the reality of her baby boy's arrest came crashing down. I could only hope this woman's situation, whatever it may be, would turn out better.

Digging my nails into my palms, I urged myself to focus on the present. "Can you tell me what kind of drugs her friends were taking?"

Washington dropped his pen, his chair squeaking as he sank deeper into the wooden frame. "Technically, no. But I'm sure she could tell you herself."

I huffed. I'd be lucky if Hope told me *anything* about

what had gone on at that party. We could talk about clothes, music, even the occasional book when she brought one home from school, but when it came to anything serious or real, she'd established clear boundaries.

Maybe I'd gone too easy on her, failing to assert parental authority by not insisting she share more information about her life. But I'd pushed too hard with other kids in the past, and I didn't want to make the same mistakes with Hope. I couldn't watch another kid graduate from the foster system to the prison system.

Balance—it's so damned hard to find.

God. I'm overreacting. It was a party. Calm the heck down, Desi.

When I met Washington's eyes again, my frustration subsided. His professional demeanor and generally calm approach to the incident were soothing.

Hope was safe and that's what mattered the most. All sorts of things could have happened to her at some wild teenage blast, things I didn't want to think too deeply about—not unless I wanted to sob all over Officer Washington's well-kept desk.

"What happens now?" I asked, my voice quiet amid the sea of noise.

"You take her home. The rest is up to you. With any luck, I won't see either of you again." He gave me a half smile, the kind someone gives you when they're not sure if they're joking or predicting the future.

"Thanks. I appreciate your honesty."

"It's what we're here for. We don't want to see teenagers in trouble. If we can reason with them *before* something serious happens, of course that's what we'll do." He stood and

I did the same. The slight change in altitude increased the potency of the coffee stench, and my head reeled for a moment.

"I'll take you to the interview room where she's been waiting. She's a smart kid, but good luck. I think you're going to need it."

CHAPTER SIX

THE LAST TIME I had driven a teenager home from the police department, it had been my foster son, Brody. Rose had been in the passenger seat, steaming mad that he had disappeared for two days. I remembered reaching for her hand, but she'd pulled away, presenting me with her back. It was the moment I had realized I was losing her.

Like last time, the drive home with Hope was long, dark, and silent. If not for the occasional glimpse of oncoming headlights, it would have been easy to mistake the quiet road for a defunct airport runway.

I'd been determined to leave Hope in peace, but after exactly six minutes, I couldn't stand it anymore.

"Hope, I—"

"Don't. Please. Just don't."

I glanced at her briefly before turning my attention to the road. With her knees tucked into her chest, her chin down, and her gaze fixed doggedly out the passenger side window, everything about Hope's demeanor suggested something had gone wrong tonight. Perhaps something more than the police breaking up her friend's party.

I considered what I could say, how I could be the parent in this situation without upsetting her. Nothing came to me.

Heck, teenagers are hard.

When Hope untwisted her body and shifted her face toward the windshield, I took that as a wordless invitation to try engaging with her once more.

"Are...are you okay?"

She whipped her head around. Out of the corner of my eye, I could tell she was surprised. Whatever she'd expected me to say, that hadn't been it.

"Are you?" I probed, wanting her to know that, despite how angry I was she'd lied to me, her well-being would always be more important than anything else.

"Yes," she murmured, her head sinking against the headrest. "Thanks for coming to get me." She sounded tired, her voice scratchy and meek.

"Of course," I replied, my volume louder than I'd intended. "I'll always come. You make sure you always call, okay?" I looked at her just long enough to see her shrug. "I mean it. I don't care if you're in a crack house, a hospital, a police station, or a Taylor Swift concert." She acknowledged my terrible joke with a softening of her eyes. "I *care*, of course, what you get up to, but I need you to be safe, and I'll come to get you no matter what you're doing or where you are."

Hope agreed silently.

Flicking on my blinker, I changed lanes, preparing to turn onto the main street through my suburb. We were almost home, and I hadn't found out how Hope ended up at a drug-infused rave when she was meant to be on a date. I'd been hoping she might be forthcoming, that I wouldn't have to pry. That had never been the case with her in the past though. I was kidding myself for even thinking it.

I bit my lower lip. I knew what I was about to ask may send Hope even deeper into whatever pit she'd been tumbling into since I collected her from the station.

"Why *did* you lie to me, Hope? You weren't where you were supposed to be."

I'd expected a sigh. Or a groan. Perhaps even a shuffling of limbs as she turned toward the car door.

Nothing. Not even a passive-aggressive sigh. Complete and utter stillness from an almost-sixteen-year-old can't ever be a good thing.

"Can you at least tell me if you were safe? You didn't take anything, did you?"

"No!" she snapped. She shot upright, her spine ramrod straight, her seatbelt outstretched. "I'm not an idiot, okay? When they brought out the ecstasy, I stalled. I went to the bathroom. I tied my shoelaces. I even made out with some guy I didn't even like to buy time."

I tightened my grip on the steering-wheel at this last detail. I didn't want to be one of those parents who expected their teenager to never get intimate with anyone until they were twenty-five. Yet, the thought of a sleazy, potentially high person groping and kissing Hope made my stomach constrict. He better not have put his hands anywhere she didn't ask him to.

"When the cops arrived..." She gulped. "When they got there, I was relieved." She rubbed her forehead and closed her eyes. "I don't want to talk about this anymore, Desi. Can you please drop it?"

"You won't tell me how you ended up there? Who put you in that position?"

More silence.

I pulled into the driveway of our house, slipped the car into park, and switched off the ignition. The two of us sat in the car for a minute or two, neither of us saying anything, yet neither one making a move to get out. The engine ticked and crackled quietly as it cooled.

My back throbbed—time for more painkillers. I reached for the door handle but stopped short when she spoke.

"I'm sorry." Hope's words were almost drowned out by the tears suddenly streaming down her face. My chest ached at the sight of her reddened cheeks and the sound of stifled sobs, her hand covering her mouth.

I reached out, inviting her to me. She shook her head and wiped at her nose. "I'm fine," she said, the words out of step with her bereft tone. I couldn't help feeling rejected.

Hope clumsily opened the door and stumbled out of the car. She was at the front door, forcing her key into the lock before I'd even had a chance to set one foot on the ground.

I wanted to chase her. To grab hold of her and hug her until all the fight drained from her system and she let me be there for her, let me comfort her.

But I didn't. I couldn't. She didn't want me to.

I'd forced a connection with Brody, forced him to let me in, and it had backfired. In the end, he'd broken every rule he could in an attempt to find what would finally force me to reject him. To try to prove his own doubts and fears about himself and about me.

I'd moved too fast for him. I'd tried too hard and been too strict, and he'd gotten scared when he started to feel something he hadn't felt in a long time; when he started to connect.

Despite how desperately I wanted to run after Hope, I needed to let her come to me. She knew she'd screwed up. She didn't need me to tell her.

What she *did* need, however... I had no idea.

CHAPTER SEVEN

AFTER THREE HOURS staring at a screen editing photographs, brunch with my sisters was exactly what I needed to reset body and mind before I went out for another shoot.

Brenna, as the only one of us with inflexible working hours, chose a cafe near the city center's government services. At twenty-five, Brenna seemed settled into her job at the Department of Youth, Parks, and Community Enrichment. Though she wasn't especially settled into most other aspects of her life.

When I opened the car door, a blast of uncharacteristically hot air flushed against my face, and I grunted. Being more of an indoor-winter kind of girl, I didn't appreciate the warm front passing through town. I was sure my hair had to have flattened against my head under the weight of the heat.

Whoever said short hair was easy to care for had clearly never had ear-length choppy layers.

During the short walk from my car to the cafe, I took in the ordered jostling of the city. With about half a million people living here, Sacramento comes alive during certain times, yet falls into a peaceful, curative sleep at others.

Bordered to the west by the Sacramento River and home to countless government workers, I've watched this place become one of the most hipster cities in California over the last ten years. With the University of California around fifteen miles away and a breadth of cultural influences shaping the growth of the metropolitan area, there's always somewhere good to eat or something interesting to see.

The unmistakable floral aroma of tea lingered in the air, followed closely by the subtle scent of maple syrup and pancakes wafting from a range of cafes around the corner.

Surprisingly, Clara had beaten me there. She waited in solitude at a round outdoor table, a large coffee mug clasped between her palms. When she noticed my approach, she stood, inviting me to her with a one-armed hug, the other hand never leaving the mug. I sat opposite and dropped my handbag between my feet.

"Now I *know* there's something different about you lately," I cooed.

Clara quirked her eyebrows. Her long auburn-brown hair flew about her face and stuck to her lip gloss as a summery gust of wind shot through the area. "What are you talking about, Des?"

"You've never been on time for brunch in your entire life. Or been on time for anything, for that matter."

She scrunched up her face, then blinked slowly, once. Clara and I had always shared an interesting dynamic. Kindhearted and fiercely loyal, she's someone who would do anything for a person she cares about. At the same time, Clara has always struggled with meeting new people, even more than I do. She much prefers fictional humans over real ones, and she can be hard to get to know. Once someone manages to break through Clara's walls, the person waiting on the other side is exceptional, smart, humble, and creative. The only people Clara lets herself be silly with are her sisters. Teasing each other is our way of expressing affection, and I wouldn't want it any other way.

"That is absolutely not true," Clara retorted. "I was on time for your thirtieth birthday party at Mom's."

I huffed. "Bullshit! You were over an hour late! You missed all of the canapes and barely made the barbecue."

"I was sixty-two minutes late, and everyone knows that's right on time for a party."

"If you say so."

She grinned. "I do. I do say so."

"Coffee?" I directed a finger toward her cup. "How many have you had so far?"

She crinkled her forehead, pretending to be deep in thought. "Today? This would be number four."

"You're a serious addict, you know."

"A caffeine addict? Yes. That's fair. But don't act like you don't have at least two coffees a day."

"Yeah, two! At most. And only if I've had tea first. Not exactly in the same league as your back-to-back espresso marathons."

An androgynous server, barely out of school by the look

of them, approached us. "Mornin'! What unusual weather, am I right? Can I get you anything? A tea? Coffee? Sparkling water, perhaps?"

I cringed inwardly. It wasn't their fault, but I'd been awake since 5:00 a.m. and was in no mood for that kind of intense cheerfulness. I forced my inner tired grouch to settle down. As a general rule, I'm not as antisocial as Clara, but I also have no talent for small talk.

"There's one more on her way," I replied. "While we wait, could I get a green tea, please?"

"And can I get some garlic bread?" Clara added.

"Garlic bread?" I gaped at her. "It's 10:00 a.m."

"Hey, don't judge me, okay?"

Good old Clara. It had been two weeks since we'd met up in person, and I'd started to miss her. Phone calls and text messages weren't the same. They didn't accurately convey her unique combination of snark and adorableness.

"Never," I said defensively.

With a polite nod, the waiter retreated.

"Right," Clara asserted, interlocking her fingers and pushing them out, though her fingers failed to crack. "What the heck happened with Sole?"

I rolled my eyes and groaned. "Really? That's the first thing you want to talk about?"

"How did you strike out within ten minutes? Desi, that woman is beyond hot. I mean, it doesn't get any hotter than Soledad Reyes."

"Then *you* date her." I poked my tongue at Clara, and she swiped at the air in a dismissive gesture. "And it was fifteen minutes."

The waiter set down my green tea and Clara's garlic

bread, then left us alone again. I had to admit, the buttery Turkish bread slices not only looked amazing, but smelled incredible.

"I can see your food envy, Des. You might as well be drooling. Much like I'm sure every person on the planet who walks past Soledad does."

"Okay, okay. Yes. She's impressive. And not only because she's stunning."

"Which she is." Clara broke a piece of bread into two and took a bite from one end.

Yes. I sighed. *She really is.* I tilted my head, avoiding a response.

"What went wrong?" Clara pressed.

"I was my usual charming self."

"Oh Jesus. Please tell me you didn't bring up climate change or police brutality." She dropped the bread and crossed her arms over her chest. "You did!"

I held my hands up as though in surrender. "In my defense, I said nothing about climate change."

Clara rolled her eyes. "So you *did* mention Black Lives Matter?"

"Smooth, right? I figure it was better to sort that out early, rather than start something up with her and work out we weren't compatible later."

"Not every person you get involved with needs to be a potential wife, you know. Besides, who's to say you can't be compatible with a cop? I figured you'd get to know her before you went into those murky waters."

I sipped my green tea, then set the cup down, tapping my fingers haphazardly along the side.

Clara had a point. Perhaps I'd been too hasty in

assuming that, because Soledad is a police officer, and I'm...well, me, we couldn't get along.

I readjusted in my seat and lengthened my spine. It didn't help to think about the possibilities now. I'd already offended her at least three times; there was no way she'd agree to another date. Not that I wanted one.

"How do you know her, anyway?" I asked.

"She's Austin's cousin."

"Seriously? You set me up with your ex-boyfriend's cousin?"

"Hey, he may be a loser, but it doesn't mean everyone he knows is guilty by association. That's been the worst part of breaking up with him. I kinda miss his family sometimes. They're good people. Especially Sole and her brothers.

"Tell me you at least Facebook stalked her? Though surely, if you had, you would've realized how ridiculous it is you're not currently chasing her down to beg for forgiveness."

"Of course not!"

Clara held one finger in the air, wordlessly telling me to wait.

Tapping at her phone, Clara brought up Soledad's social media profile. When she flipped the screen, my breath caught in my throat at the sight of Soledad Reyes in a clingy tank top, hanging from an indoor climbing wall by one well-muscled arm.

Though her form impressed me, it wasn't her physique that most captivated, but rather the courage and resilience emboldened across her entire being. The soft curl of a half-smile tugged at her lips, contrasting the tense determination of her body.

The woman in the photograph didn't exercise to make herself more attractive or because she'd been dragged into participating in one of the many fitness fads by her friends. No. This was the demeanor of a woman who cultivated and savored her own vitality, her own tenacity. I hadn't noticed any of that when we'd met at Lucca's. Perhaps I hadn't let myself truly *see* her.

"I know, right?" Clara said, returning the phone to its previous facedown position on the table. "Come to think of it, you wouldn't have been able to find her online anyway. She uses a fake name. Police work and all that."

I gave a noncommittal "mmm-hmm."

"Really? That's all you're going to say?"

"Clara, you're my sister, and I love you, but I don't need a girlfriend. And I certainly don't need a girlfriend who's in the police force. My life is fine the way it is."

"Ha! What price are you selling that lie for? I don't buy it. That you're fine, or that you aren't interested in Soledad. You're a hopeless romantic and we both know it."

I swallowed, eager to change the subject. I'd come way too close to admitting to my far-too-pushy sister that perhaps I should have tried harder to find common ground with Soledad, that perhaps I'd given up too readily. Clara had never been this determined to set me up with a specific person before, and maybe she had good reason for doing so now.

No. My life was good. No need to mess with stability.

I cleared my throat. "Your turn. How's it going with Evie?"

The grin that bloomed on Clara's face stretched so wide I wondered if she might pull a muscle.

"Wow. That good, huh? Even though she's in Australia and you're here?"

Clara uncrossed her arms and rested her elbows on the edge of the table. "I'm surprised too. I honestly thought she'd go back to droving, I'd go back to data entry, and we'd end our little fling with some nice memories and a few platitudes. But since I've come home, I keep thinking about her."

"And she's thinking about you, I take it? It's so nice to see you like this, after what happened with Austin."

Clara bit her bottom lip as her eyes became unfocused. She was absolutely picturing her Australian cowgirl, though doing *what*, I didn't want to know.

"Oh God," Clara said, her tone gravelly as her expression darkened. "Speak of the devil."

Following her gaze, I glanced over my shoulder. Austin, the idiot who'd cheated on my sister for months, sauntered into the cafe, his arm wrapped around a small-waisted girl who, had she been older and had even half of her innate charisma, could have been Gina's twin. A slightly shorter, less intelligent-looking Gina, that is. My boss wasn't someone most people could hope to match on that front.

A normal person, when he caught the eye of his ex-girlfriend and her sister, might have quietly backed away and gone somewhere else for his midmorning coffee. But not Austin. Instead, he smirked at the pair of us and guided his companion to our table.

"Austin," Clara said, shielding her eyes from the sun as she looked up. "Out for a stroll?"

"Yeah, something like that," he replied, tugging the woman closer. "This is Lena."

"Lena?" I asked, incredulous. "Already moved on from the one you were screwing when you were in a relationship with my sister?"

His expression hardened and Lena's eyes narrowed. "We never said we were exclusive," he said through gritted teeth.

Clara scoffed. "You're a piece of work, Austin. Well, good luck to you, Lena; you're going to need it."

Austin pointed at Clara with his index and middle fingers. "Hey, just because you're bitter doesn't mean you get to talk to her like that. You were the one pulling away from me. And from what I hear, there's a good reason why. Maybe now you've got a piece of female ass, you'll pull that pole out of your *own* ass."

Clara and I shot out of our seats in unison. Austin and Lena, startled, stepped away, Austin almost tripped over his own feet.

"What the hell?" he said. The muscles in his face tightened.

"Hey!" I snapped. "Clara's relationship with Evie—who has at least fifteen more IQ points than you, by the way—has nothing to do with you. Bisexuals are a thing, Austin, or are you that obsessed with yourself you haven't noticed other people actually exist?"

The color drained from his face, and Lena drifted away from him, his arm left hanging.

Austin rubbed at the spot between his eyebrows with his thumb, apparently lost for words. As we stood there with my chest puffed out and people staring at us, it felt like we were all one finger snap away from breaking out into an antagonistic song like characters from *West Side Story*.

"Go away, Austin," Clara said. "You can show off your new girlfriend to someone who cares."

He scowled, then spun on his heel and exited the cafe's outdoor area, moving toward the street.

"Sorry," Lena mumbled, before following after him.

When Clara and I made eye-contact, we both broke out into laughter, though I'm certain neither of us had found the encounter funny. I dropped into my chair and took a few light sips of tea as Clara settled into her seat. "I can't believe you dated that fine example of an archaic *Homo Erectus*."

"To be honest, Des, he wasn't all that good on the *Erectus* front."

I laughed and almost choked on my tea. I hit my chest with my fist, urging the liquid to dissipate.

"Come on, you made that far too easy," Clara teased.

"True." I looked around. "Where on Earth is Brenna? I'm hungry."

Clara nibbled at her garlic bread. "Stop being so polite and order something."

"Some of us have standards of etiquette."

She grinned before pushing another square of food into her mouth, then chewed deliberately, mocking me and my rumbling stomach. Her expression changed as she swallowed, like a thought had struck her. "Okay, so if you won't call Sole, how about you come to a party with me on the weekend?"

"A party?" I frowned. "When I need to be around for Hope? I don't think so."

"Oh, come on." The words had a slightly childish lilt. "You need to make some friends other than me and Bren."

I held a hand up defensively. "Hey! I have friends."

She raised both of her eyebrows. "Name one."

"Gina."

"That doesn't count. She's your boss. You only see her for work and the occasional obligatory work social."

I scrunched up my face, unable to respond fast enough to avoid Clara's *I-told-you-so* smirk. "I'm busy, okay?"

"Uh-huh," she said. "Busy. Sure."

"You don't like parties either, you know."

"Not true. I don't like *certain* parties. I'm selective. Not one hundred percent antisocial. This party will involve the perfect mix of shots, pizza, and board games. Think about it; how often do you hang out with anyone you don't share DNA or a house with? I bet you haven't made a new friend since Rose left."

Ouch. That one hurt. She knew I didn't like to think too much about Rose. "It's bad timing; that's all. Hope is genuinely going through something right now, or she wouldn't have gotten herself into trouble. I should be at home more often in case she needs anything."

My handbag vibrated between my feet, and I reached for my phone.

"Oh, dammit," I mumbled as I read the text message. "Can you tell Bren I'm really sorry? I need to go."

Clara frowned. "What's wrong?"

I sighed. "Oh, nothing major. Gina needs me to start today's shoot earlier because the client's work schedule changed. This one apparently doesn't want to leave us there alone, which means not only do I miss brunch, but I'll be followed while I take the photos. Wonderful."

At least the message wasn't about Hope. After our truncated and fruitless discussion last night, I'd been craving a couple of hours free of parental anxiety to try to unfurl the knots lining their way up my spine.

"I'll be thinking of you when I order my next course," she replied.

"You suck," I said as I rose.

"Only when I'm in a good mood." She huffed at her own joke.

I rolled my eyes and laughed soundlessly.

"See you, Des."

I blew her a kiss, dropped a five-dollar bill on the table, then headed to my car.

CHAPTER EIGHT

THE ADDRESS GINA gave me was in South Oak Park, not far from Temple Avenue Park. Given the active church groups in the community and the rich diversity of the area, it's not a bad place to try to sell property, though most people nearby were renting.

Unlike the last one, I found this house without any problems.

A generous driveway led to a Californian bungalow with a wide, prominent porch and a gabled roof. A modest-looking building, the single-story home seemed well cared for and had a welcoming character about it, stemming from the manicured lawn and charming Japanese maple in the front yard. Coupled with the glass panes lining the top of the door, and the earthy brown and green tones of the gutters and roof, the front of the property would make for some lovely pictures, and I began planning before I'd even opened my car door.

Gina exited the house with a woman in her late fifties or early sixties—the homeowner, I assumed—the pair deep in conversation as the woman gestured at various windows. Gina's shoulder-length corkscrew curls, stunning in the daylight, bounced as she descended the porch steps.

The client, a tall woman with long, charcoal hair framed by gray edges, noticed my approach before my boss did. Gina turned.

"And here's my fabulous photographer," Gina announced, her arms outstretched. I shook my head at her whimsically as I stepped onto the porch.

"What a lovely home," I said to the woman.

"Thank you!" The client smiled with a rare sincerity, her eyes welcoming. Now that we were standing closer, I could take her in properly. The thin streaks of gray through her dark hair matched the color of her pencil skirt. She wore a light-pink blouse and comfortable-looking black slip-on shoes. A prominent, rounded pendant drew attention to the warm beige and time-worn skin of her neck. Her chin, slightly squared, gave her a regal appearance, like she belonged in a classic film.

"We've lived here for over twenty years, but, as is often the case, the nest has become empty, and the time has come to move on to something more manageable." She spoke with an accent I couldn't quite place, but I guessed she had been born somewhere in South America.

"Desi, meet Claudia," Gina chimed. She waved her hand in front of me as if I were a prize on *Wheel of Fortune*, and I let out a short laugh. "Claudia, this is one of the best damned real estate photographers in California."

For plenty of agents, the way they spoke in front of a client was different to their true manner. But not with Gina. She had an authenticity about her that, some might argue, could have undermined her professionalism and stunted the growth of her business. In reality though, most clients found her lack of pretense refreshing. Plenty of people had cited Gina's unapologetic and unrestrained manner as the main reason they'd decided to hire her, despite the commission rate being slightly higher than some of our larger, more influential competitors.

I offered Claudia my hand and shook hers gently when she accepted it. "Lovely to meet you, ma'am."

"Oh please," she replied, swatting at the air. "Claudia is perfect, my dear."

I readjusted the strap of my camera bag, which had been digging into my collar bone. "Of course, Claudia."

Unlike Gina, I never felt as comfortable dropping the veneer expected by most people in this industry, so I found myself, once again, speaking like some sort of robot.

"Thanks for making it over here on short notice, Des." Gina gave my hand a gentle, appreciative squeeze before moving close to the front door. "Now, you said your daughter wanted to be present for the photos, Claudia?"

I suppressed the urge to roll my eyes as a silent groan rumbled in my chest. Most clients preferred to leave the house for a couple of hours to let me work. It made my job easier, not having to stumble over other people, or worry about them second-guessing the angles or rooms I chose to photograph. Explaining why a family's oh-so-gorgeous living room was too narrow to make for a commercially viable shot or why I didn't want the family dog licking itself to be a key feature of an external landscape slowed things down.

I don't mind interacting with new people. I don't love it, but I don't hate it either. Unless I'm trying to work. I need space to think, to move, to create. That was something Hope and I had in common. I briefly wondered how her day was going and, deciding to text her soon, let the thought drift into Parent Desi's sphere where it needed to stay while Work Desi did her thing.

"Yes," Claudia said to Gina. "My daughter is very attached to this house, and I think it'll help her begin to let go." She took up position next to Gina and opened the door, holding it so everyone could enter. "Plus," she added as I stepped into the entryway, "she's a police officer and, truth be told, I think she may be worried about leaving strangers in the house. And I have too much to do today to stay."

I gulped. Like, really gulped. Such an obvious and exaggerated gesture that I resembled one of the kids from *The Little Rascals* when they'd been caught in some act of mischief.

Claudia's daughter was a police officer. And she was Latinx...

"Desiree Adler."

Before I'd even turned toward the voice, I knew it was Soledad Reyes.

She leaned casually into the frame of the entry to the dining room, and my stomach clenched at the sight of her roguish smile and cascading brown hair. Totally at ease, her thumbs hooked into the belt loops of her torn black jeans.

Her bright-orange tank top left her toned biceps exposed. I could have sworn the temperature in the house was at least five degrees higher than it had been moments earlier.

This was absurd!

One coincidence with this woman was unlikely, but two? Inconceivable! Maybe that word didn't mean what I thought it meant.

Gina's eyes widened. "You two are acquainted?"

I opened my mouth to speak, closed it again. Unable to construct a sentence from the misshapen, incomprehensible syllables floating around in my head.

Claudia clapped her hands together. "Okay," she said, her eyes sparkling as though she were in on a joke that had gone right over my head. "I'm off to the grocery store. Thank you again, Gina. I'll be seeing you soon." She approached Soledad and kissed her on the cheek. "I'll see you later, my little *paca*."

Soledad gave her mother a knowing smirk. "Te quiero, Mamá. I'll see you tomorrow."

Claudia said something in Spanish, a playful tone to her voice, her eyes widening. Soledad lifted her hands as though feigning innocence as she replied, "What? It's fine. Go, go," Soledad said, shooing her mother with a gentle, fluttering gesture.

As Gina and Claudia exchanged pleasantries out on the porch, I fixed my attention on Soledad. "This seems like an unlikely accident," I said, slipping my equipment onto the floor.

"Then it probably isn't."

"Isn't what? Unlikely? Or an accident?"

Soledad stood to her full height, and I remembered how

impressive I'd found her when she had first sashayed her way alongside my car. "It wasn't an accident." She glanced past me and waved goodbye to her mother and Gina. I followed her gaze and did the same, smiling through tight lips as they both made to leave.

I lifted my chin slightly and crossed my arms over my stomach as I gave my attention to Soledad. My fingertips tingled, but I couldn't be sure if the sensation came from frustration or excitement. "You knew I'd be here?"

"I didn't know for sure, but it seemed like a strong possibility."

I closed my eyes as I realized what had happened. "Clara. Right. Your mother is selling a house. You're friends with my sister and she recommended Gina's agency."

She sucked her cheeks in ever so slightly, as though pleased about something. "And, of course, she told me you're the one responsible for the photos on the website and in the brochures."

A brief spark of electricity in my chest caught me off guard, and I cleared my throat, hoping she wouldn't notice the blush blooming on my face and neck.

"Hmm" was all I could manage by way of a response.

I returned to my equipment and picked up the bags, appreciating the pause in our conversation so I could retrieve my capacity to think straight.

I couldn't understand why everything became so foggy around her—my brain overloaded like a circuit breaker and shut off. The only interactions we'd had so far had been, at best, awkward. At worst, they'd been outright unpleasant. So why had my skin warmed? Why had my throat gone dry? Why was I happy to see her?

I blinked rapidly to dispel any unwelcome answers to those questions and adopted my work face, determined not to let her see the confusion churning inside me.

"I usually set these down in the dining room or the kitchen to begin with. Is that okay?" I asked.

"Absolutely," she replied. She moved deeper into the dining room, inviting me to follow. "I'm still impressed by how tidy my mother managed to make this place for the photos. You should see it normally. The cupboards must be almost bursting."

"She's a bit of a collector?"

Soledad hmphed. "More of a hoarder. I think it might be genetic. My brothers do it too. They sometimes joke that perhaps I'm adopted since I haven't covered every free inch of space in my apartment."

Soledad watched as I unpacked my gear, laying lenses and flashes out along the rectangular, trestle-based table. The smooth, mismatched pieces of wood in her mother's furniture gave the room a contemporary, industrial character heightened by the naked metal frames of the hardwood chairs tucked neatly about the table. This room belonged to a large family that liked to spend time together. At least, that's how it felt.

When Soledad's curious gaze had all but burned a hole in my skin, I slipped my camera strap over my head and turned. "You changed the appointment time so we'd run into each other," I said, my tone leaving no room to interpret my statement as a question.

"I did," she admitted, her voice clear and unapologetic. Her unbending confidence reminded me of my youngest sister, Brenna. I'd always admired women quick to own their feelings, to announce their thoughts and do so without hesitation. I had moments where I could do the same, but they were few and far between, and they almost certainly never came when I spoke to a woman I found attractive.

Not that I was attracted to Soledad. Nor did she—I suspected—feel an attraction to me, for that matter. Why would she? I lost my senses every time I saw her, my ability to construct coherent sentences free-falling straight into those brown eyes. *Stop it! Not attracted, remember?*

I switched the camera on and removed the lens cap. When I spoke again, I kept my eyes on the camera screen, pretending to check the battery level, though I knew I'd charged it. "Why...why would you line this up?"

She took two steps and suddenly we were so close I could smell the intoxicating, crisp scent of freshly washed hair, her body mere inches from the edge of my camera, a camera that now felt like the only layer of safety left between she and me.

Fine. Maybe I was attracted to her, but if that was the case, it was a purely physical reaction. I was sure of it.

"I needed to apologize."

My gaze dropped to the floor as a sense of guilt kindled in my gut. "It's me who should say sorry. I know I can be intense. I tend to release my thoughts in these impassioned torrents, rather than pacing myself. At least, I do when I'm—"

"When you're what?" Her eyes sparkled expectantly. "When you're nervous? Did I make you nervous?"

Another spark of electricity. Another dry throat. I wanted to answer Soledad, to give some witty retort like Clara might, or outright own up to my inner thoughts like

Brenna. But I wasn't brave like either of my sisters. Not when it counted. Instead, my attention fell to her full lips, lightly coated in a clear gloss, and I wondered what they'd feel like sliding against my own.

Soledad hadn't simply made me nervous both times I'd spoken to her yesterday. She'd invaded my thoughts throughout all the hours between, a fact I couldn't deny now that she stood right in front of me, regardless of how convinced I was the two of us were incompatible.

Soledad reached out and rested her hand on my forearm. Goose bumps raced along my skin, radiating from the spot where she touched me. "You were trying to be honest, and I could see you were finding it hard to explain your views. I could have made it easier." She ducked her head, compelling me to look up, to make eye contact with her. Her wide eyes left no doubt as to the sincerity of her apology. "I shouldn't have let you walk out. I should have asked you to stay so we could talk some more. So we could at least finish the night on a less sour note." She paused. "Am I forgiven?"

"Would you go out with me again?" The words had spilled from my mouth of their own accord, and I couldn't do anything to change it. "I mean, it doesn't have to be a date, though."

What the hell am I doing?

That wasn't like me. Not one bit. I never asked women out. Not in such a direct way. I flirted and I waited. If I was especially eager, I'd send a noncommittal text message, fishing more than drawing in, hoping the other person would be braver than me and make a move. And I hadn't even done that for over a year. Ever since I'd broken up with Rose, my expectations had been pretty low.

Soledad shifted her weight to one hip and slid her hands into the pockets of her jeans. She tilted her head, and the edge of her mouth curled into a delicious lopsided smile. "Absolutely."

"That's okay. I didn't think you would, I just..." I stopped, waited as my mind caught up with my mouth. "Wait. Did you say yes?"

Her smile melted into a coy grin as she closed the distance between us. "I have no idea why. Clearly you don't like cops, and your driving record isn't quite up to the standard I'd like, but..." She drew the word out, a habit of hers I was beginning to like. She lifted her hand, gingerly, and brushed a thin strand of hair away from my face, my abdomen clenching as she did.

"But what?" My voice cracked, and I shied away from her touch, though every nerve ending in my body rebelled as I sank against the refrigerator, away from Soledad.

She dropped her hand to her side. "But...I want to spend time with you. We have some more things we should talk about. And I want to see where that wonderful combination of fire and ice comes from."

Fire and ice. I'd never heard anyone describe me so accurately, let alone someone I barely knew. But between my sometimes-uncontrollable urge to take on the whole world with one arm tied behind my back and my deep appreciation of a quiet night in rewatching episodes of *Orphan Black*, she'd been spot-on with her summation.

"Are you busy tonight?" she asked.

"No, I'm not." I smacked my lips as I remembered the game. "Oh wait. No. I'm wrong. We have baseball tickets."

"The River Cats?" Her face lit up, as did mine at the

thought we may have found some common ground.

"Yes!" I coughed lightly, trying to backpedal on that obvious display of excitement. "You follow them?"

"I do," she replied. "I had a friend in high school who turned me into a fan. Well, perhaps another night?"

Disappointment washed through me. Then, I remembered we had too many tickets. "We have an extra ticket. I mean, that is, if you can cope with my sisters and my foster daughter. My youngest sister's new boyfriend was meant to be coming, but he has work."

"Is that what you want? I already know Clara, but your other sister, and your foster daughter?" She didn't sound hesitant or unwilling, only concerned, perhaps worried about putting me in an uncomfortable position—something I had quite the talent for doing all on my own.

"Safety in numbers, right?" I hoped she knew I was joking. The quizzical look on her face left me unsure. "Sorry. That wasn't funny."

"You second-guess yourself a lot," she asserted. "You shouldn't. You shouldn't apologize for your views or your thoughts. They all seem quite sound to me, so far."

"You've got me all worked out after only a few conversations?"

She quirked an eyebrow—again—and my throat caught fire. "You learn a lot about a person when you see how they react to a traffic infringement."

"Or walk out on a date?"

She crossed her arms. "That too." She tilted her head slightly. The gesture sent shiny strands of dark hair across one side of her face and neck, and something unfamiliar and fizzy bubbled in my core.

"Safety in numbers is fine with me," she said. "Besides, there's no pressure here. We may end up friends. We may end up never seeing each other again—but at least there'll be a more reasonable resolution than what happened last night."

Or we may end up... No. Stop that. Not helping, inner Desi!

"I better tell Brenna we need that last ticket after all," I said. "But first, would you let me take these photographs?" My voice sounded more confident than I felt, a fact for which I was grateful.

"Absolutely," she replied. "So...friends?" She extended a hand.

"Of course. Friends," I confirmed, shaking her hand. I dropped my gaze to our connected fingers and, when I looked up, I could see she'd done the same. My smile faded as I let go and ran a hand through my hair. I'm sure I was about as subtle as Danny Zuko pretending he wasn't head over heels for Sandy Olsson in *Grease*.

Soledad turned to the kitchen bench and shuffled envelopes in a small wicker basket. We agreed on one thing: the conversation had come to an end, for now.

As I adjusted the settings on my camera and prepared to move to the front lawn for exterior shots, I did my best to convince myself that making a new friend was all I wanted, that Soledad Reyes hadn't sidled her way into my subconscious and made me wish for something else. Something I'd given up on around the same time my chronic pain had forced me to quit my old job. Something...magical.

CHAPTER NINE

HOPE CAME HOME from her friend's place in an atrocious mood. When I asked how her day had been, the only reply she gave sounded more like some sort of animalistic mating call than actual words. If I still had any doubts about her disinterest in having a conversation, the thunderous slamming of her door snuffed them out.

I stood in the kitchen, staring through the window. The weather had turned sometime after three, and as I gazed out at the angry blanket of gray and purple sky, I wondered if the River Cats game would be canceled. I sincerely hoped not. Not only because it meant I wouldn't have a chance to see Soledad again, but because Hope needed this—a distraction from whatever bothered her, time with people who cared about her.

When I'd told my sisters I wanted to become a foster carer to teenagers almost ten years ago, they'd been nothing but supportive. Unlike some of my friends, Clara and Brenna hadn't shaken their heads at me and asked with a pointed tone, "*Why?*"

Clara and Brenna had fully committed themselves to their roles as foster aunts, and not one child I had cared for could have accused them of neglecting their duties. Public embarrassment in the form of overly enthusiastic hugs or awkward questions about their love lives? Yes. Disinterest? Absolutely not.

I filled a glass with tap water and took slow sips as I continued to stare absently at the sky. My temples were tightly wound bolts, and I grabbed a couple of Tylenol from a bottle by the sink. I'd only had one cup of tea today, silly really, given I knew if I didn't have at least two caffeinated beverages I'd have a headache by the midafternoon. I supposed there were worse things I could be addicted to than caffeine. When I'd first met Rose and she'd encouraged me to quit smoking, I'd made a deal with my future-self to take better care of my body and, aside from a few painkillers and too much caffeine, I'd mostly managed to keep that promise.

Finishing off my water, I slipped the glass into the rack and clicked the dishwasher closed. Then I made my way toward Hope's room. The floor vibrated as I drew nearer, loud music thumping from within. As usual, I didn't recognize the band, but I did recognize the sentiment. Though muted by the door, the voices and instruments were angry, frustrated, and disenfranchised.

Standing outside her door, I hesitated, not quite sure if I should try talking again or leave her alone. No, I decided.

I'd given her space after last night. It was time to address this.

I tapped lightly at her door. No response. I tried again, louder this time. There came a banging noise. Footsteps. The volume of the music dropped.

"Hope? Can I come in?" I rested my forehead against the smooth painted wood as I waited for a reply. After a few seconds, the lock clicked, and I stepped back as she opened the door.

"I guess," she said, leaving a gap so I could enter.

The scent of lavender permeated the space, a thick rounded candle alight on the dresser. Her room was neat, as usual. No teenage clichés here. The various bottles and ornaments on her dresser perched in orderly groups. Her lilac comforter pulled tight across the mattress. Sheets were tucked with military precision. Her floor was clear of clutter save for a pair of black ankle boots beneath the curtained window, where she always positioned the shoes she intended to wear when we had an outing planned. Acclimating to habits like these are one of the less well-known quirks of looking after someone else's children. There's no way to know who instilled this almost obsessive sense of cleanliness upon Hope, nor if the way they did it had been constructive or scarily toxic.

Every child is different. Some have never had anyone to teach them personal hygiene or what it means to be considerate when you share a living space. I would never forget poor Emily and the embarrassment painted on her face when, at seventeen, she was told how to dispose of a tampon properly for the first time in her life.

Others were so particular about how their belongings

were stored it could break your heart imagining the possibilities of what had happened to make them nervous in that way. Like Fotini, who had hidden food in every place she could and hated to leave her room in case her shoes went missing.

Fotini would always stand out in my memory because, on the first day of her emergency placement here, she had said, in complete earnest, "Will we eat today?" It had taken everything I had not to fall into a heap right there in front of her. Through tight lips, I'd nodded and blinked away threatening tears as I led her to the kitchen.

Hope didn't seem to have been denied regular access to food. Nor did I believe she'd had any of her things disappear on her when she wasn't looking. But I did wonder about the intensity with which she maintained her room. That intensity didn't extend to other parts of the house. She could leave a dirty cup out or forget to empty the trash as easily as the next person, but never in her room. No. That space was immaculate, almost as though she were scared something bad could happen if even a speckle were out of order. If we had an appointment or a reservation and something needed cleaning, I knew we'd need to be late. It didn't bother me, but it did leave me wondering.

Hope flopped onto the bed and crossed her legs. She glanced at me, then focused on her phone. "Is the game still on?" she said as she thumbed the screen.

"The weather only seems to be threatening so far, no actual rain. I've got my fingers and toes crossed," I replied, inching forward. When a few moments had passed and I could be sure she wouldn't object, I sat on the opposite end of the mattress. "I wanted to give you space, but you need to tell me why you were at that party. Why you were carrying around cash for someone selling drugs."

Hope's features tightened and the movement of her thumbs slowed, but she didn't look up. "How much trouble am I in?" she said, her voice low and her tone unreadable.

"It depends. Is this a regular occurrence?"

"No!" She dropped her phone onto the nightstand. "I've never gone to a party like that before. I didn't know they'd be acting..."

"Acting like what?" I urged, dipping my head.

She collapsed against her pillows. Light streamed through the blinds, casting strips of shadow across her torso.

Frustration sizzled inside me. "Okay, you don't have to talk if you don't want to," I said. "But you need to be safe. Stay away from whoever you were with."

Her eyes narrowed as she cut me a look. "What? All of them?" She sounded worried and mildly angry too.

"If you aren't going to tell me what led you there, and who exactly you were helping, then I can't narrow it down." I slid my hand along the comforter, not touching her, but closing the distance between us. "I'm going to have to trust you to know who you should spend time with. But, for now, you're grounded. Aside from going places with me or one of the aunts, you need to be at home."

Hope closed her eyes and sighed loudly, drawing her knees toward her chest.

"You're lucky there aren't more consequences, Hope. Don't forget, I picked you up from a police station of all places."

"I know," she retorted. "I was there, remember?" Her

attention fell to her lap, and I could see the remorse on her face. She knew she'd put herself in a dangerous position, and she knew she'd been rude just now, but her silence made it clear she had no intention of verbalizing as much.

"All right," I said as I stood. "I care about you. You know that, right?"

She nodded but her eyes seemed vacant.

"Assuming it doesn't rain, we'll head out in about an hour. And assuming you don't mind, but...I'm bringing a friend."

Hope's pale-blue eyes snapped to me, curiosity flashing within them as her nose crinkled. "A friend?"

I slipped my hands into my pockets. "Yeah. The woman I had the blind date with. I ran into her today and, you know, it turns out she likes our team as well, and we had that spare ticket going to waste. Do you mind?"

The skin around Hope's eyes and mouth softened, and she shook her head, the tension thick in the air moments earlier melting away.

"Thanks," I said.

"Hey, Desi?" she murmured as I turned to leave.

"Yeah?" I glanced over my shoulder.

"Did you call that plumber yet?"

I groaned. Not at Hope, but at myself. "Dammit."

She gave me a withering look, then resumed playing with her phone.

As I walked sluggishly down the hall, I resigned myself to yet another cold shower, preparing for a night out that was definitely *not* a real date.

CHAPTER TEN

IF I COULD bottle the atmosphere of Raley Field and take it home with me, I'd have a cure for almost any low mood I could ever experience. The magnificent mixed scents of warm beer, pretzels, popcorn, and rich green grass transported me from a realm of parental anxiety, intermittent bursts of pain, and social awkwardness to a place where everything simply made sense.

After our dad left when I was about thirteen and we moved to Sacramento, Mom brought the family here whenever she could, making sure the four of us had at least some time as a family. She had to work hard to pay the bills, but baseball games were one way she ensured we didn't lose touch. We may not have always been together for dinner or have been able to get to everyone's school presentations or whatever else, but at least we had Raley.

"I see you managed to get my stubborn sister out of the house," Clara said to Soledad.

I narrowed my eyes at my sister in a shut-the-heck-up expression she'd seen enough times that there was no way she could misunderstand. But when Clara's reply came in the form of a long, loud slurp as she sucked soda up through a straw, I knew I'd need to let her get this line of teasing out of her system. I'd save bringing up the fact she herself had been disconnected from the world of social interactions until her trip to Australia. Like any good sister, I'd keep my retort to myself until the best possible moment to ensure maximum impact.

Soledad gifted me a gentle, sympathetic look before answering Clara. I could have kissed her for that. Well, not *kissed*, but I appreciated her understanding.

"Well," she started, "I'm the one crashing your family outing, and technically she invited me. So, I'd say it was Desi who got *me* out of the house."

"Yep," Clara declared. "You two are getting married one day. I can tell."

I reached across the empty seat between us and smacked her bicep with the back of my hand. "Clara!"

She smirked and took another sip of her drink. "What? This is clearly a done deal. I can tell." She looked at her cup accusingly. "You know, the fact there's no bourbon in this is disappointing."

"A done deal?" I scoffed. "That's hilarious coming from you! Even before we found out what a loser Austin is, you didn't believe in the whole marriage thing and now you're marrying me off to your friends?"

Clara raised her eyebrows and pulled her lips together as though blotting her lipstick. It took me a second to realize what I'd done. *Oh shit. Austin is Soledad's cousin.*

I turned my head to the left and met Soledad's eyes. They were unreadable. "I'm so sorry. I forgot he's—"

"It's fine," she replied as she rubbed her palms along her thighs. There was no judgment or malice in her tone.

The heat in my cheeks flashed brighter for a moment. "You're not mad?"

She shook her head. "Definitely not. I love Austin, but just because my father and his mother are siblings doesn't mean I don't see what a jerk he can be. If someone cheated on my sister, I'd be furious. My whole family has told him so. Quite the Reyes-Mitchells family scandal."

"See," Clara interjected. "I told you she's quality." Clara sank into her seat as though removing herself from the conversation and giving us space.

Almost immediately a strange sense of closeness enveloped me, as though Soledad and I were walled off from anyone else. I tried to swallow the dryness in my throat, but it didn't help. I focused my attention on the field, scanning the diamond like I hadn't been to at least fifty River Cats games in my life.

The sun had almost disappeared behind the stadium's walls, and splashes of blue, green, and yellow stretched between the dispersing cloud cover. By the time the game ended in a couple of hours, the outside world would be dark, quiet, and winding down. Raley Field, however, would thrive beneath flooding lights and the emphatic energy of the crowd.

What was taking Brenna and Hope so long? Surely the

line for the bathroom couldn't have held them up for *this* long.

As though the universe wanted to give me a break, they turned up before it became too obvious I'd been embarrassed by Clara's comment about liking Soledad.

"Excuse us," Brenna said as she shimmied between our knees and the seats in front of us to take a spot on the other side of Clara. Hope slipped quietly into the empty seat between Clara and me, hot dog in one hand and giant soda in the other. "Hope you don't mind, Des, I got her some food."

I pretended to sniff the hot dog and retreated in disgust. "You call that food?"

Brenna looked heavenward and shook her head. "Absolutely." To prove her point, she bit into the end of her own hot dog, a small spot of ketchup catching on her upper lip. "Mmm-mmm-mmm," she hummed as she chewed more zealously than the processed meat would have required.

"Are you a vegetarian?" Soledad asked.

"I am," I replied. "You?"

She dipped her head from side to side as though swishing a thought about. "I'd be lying if I said yes. But I don't eat much meat at all. I prefer meals based on vegetables, beans, lentils…that sort of thing."

"Why not go for the full vegetarian lifestyle?" I asked. Maybe the spasmodic yells and rise and fall of the crowd's cacophony helped somehow, but I felt myself slipping comfortably into an effortless conversational rhythm with her for the first time since we'd met.

Soledad bit her lower lip self-consciously. "Would you hate me if I said it's because I love burgers too much to make that kind of commitment?"

A warm and natural laugh tumbled from my body and out into the world.

Soledad released her lip from between her teeth. The sheer magnificence of her face brought my laughter to an abrupt halt. We stared, neither of us blinking.

"Plus," she added, breaking the moment, "I'd be the talk of my family if I swore off all meat. Have you ever eaten from an asado?"

I squinted, demonstrated my unfamiliarity with the word.

"It's a barbecue. We have house parties sometimes; they're a real test of stamina. In our family, you dance, you drink, you laugh, and you eat meat straight from the grill."

"Sounds incredible."

"Yeah," she replied, falling into a memory judging by the expression on her face. "It is."

"Hey, Des?" Hope's hail dragged me out of whatever maze Soledad and I had wandered into. I twisted in my seat to face front, then looked at Hope. How did I end up at a baseball game with my foster daughter on one side of me, and my...well, new friend, on the other? I flicked my attention past Hope to Clara for a moment and saw her grinning at me with another *I-told-you-so* expression. "Would you kill me if I got my cell phone out?"

I sighed. "Do you have to?"

Her shoulders rolled in, hollowing her chest. "I'm sorry," she said with a childlike apologetic tone, exaggerated but sincere. "I've tried to like this whole baseball thing, but I don't get it. I'm here, right? I'm with the family and all that. But do I have to watch?"

"Can I make a suggestion?" Soledad asked. Hope's

eyebrows shot upward. She'd been introduced to Soledad, and they'd exchanged a polite greeting when we'd first arrived about twenty minutes ago, but they'd not spoken since.

I was surprised at how easily and confidently Soledad spoke to Hope. Plenty of people found it hard to know what to say to my foster kids, and it was rare for anyone to instigate a conversation so soon after their first introduction. I thought it was partially because people didn't want to say the wrong thing—like they thought kids were made of glass, when in actual fact they were made of much tougher stuff. But largely, I suspected it was because my kids were always teenagers, and teenagers weren't exactly hard to offend. I certainly hadn't been; that was for sure.

"Sure," Hope replied, her features drawn into a curious leer.

"I don't think this game is much fun if you don't have a player."

"What do you mean?"

Soledad leaned into her arm, the one dangerously close to the side of my body. "Well." She rolled her other hand through the air. "A player that's yours. At least one who's name and number you know, whose stats you follow. I bet Desi has one."

In eerie unison, Clara, Brenna, and Hope all said, "Daric Barton."

Soledad gave a short, bubble-like laugh. "Right. Exactly. You need one of your own. Because no way does anyone want to track the same player as their carer or parent."

"Finally," Hope asserted, one hand chopping the air. "Someone who understands. Des has been trying to get me into Barton since I moved in. But the guy doesn't even play anymore."

Soledad gave me a slow shake of her head, accompanied by a playful "tsk-tsk." Her face softened. "Well, all that's left now is to pick your player. But don't be too hasty. I mean, this is a long-term commitment you're making here. You don't want to rush into anything."

The corners of Hope's mouth pulled outward into the kind of noncommittal expression someone has when they're trying not to smile. "Yeah. Yeah, okay. That makes sense." Hope clasped her fingers together in her lap, enfolding her cell phone as though declaring she'd ignore social media for a while. "But, so you know, this could go either way. There are two teams in this game."

"Oh no," I retorted, my voice grim. "Absolutely not. River Cats or bust, kiddo."

Hope fixed me with a coy, lopsided look. "We'll see." The crowd burst into cheers at the signal the game was about to start, and she turned her attention to the field.

The stadium became too loud, and so I thanked Soledad silently, mouthing the words. She dropped her eyes for a moment, then returned her gaze to my face. Was that a blush? Did I want it to be? Gazing through the open roof of the stadium, I could sense her eyes on me, sense her watching and thinking, and my toes tapped nervously, seemingly of their own free will.

A huge swell of noise suddenly flew up from the crowd with the fervor of a fighter jet in motion. I hadn't realized I'd detached from reality. I jolted in response to the abrupt cacophony and clamor as people jumped to their feet.

"Far out!" Brenna yelled.

"Did you see that?" Clara called out, looking down at me.

I stood, my brain trying to catch up. The leading batter had absolutely obliterated the ball! He rounded second. The stadium practically shook with excitement as he pounded his way to third.

"Throw the ball!" I yelled.

"Stop him!" Soledad called through cupped hands.

I cringed as the outfielder pelted the ball to one of the in-fielders at the same moment the runner rounded third and made for home. No way could that be a safe play. The River Cats, *my* River Cats, would make sure the ball beat him there.

The ball sliced through the air, hurtling toward the catcher as the batter made his last, feverish play for the home plate. I clenched my eyes shut.

"Safe!" Clara yelled.

"He's safe!" Hope echoed.

I opened my eyes. "What? No way." The player stood, dusted off his legs, and waved at the appreciative crowd. What a start to the game!

Soledad's hands flourished through the air. "It was a bad throw to the catcher. He had to jump off the plate, and that was just long enough to slide underneath."

"What kind of pitch was that, Anderson?" Clara huffed as she slumped into her seat.

A calmer, buzzing murmur filled the stadium as people sat, mumbling at one another about the rather spectacular start to the game. *Spectacular*, I thought, *and deeply disappointing*.

"They should've started with Connolly," Soledad said. I

agreed. "Thanks for the ticket, by the way. And now we're kind of even. I gave you a ticket. You gave me a ticket...all square now, right?"

"Uh-huh," I replied, mock indignation in my tone.

"But really, this is fun. I'm glad I came."

I tried to suppress a smile, but my face had a mind of its own and I knew I was beaming. I was glad she'd come too. Not only did she know the team as well as I did, but she had managed to connect with Hope faster than even my sisters. Or, truth be told, me. Soledad had an inextricable kind of honesty about her, an assertive radiance that shone through her eyes and framed every word she spoke.

"You're a lot quieter than you were at the restaurant," she said, nudging me gently with her elbow. I dropped my head, trying to conceal the shadow of embarrassment I felt blooming across my cheeks.

"I guess I didn't expect..."

"To like me?"

Damn. This woman was not going to let me off the hook, was she? How could she be so forward, so forthright about a situation? Everything in my world, at least my romantic world, always seemed so hazy.

"Something like that," I replied. "But I also realized I hadn't given you a chance to tell me your reasons for being a cop, or to tell me your views on much of anything. That wasn't fair."

"Thanks for saying so. I would like to share all that with you. I was caught off guard, I must admit. It's unusual for me not to have a fast response. But can we try that discussion again sometime. Soon, maybe?"

I nodded.

A loud crack sliced the air as another ball was smashed violently across the field by a batter. I wasn't even watching the game. Normally I'd be fixated, not even looking away when I'd throw popcorn at Clara or talk rubbish with Brenna.

Soledad leaned into me, close enough to whisper in my ear and make sure I could hear her despite the waves of emotive sound erupting from the spectators. My pulse thundered when I realized how close her lips were to my neck. And how much I wanted them to be even closer. "In that case, will you go out with me again? Only the two of us?"

Just when I thought my heart couldn't pound any harder, my body proved me wrong.

"Okay."

CHAPTER ELEVEN

CHRISTIAN LYNETTI HAD been my doctor since we'd first moved to Sacramento. Though I'd had some frustrating moments with him over the years, the fact that he treated my mother, my sisters, and that he'd been so understanding during the embarrassing acne affair of '04 meant I'd be sticking with him until the day he retired. Which, by the look of his receding hairline and deep-set skin furrows, couldn't be too far off.

"The IUD is helping, then? That's wonderful news." His voice was as calm and pleasant as lapping waves. Everything about Dr. Lynetti was calm; even his bushy rust-colored eyebrows somehow projected a sense of tranquility.

"The cramps and aches are less intense than before. It's refreshing not to spend most of the hours of the night stalking up and down my hallway or basically burning myself with heat packs to try to get comfortable."

"Good. That's really good. Have you cut down on the anti-inflammatory drugs?"

I shook my head once, as though I were a small child in trouble with their favorite teacher. "No. I still seem to need them a lot. But they work most of the time now."

He swiveled in his chair, typed something into my patient file, and returned his attention to the conversation, his expression sympathetic. "I'm hopeful that after the laparoscopic surgery, and with continued use of the Mirena device, you won't need the pills anymore. Long-term use isn't good for anybody."

"I know," I replied, my tone soft and my volume quiet. "I'm still on the waiting list for the surgery. They can't even give me a date yet."

"Did you read the materials I printed for you about the keyhole procedure?"

Of course, I'd read them. At least ten times. They'd start with a tiny cut close to the middle of my belly button, then send a scope inside to check for signs of endometriosis. If they found any tissue where it wasn't meant to be, they'd likely make two more cuts lower on my abdomen, take a biopsy to (finally!) confirm the diagnosis, and if they could, remove or burn the endometriosis. If I was lucky, the IUD would stop any more from returning, or slow it down so that it would at least be a decade until I'd need the surgery again.

Surgery was scary. There were always risks. I could end up with internal scar tissue far more problematic than the original symptoms. The surgeon could damage my bowel or my bladder if they needed to cut or burn endometriosis away from those organs. Or, and perhaps still insidious in its own benign way, nothing could improve. My experiences could remain exactly the same once the surgery was over.

But I didn't care. Not yet, anyway. I had been desperate for a diagnosis for so long that any fears lurking within me were overshadowed by an intense excitement. A diagnosis meant validation. It meant no more "suck it up, it's period pain" comments from colleagues, or arched eyebrows from friends when I'd turn up to an event on the bus because I didn't trust myself to drive that day.

I'd have a name for my condition. Despite society's best intentions when it came to acceptance and empathy, I'd come to learn that—for most people—only when they could label your illness could they begin to acknowledge and understand your experiences.

"I'll take that far-away look as a yes, Desiree?"

I blinked a few times, dispelling the dazed state I'd fallen into for a few moments. "Yeah," I said, clearing my throat before continuing. "Of course. I just want it to happen already. I'm not generally an impatient person, but I am when it comes to this."

"Yes," he said as though in agreement. "It took far too long for your insurance company to approve the operation, and now you're in what seems to be a never-ending line of patients. I am sorry."

I shrugged. "I know I shouldn't complain. Plenty of other people in the world wouldn't have access to health care at all. Even if ours does need a massive overhaul—at least it exists."

Who was I kidding? The system sucked. And if it had been a person, I would have slapped it silly, all the while screaming *"Get your crap together! Nothing about you makes any sense!"* And still, I was one of the lucky ones. At least I had insurance. In a country where about a third of the population didn't have the same sort of security, my privileges were nothing to be scoffed at.

"Okay, Desiree," he said, a touch of whimsy in his tone as he tapped his thighs. "Your check-up is all done. Is there anything else you need?"

Aside from a plumber who could come to my house sometime this century, a better knack for navigating teenage mood swings, and a nice outfit for my next date with Soledad? "Nope," I replied, looking down at my hands. Geez. I needed to stop chewing at my fingernails; I'd destroyed the cuticle on my pinky finger. "Thanks, Doc. I'll see you next time."

CHAPTER TWELVE

AFTER I'D FINISHED with Dr. Lynetti, I made my way across town for my weekly catch-up with Mom. I tended to do work most Saturdays and at least half of every Sunday because I needed to operate around the times that best suited Gina's clients, so Monday was a day just for me.

Sometimes Brenna would be able to start work early so she could have an extended lunch break and join us, and those days were my favorites. I adored Clara, but I didn't see Brenna or Mom nearly as often, let alone at the same time. And last night at the game, Brenna had been sitting three seats away in a stadium so loud she may as well have been a mile away. Admittedly, even if we'd been side by side I wouldn't have noticed. Not with Soledad there.

I couldn't stop myself replaying the night as I drove to

my mother's house. Every interaction, every comment. Nor could I stop picturing her lips, painted crimson red, bright and confident against her white teeth and complementing the striking tank top she'd been wearing.

How had this woman had such a profound effect on me so quickly? The police officer who'd pulled me over, the blind date I'd missed the mark with, had somehow gone from an uncomfortable anecdote in my memory, to a pervasive fantasy I couldn't shake. And I didn't only mean fantasy in the physical sense, though I was most definitely attracted to her. I was also thinking about things we could talk about besides baseball. Places we could go. Even things we would disagree on. I started to consider how I'd react the next time her profession came up in conversation.

I slid my hybrid car into Mom's driveway, moving as close to the garage door as I could safely manage so Brenna would have space to park behind. As usual, my mother's front lawn, small as it was, needed to be mowed. The uneven hedges lining the fence threw their limbs outward like excited children, waving at me as an assertive wind blew through the yard. Ill-matching potted plants dotted the grassy area in a haphazard fashion that seemed so erratic it could almost be mistaken for a pattern. I weaved between them and approached the front door where I paused.

Looking over my shoulder, I smirked to myself. If landscaping were anything to go by, my mother and Soledad's mother couldn't have been more different. One attentive to every minor detail, each blade of grass fresh, crisp, and manicured. The other, blissfully unaware of her own chaotic universe and the sideways glances her neighbors flicked her way each Monday morning when they noticed she'd, once again, let another weekend pass without working on her garden.

I thought my mom and Claudia Reyes would get along well. It was early to be planning a parental meet-and-greet though, so I inhaled, reset my brain into Mom Mode, and slipped my key into the lock. With a gentle creak, the faded burgundy door gave way and I shuffled inside.

"Is that you, Bren?" Mom's words floated through the house from the kitchen, her voice as breezy and carefree as the garden out the front.

"Nope," I called. "It's the other one."

A brief cackle and a few loud footsteps later and my mom appeared at the other end of the narrow corridor leading from the front door to the dining room, with one hand on her hip and the other loosening her checkered orange apron. "You look tired, Des."

"Thanks, Mom," I huffed. "You look great too."

In her early sixties, Abigail Adler was a rotund woman with ear-length auburn hair that always seemed a touch unruly. Her hazel eyes were endless in their own way, as though she'd lived many times and loved deeply in each and every one of those lives. She'd certainly always loved us.

Finally free of the chocolate-smeared apron, Mom held her arms out, inviting me to her. I fell into her round, fleshy body and breathed in her rich scent: cookie dough, fresh bread, and coffee. "You know what I mean," she said, drawing back and rubbing my arms like she was trying to warm me on a cold day. "More tired than usual."

"Yeah, I know," I replied, tilting my head. "I'm fine. Just the whole grown-up thing. Why didn't anyone tell us as kids how exhausting it is being an adult?"

"Ha!" she blurted, her cheeks reddening for a moment. "We *did* tell you!"

I shook my head at her as we passed through to the main area of the house, an open-plan kitchen and dining area that had been renovated about three years earlier.

The rest of Mom's place, sagging, sighing, and a little sad, didn't at all match this central zone with its gleaming stainless steel, sleek cabinets, and recessed lighting. She'd wanted to create a warm, inviting space for family events, she'd said. I suspected the expensive remodel may have been a sign of anxiety about her girls growing up—a reflection of her concerns that we wouldn't visit often enough. No doubt when Hope reached her twenties, assuming nothing went wrong before, I'd feel the same way.

I plunked unceremoniously onto a stool by the breakfast bar, my tasseled vegan leather bag sprawling like a starfish on the bench in front of me. Being the mind reader she was, Mom presented me with a mug of berry-infused tea, already at the perfect temperature for drinking. After a few quiet sips, I looked up her, an indication I was settled and ready to catch up.

"Any interesting projects coming from Gina?"

I squinted as I contemplated the definition of the word *interesting*. None of the houses I'd photographed over the last couple of weeks had been especially unique, though one of the clients had certainly surprised me.

"I know that face," Mom asserted. "Something's happened." She'd been standing, erect, at the opposite side of the bench, whisking a delicious sugar-scented concoction in a bowl. Now, however, she set aside the mixture, planted her elbows on the countertop, and cradled her chin with her palms. Her hunched body and inward slanting eyebrows made it clear her words had been a question, a question for which she'd insist upon an answer.

"Sort of," I replied, my words drawn out and reluctant. "It might. I'm not sure."

"Who is she?" Mom asked, not missing a beat. "You met her through work? One of Gina's clients?

I shifted on my stool and stared at the gentle curl of steam rising from the mug. "Not quite. She pulled me over the other day." I looked up; my mother's eyes narrowed, and she tilted her head, which still rested atop her clasped hands. "She's a cop. I got a ticket."

Mom stood to her full height and tapped her short, well-kept fingernails against the sand-colored countertop. They clacked against the granite, insisting I elaborate. I drew in a slow, prefatory breath before recounting my interactions with Soledad. Everything from the initial conversation on the side of the road, the dreadful blind date a few hours later, her ploy to run into me again at her mother's house, and finally, the baseball game. A game I remembered little of, thanks to the steady flow of tension that had trickled into my stomach from that first accidental brush of her arm.

When I finally stopped talking, my tea had gone cold, but I drank the floral concoction anyway. It was all I could do to escape my mother's knowing grin. She'd fussed about the kitchen while I'd been speaking, preparing lunch and dessert, and giving me some space, but now that I'd come to the end of the story, she had stilled, her eyes spearing me with their hopeful yet teasing sincerity.

"Sounds promising," she said at last.

I set my mug on the counter and wiped at the side of my

mouth though nothing was there. "Hmmm," I replied, non-committal.

"Does she know you've stood outside her police department with protest signs?"

"I blurted out all this stuff, Mom, about how I feel about the police, but I didn't really give her a chance to respond properly. I feel like such a jerk. I try to be the best ally I can, to be conscious of my own privilege and not judge, and then I act like *that*." Sighing, I shook my head. "Looking back, I don't think she wanted to respond, though. We'll talk about it properly soon, I think."

Mom murmured her own noncommittal "hmmm." Clasping her hands together, she said, "Yes. I think you should. And maybe you should explain how it is you became so passionate about Black Lives Matter? She'd be able to see already that it's about morals—as it should be for everyone—but it might help to tell her about what happened. To tell her about Jason."

"Yeah," I said softly. We would need to go there, at some point, if Soledad and I were going to reconcile the differences I'd so clearly asserted at that restaurant. But it was never easy talking about things that are so awful, so confronting.

"It's good," Mom said.

"What do you mean?"

"That you've been out with someone. I've had to watch you quietly withdraw from your life for ages, Des."

"Oh no, don't you start too. Clara has already lectured me." I tucked a strand of hair behind my ear, avoiding eye contact.

"Smart girl, our Clara. She's not wrong. After Rose

walked out, you found your own emotional hiding space and you've stayed there far too long."

"I don't need to have a girlfriend to be happy, Mom. Things are fine exactly the way they are. I look after myself, I look after Hope, and things work. Besides, it's not like I've totally cut myself off from a new friendship. I asked Soledad to the game, didn't I?"

Mom shot me a look that said she wasn't convinced that was enough evidence to prove my point.

As though her sister-telepathy had been set to Rescue Mode, Brenna called out from the entryway. "I'm here, Mom!" She almost fell through the open doorway into the kitchen, weighed down by canvas shopping bags that seemed to hang off every limb. Brenna cringed as she plunked one of them on the counter, only to be met by the sharp tell-tale crack of splitting glass. "Blast," she said, her face red with the effort of easing the remaining bags down more gently. By the time I'd slipped off my stool to help her, she'd already unloaded all she'd been carrying.

"Geez, Bren," I said, lifting one of the bags from the floor and repositioning it on the counter so the contents could be packed away. "Did you buy the whole damned grocery store?"

"I knew Mom would cook everything she had in the house even though it's only the three of us, so I figured I'd better replace some of it."

I gave my baby sister's shoulder a gentle squeeze before hugging her. She'd always been a thoughtful soul, our Brenna. Clara's strongest traits included her honesty, her integrity, and an uncanny ability to turn almost anything a person said into inappropriate innuendo. Clara was strong, and intelligent, and generally incredible, but she wasn't much of a people person. Brenna, on the other hand, personified sweetness. Rarely did she do anything not fueled by a sincere desire to help another person. The small joy to come from another's genuine warmth, moments of kindness; these things energized and motivated Brenna. The only problem, however, was that she gave so much of herself to other people that sometimes she'd get in her own way. She'd wave away opportunities, anything from a job prospect to a romantic connection, if she thought a friend of hers might lose out because she'd stepped in their way.

When we disengaged from our hug, Brenna and I took up our usual positions at the breakfast bar, she on the left and me on the right. Mom blew Brenna an air kiss then turned away to wash her hands. We spent a few minutes exchanging the usual updates. How was work? Anything exciting to report? How did we all cope with that heat wave last week? Inevitably, the topic returned to Soledad.

"She is stunning, Des. And I don't just mean that gorgeous face of hers!" Brenna cooed. "Mom. You have *got* to meet this woman. Even Hope liked her. And it took me at least a month to get Hope on my side."

"Hope!" Mom exclaimed, as though she'd had a revelation. "Geez, I didn't even ask you how she's doing. What a terrible foster grandma! How's things with her?"

I stretched the side of my neck before replying. "She's..." I wanted to explain the strange vibe I'd been getting from my foster daughter lately, but it was hard to articulate that sort of intangible, instinctual sense that something was wrong. "She's okay in a lot of ways. I mean, we get on well at home most of the time. There's even banter on occasion."

"Oh, I love banter," Mom said

"We know." Brenna and I laughed at our unified response.

The oven buzzed, and Mom held one finger up in a hold-that-thought gesture. The savory aroma of baked vegetables and freshly made bread wafted into the room as she exposed the food she'd put into the oven when I first arrived. Until that delicious scent reached my nostrils, I hadn't realized how hungry I'd become.

"Yum!" Brenna said.

"Let it cool for a minute." Mom set the tray down on the stove top. "Now," she announced. "Back to Hope. It felt like there was more to say."

"You already know what happened with that party she went to." I rubbed at the space between my eyes as a pang of frustration asserted itself at the memory of our drive home from the station. "But it's obvious something is bothering her. Something with her friends, maybe. I thought she'd settled into the school now, but who knows? Could be friendship stuff. Could be family stuff. I have no idea."

"She won't tell you anything," Brenna added in a half-questioning tone. My face gave her the answer. "What did you do about the situation with the arrest and all? I haven't had a chance to talk to you properly since then."

I swiveled on the stool. "Not a lot, I guess. I asked her to be safe in the future and, naturally, she's grounded."

"Grounded?" Mom's jaw hung loose in disbelief. "That's all?"

"Mom," Brenna said, a hint of pleading in her voice. "Don't push."

Mom started to dish up the food.

I knew what was coming. I could have scripted the whole speech myself. "I know I always tell you to pick your battles, but she needs boundaries, Desi. She's a great kid, we all know that, but even the best of teens needs strict lines they know not to cross. Why not take her phone away? Or change the Wi-Fi password? Make it harder for her to make plans like that, plans that put her in harm's way."

I sighed. I agreed with everything she'd said, of course. But she knew why I didn't do any of those things, and the fact I had to remind her anyway made the tips of my ears burn red. "Because I'm not going to push her away!" I snapped.

Brenna gave my shoulder a gentle, reassuring pat. "She isn't Brody," she said in a soft voice. "Things won't turn out like that. Not this time."

I hanged my head and pressed my fingers against my temples. The pressure brought a small measure of alleviation.

"I know," I admitted. "They're different people. Different personalities. But both Brody and Hope went through way too many homes growing up. Both have mothers that play their emotions and loyalties like yo-yos. I want her to trust me. To come to me if she needs help. I'm not going to scare her off. Not like I did with him."

Mom, plates in hand, faced us once more, her features awash with understanding. The slack skin around her eyes and mouth relaxed as she looked at me. After setting the food down, she reached across the bench and took hold of my hands, bringing them to her lips and kissing them like she had when I was a child. "I know," she said. "I'm sorry.

It's hard to strike a balance between providing boundaries and being too harsh. I get that. You love her, and you don't want to lose her. We all understand."

I blinked away a few tears. I didn't know what affected me more. Mom giving voice to the notion that, like any foster child, I could lose Hope to the system one day, therefore making the situation all the more real, or Mom's empathy, which soothed me like a weighted blanket. "Thanks," I said.

"You've got such a big heart, my girl," Mom said. "Not a lot of people could do what you do."

I smiled mirthlessly. "Screw up, you mean? Over and over. My foster kids. My girlfriends. I'm not very good at holding on to any of them, it seems."

"Hey," Brenna said hopefully. "Things can change. I *know* it's different with Hope. And maybe this super fit cop will be different, too. She seems way more understanding than Rose was."

I huffed, dismissing Brenna's words for the most part. Rose, someone I'd been with for three years, had left me, and I hadn't dated anyone—not properly—in the time since. Heck, I hadn't even managed to build any new friendships.

Deep down, though, a small piece of me wanted to nurture some kind of hope that Brenna was right, that her optimism was prophecy, rather than naivety. "Maybe," I conceded.

"No maybes about it." Mom removed her oven mitts and smacked them, somewhat dramatically, onto the counter. "Your sister's right. Now, let's eat. And you can tell me about this second date you and Soledad have planned."

CHAPTER THIRTEEN

I CAST MY attention about the room for what felt like the fiftieth time, my eyes narrowed and my teeth clenched. There had to be some piece of evidence I'd missed, a clue that stubbornly refused to reveal itself. Who the hell broke in and stole all that cash? I had to know.

"You're taking this more seriously than most of the cops I work with," Soledad teased, her analytical gaze passing over me.

"Listen, Officer," I quipped. "You can't just take me to an escape room, lock me inside for sixty minutes, and not expect that I'll apply myself to the task of solving this rather insidious crime."

Soledad blinked at me, her penny-colored eyes eerily reflective in the dimly lit space. "Insidious?" She flopped into a creaky rocking chair perched in the corner of the room, then held up the clipboard our host had given us before we started the game. "Our main suspects include Mrs. Jenkins, an elderly lady who makes porcelain cups; George, the chauffeur; and a six-year-old who may or may not be a mathematical genius."

I angled my head, a challenge to her *you-must-be-kidding-me* expression. "Come on." I waved at the lunar calendar painted on the wall. "I'm not too bad at puzzles and riddles, and I can't work out what Mary-Sue is trying to tell us with this calendar. Obviously there's a pattern that'll give us the code to unlock this stupid box." I gently kicked at the wooden chest by my feet. "But I don't know how to solve it. Clearly, this child is a prodigy. And quite frankly, Officer Soledad Reyes, given we're only on the second puzzle and we've lost twenty minutes, I don't think you're taking your duties seriously enough."

She stood with a decisive air. Her features were stern, but playfully so. Though we weren't physically touching, she was near enough that the heat from her skin gave me goose bumps. Discomfort and excitement churned in my stomach as she looked at me with searching eyes. I couldn't hold eye contact and my attention fell to her lips. I imagined dropping my head, drawing her in, and kissing her. I wanted to experience the firmness of her embrace, feel the softness of the skin of her neck, and discover the taste of her mouth.

But I didn't.

Instead, frozen by my own doubts—hamstrung by my whole personality, really—I exhaled loudly, my head turned toward the wall. She pressed against me, reaching beyond my body. When she drew back, she presented an antiquated key on a copper hoop, dangling from her index finger. "I'm taking my duties seriously," she said. "But I think we have different mission statements in mind."

I swallowed, which was difficult given the boulder lodged in my esophagus. "Oh?" I said after a silence that was long enough to feel clumsy.

"Yes," she replied, slipping the key into my palm, her fingertips gently caressing the inside of my wrist. My eyes closed involuntarily as her touch sent shivers through my torso. My spine seemed to lurch as though I were aboard a ship that had crested a wave before dropping again. "Watching you is far more fun that solving the puzzles. I mean, how long might it be before I get you alone in a dark room again?"

I couldn't believe this was happening. How did I end up in this place, at this time, with this incredible woman? My life was settled, overall. I worked for a fiery real estate agent, spent time with my sisters, did my best to give Hope a safe and supportive home, and I worked through episodes of pain while I waited for my surgery. It had been a long time since I'd even considered a new relationship, let alone taken steps toward connecting with a specific person.

It didn't feel like I deserved this much attention from someone so extraordinary.

Soledad was confident, intelligent, funny, and every time she touched me, however briefly, my knees threatened to give way. I could have been a cliched heroine in a romantic comedy with how enamored I'd become. I'd never wanted a woman so badly after so little time together, and I didn't trust myself enough to give in to the fantasies fizzing away in my mind. Surely I'd screw up, somehow. Say the wrong thing. Or do the wrong thing.

There was always the possibility that I wouldn't be able to juggle my commitments to Hope, to work, to my sisters, and then manage to add someone new to the equation. Imagining what I might look like through Soledad's eyes, I had started to understand that this was why Rose had left. She hadn't wanted to share me with the foster care system anymore. I guess she didn't think I had enough love and energy to go around. Maybe she was right.

I also still had to consider the fact I struggled to picture myself with a police officer in the current social climate. What was Soledad's life like? How much danger did she face every day, and could I even cope with the constant worry that comes with being the partner of a police officer? Would she ever misread a situation like some of her colleagues and end up on the six o'clock news because she'd fired at an innocent teenager? Would she help cover for a colleague? So many of them seemed to close ranks after a tragedy. The possibilities were as endless as they were terrifying.

"Oh, and by the way," Soledad said as she reclaimed the key in my hand. The delicious silkiness of her voice brought my unruly thoughts to an abrupt halt. My anxieties fell into a frazzled heap, overshadowed and surpassed by her easy nature. No. This wasn't a woman who fired first and asked questions later. She couldn't be. "Soledad is fine, but it's okay to call me Sole. If you want to."

I knew we'd crossed an invisible line from flirty acquaintances to something more—a development I felt equally happy and horrified by. Was I ready for anything to happen with Soledad? With someone who felt so far above me? But not only that, someone who was so connected to an institution that, time and time again, perpetrated race-driven violence and provoked fear in many communities?

There's no way I'm attractive enough or interesting enough for this woman. And there's no way I can ever understand how she can be a cop, a cop in Sacramento of all places. What am I doing here?

"So," I said. Not a subtle or effective attempt to carve through the tension fluttering between us. "I missed a key right in front of me, apparently. Where does it go?"

She screwed up her face in a childlike expression of confusion. A positively adorable expression, I might add. She had so many of those. "That part I'm not sure of," she admitted. I sent my gaze to the floor, her unwavering attention too hot for me to handle much longer.

Something caught my eye. We both stood on a round mat and, around the edges of that mat, there was a thin strip of clean floor contrasting a light layer of dust splashed across the rest of the room.

I squatted and peeled the edge of the mat from the floor. I flipped the fabric over and found a tic-tac-toe-style design fixed on the reverse with masking tape. There were numbers inside some of the squares.

"Nice work!" Soledad gave my shoulder a light squeeze as she knelt next to me.

"Looks like we can use that to decode the kid's lunar calendar!" I made to pass her the mat, but something else grabbed her attention.

"Hey, check that out." She pointed at a lock embedded in an envelope-sized hatch on the floor. "And that's where the key goes."

Stating the obvious was way more fun in an escape room than out there in the real world. I slid the key into the lock and retrieved a small, faux-leather pouch from a tiny crevice while Soledad examined the clues painted on the far wall. I moved close enough not to crowd her but to watch as she thought her way through the patterns in front of her. Two thin lines formed between her eyebrows when she was concentrating, and she cupped her own chin whenever she got close to piecing something together. I loved watching her. I couldn't keep pretending I didn't.

"I've got it," she announced, triumphant.

"Seven... Nine... Three... One." Sole silently mouthed each number as she worked the combination lock on the wooden chest. The *click* that came when the latch released was surprisingly satisfying. Inside the chest we found a modest collection of casino chips and a faded photograph. More clues to decipher.

"What's inside?" Soledad asked, indicating the pouch I'd set between my feet.

I passed the bag to her, and she drew a slip of folded cardboard from within. On the card we found an image of a clock with thirteen hours, the minute hand pointing at the six and the hour hand pointing at the two.

I sighed ruefully. "Sole, do you make all your dates work this hard? My brain hurts."

Before I'd registered what was happening, her lips were pressed against mine, the sweet yet subtle taste of vanilla gloss clouding my mind and drawing me into a storm of formless, hazy sensations. My thoughts lost all shape and meaning. I couldn't form words inside my head to properly react.

Sole's fingers curled over the back of my neck, gently guiding me closer, deepening the kiss as she gradually parted her lips, teasing the tip of my tongue with her own. After a few moments—or, at least, I thought it was a few moments, I couldn't tell—she gave my lower lip a soft, chaste kiss and opened up a small gap between us. My head whirled like it did as an elevator comes to a stop, dipping for a second before settling into place.

"Does your brain still hurt?" she asked, guiding my hands into her own. It took me a second to remember what I'd said before she kissed me and, when I did, I shook my head. Once again, Sole had left me speechless. "That's a relief."

I glanced at the digital timer above the door, glaring red numbers that announced we only had thirty minutes left. When Soledad had asked me to meet her here, I'd been less than thrilled about the prospect of an "adventure date." But I had to admit, this was fun. Each discovery we made, each riddle we unraveled, sent a wave of adrenaline and excitement coursing through me. I hadn't enjoyed myself this much in a long time. The kiss was a bonus. A delicious, intoxicating bonus that would keep me awake. But I wondered whether this was a good time to bring someone new into my life, given Hope was going through something at the moment. Something hard. I swallowed, tamping down my concerns, knowing I'd need to face them more directly soon enough.

"Should we, umm, try to work out this thing with the thirteen-hour clock?" I asked.

Sole drew a circle on my hand with her thumb. "Probably," she replied. "But can I check, is it all right that I did that? That I kissed you?" That moment of wavering confidence surprised me, but it was good to know I wasn't the only one who questioned the way things were panning out.

By way of reply, I entwined my fingers with hers, letting our arms hang between us as I touched my forehead to Soledad's. "*All right* might be an understatement," I said, my words softer than I'd intended. "I might be becoming a tiny bit addicted to you."

"Careful," she purred. "I'll start to think this could go somewhere."

I sighed. Not because what she'd said had been wrong, but because so much about her had started to feel so incredibly right. And that scared the heck out of me.

CHAPTER FOURTEEN

IT WAS STILL light outside when I arrived home, though it felt as though hours had passed since I'd walked out the door sometime around three o'clock. The escape room had a firm sixty-minute time limit, and I'd avoided making any plans for dinner with Soledad in case things hadn't gone well. Or, maybe, in case they had. Either way it had been a good idea not to commit to an afternoon with her that turned into an evening. There was no telling where that could go, and I needed some time to let a few things churning in my mind marinate. To adjust to the new flavor of my days. To adjust to the reality of Soledad.

I tossed my keys into the basket on the hall stand, kicked off my sneakers without untying the laces—I liked to live a little dangerously every now and then—and sifted through the mail as I meandered into the kitchen.

"Bill," I mouthed silently to myself. "Another bill." I tossed the pile aside and jammed my hands into the front pockets of my cargo pants. I had no idea what to do with myself. Gina needed that new crop of photographs edited by tomorrow afternoon, but I'd already done about three-quarters of the job and wasn't particularly in the mood for another couple of hours hunched in front of my computer. That could wait until tomorrow morning, or at least until after dinner.

I made a few calls and, after about fifteen minutes, found a plumber who could come to check our water heater within the next forty-eight hours. Apparently, miracles did happen.

After that, I headed out to our modest backyard and steeled myself for the onslaught. Within moments, Ginger Snaps bounded toward me, launched off the ground, and threw her whole weight into my body. I laughed as I slipped into a half-crouched position and caught her. The Labrador showered sticky kisses across my neck and cheek as I eased her back to the earth.

With my puppy's feet on the ground where they belonged, I rubbed vigorously at her ears and neck. "There's my girl!" I laughed again as she nudged at my chin with her nose, then fixed me with another sloppy dog kiss. When I reached for the leash hanging off the back door, she reared up in a gesture of canine approval. "Yes, yes," I assured her. "Walk time."

As excitable as she was in the yard, Ginger Snaps was well behaved on the leash. The poor thing didn't get walked often enough, and as we strolled past the unpretentious, boxy homes along my street, I committed myself to taking her at least once a day. Even if it was only a short walk.

My mind wandered along with my feet. I replayed several key moments from this afternoon. Not least of all that kiss. And geez, what a kiss! I'd never been as cynical about love as Clara became after that whole situation with Austin, but I'd never been quite the romantic Brenna is either. Though I wasn't the middle sister, I seemed to have become a symbol for the middle ground in our sisterly trio. And so, given my usually slow and sensible approach to relationships, the fact I was already picturing Soledad as a permanent fixture in my life made me uneasy.

"What a gorgeous dog!" A cheerful, round-faced man with an equally cheerful rainbow T-shirt knelt to Ginger Snaps' height. His copper skin wrinkled and his hazel eyes softened as he gazed at the pup. "Can I pet her?"

I always appreciated people who were sensible enough to ask before lathering hugs and kisses on a dog they didn't know—and that didn't know them. "Sure," I replied. "She's super gentle."

Being the star she was, Gingey, as I called her sometimes when Gina's son wasn't around, indulged the stranger's apparent need for furry-friend attention. My thoughts turned to Daxton, who'd come up with the pup's name.

At four years old, Gina's son was an endearing ball of sweetness with a tiny splash of age-appropriate sass. His father, Elliot, had seemed like a generally great human being when Gina had fallen in love with him. Elliot was one of the only men to make Gina laugh. Like, *really* laugh. Gina had been so hurt when Elliot walked away with barely any notice, leaving her and their infant son behind. Gina may have a spine of steel, but even steel buckles under enough force. For a short time, she'd had a full glass and an empty heart.

Why did people start relationships with enthusiasm, consideration, and love, only to end them with everything but those things? If someone had fallen out of love, or become unhappy, why couldn't they be open? Sure, telling Gina that he'd never wanted to be a dad would have been indescribably hard for Elliot, but I didn't see how owning up to a string of meaningless one-night stands was much better—one of the first things he'd said when he asked for a divorce.

Screw *that*. I would not fall in love with someone like our dad, Elliot, or Austin. Nor would Brenna. And Clara sure as heck deserved a fresh start. All three of us were good people, and we could find good people to be with. *Right?*

Clara had already met Evie, and things there seemed to be going well. And I...well, I'd met Soledad. Quick-witted, assertive, magnificent Soledad. Those things couldn't all be an act.

"Sorry, did you hear me?" The middle-aged man's voice sounded concerned.

"Oh," I said, waving away a nonexistent fly. It went some way to dismiss the fog becoming a permanent fixture in my brain lately. "Excuse me. I tuned out. What did you say?"

"I asked her name." He scratched at that sweet spot behind Gingey's ears, and her tongue lolled out of the side of her mouth. She was in doggy-heaven.

"Ginger Snaps."

He looked at me, a questioning grin pulling at one

corner of his thin mouth.

"Yeah," I conceded. "It's odd for a puppy. But who am I to argue with a preschooler?"

"It's sweet," he said. "Literally."

As I peered down at this total stranger practically salivating over my dog, I realized something.

Mixed in with the constant concern and worry that came with being a parent—a worry that had taken up residence like a paradoxical anchor the moment I became responsible for another human being—I felt happier than I had in a long time. I'd been living my life, of course, but I'd been doing so from behind a thin veil that kept me insulated from feeling anything beyond the superficial. A veil I sensed melting away. And there was no doubt that Soledad Reyes and her delightful kisses were a significant part of the reason. What worried me though, was what exactly might exist on the other side of that veil. Relationships could go so wrong. But they could also be beautifully *right*.

I groaned as I registered an all-too-familiar sensation. Having the implant in my uterus meant it didn't happen anywhere near as often as it used to, but hadn't fully stopped the unpleasant and disproportionate gushes of menstrual blood that hit me from time to time. In the past, I'd be lucky to get through two hours without having to swap out both a tampon and a heavy-flow pad, so I swallowed my embarrassment and reminded myself things could be worse. I had black pants on, I wasn't at work, and I could easily access a change of clothes. *Bring on that surgery, Doc.*

I rubbed at Gingey's ear, accepting my introspective moment of peace and quiet was over for the day. "Sorry, pup, time to go home."

Chapter Fifteen

FOR THE NEXT week or so, Soledad and I exchanged text messages that I could only describe as desperately flirty. I'd been eager to see her, but she'd been putting in a lot of hours at work, and I had taken on extra freelance jobs for Gina to distract myself from the unfamiliar yearning bubbling within. Was this how I'd felt with Rose? Distracted and excited and hopelessly mirthful? Constantly checking my phone in case she had been in touch in the twelve seconds since I'd last looked? It had been so long since Rose I couldn't remember anymore.

As the suggestive double entendres gave way to more meaningful discussion, Sole sent me updates about the interesting characters who'd come to inspect her mother's house, and I told her about the ongoing argument I'd been having with the clarity and lines of some particularly troublesome photographs from my last shoot. No one would have even noticed the imperfections, but I could be a stickler and I didn't want the pictures published until I'd gotten it right. Her stories were more exciting than mine, but she entertained my rambling description of software settings regardless.

From there, we opened up pretty quickly. She asked me how many foster children I'd looked after, and I explained that, in total, eleven had passed through my house, but most of the children had only stayed for a few days on their way to a more suitable long-term situation. I mentioned Brody, but even via text message she seemed to sense my conflicted feelings about him, and she didn't press for any more information than the basics I'd provided: he'd lived with me for eighteen months. Charming, affectionate, and articulate at first, but things had ended badly.

Sole told me she'd been a cop for eleven years and had no intention of trying to become a detective anytime soon. She loved her beat too much. She knew the people. She'd earned the trust of a lot of folks who'd never trusted a cop before in their lives, and no career opportunity was worth giving up those relationships. If I hadn't liked her before she told me that, there was no hiding my admiration after. I still hadn't asked her exactly why she'd become a police officer, or whether she'd been involved with any situations related to police brutality, or known others who had been, but we were inching our way closer to acknowledging that elephant in the room.

I'd finally finished the batch of pictures from the Huynh house when my phone buzzed. Grinning, I opened messenger.

Dinner?

I bit my lower lip, glad to receive even one word. A word that held a great deal of possibility.

I can't, I replied. *I'm having an early dinner with Hope before she heads to the movies. But I could meet up for a drink later on, if you like?*

You're on. My place. Whenever you're ready.

She sent her address, and I could barely read it I was so excited. Dinner with Hope was already something nice to look forward to, but now my night had reached a whole new level of excellent. My fingertips tingled as I clipped my phone onto the charger plugged into the computer. I ran my hands through my short hair, trying to snap into reality and wipe the no-doubt idiotic expression off my face before making the shift into parent mode.

"Hope, are you awake?" My voice traveled along the short corridor of our home to be met only by silence. Like a lot of teenagers, she often slept for a while after school before staying up way later into the night than I had the stamina for. "Hope?" I repeated, drawing the vowel out.

"Yeah?" Her response was unenthusiastic to say the least, and from even that one word, I could tell that she hadn't had a good day at school.

"Ready for some dinner?" I took a few steps and tapped lightly at her door. "It's homemade pizza." I smirked as shuffling sounded from the other side of the door. Couldn't go wrong with pizza. I made my way to the kitchen and started to serve dinner. A thick doughy scent filled the air, punctuated by the rich sweetness of tomato sauce.

Hope flattened her palms against the countertop and

speared me with an incredulous look. "It's vegetarian, isn't it?" She eyed the cheese and spinach toppings like they were dubiously old leftovers, rather than the fresh, delicious ingredients they were.

"Come on, pizza with fewer toppings is the best way to eat it."

She smacked her lips and responded with a satiric "uh-huh."

"Okay, okay." I released the door of the oven once more, withdrawing a second pizza packed to the edges with ham, pepperoni, and red pepper. "Better?"

The wrinkles in her forehead smoothed, and she nodded approvingly, though her tone remained the same. "Much."

"Good!" I sliced the food, tossed a couple of slices on each of our plates, then carried them to the small, square dining table nearby. Without prompting, Hope retrieved two glasses from the cupboard and filled mine with sparkling water and hers with Diet Coke. For a few minutes, we ate in silence, her thoughts apparently buried somewhere deep in her lap because she barely looked up even to lift and set down her glass of soda.

"How was school today?" I asked, immediately regretting the question. Could I be anymore cliché? Parent of the year, right here.

"Fine," she said in a noncommittal tone before dropping a sliver of crust onto her plate.

And that was why you never asked a teenager a close-ended question if you wanted to start a conversation.

"Did you find that trigonometry stuff made any more sense today?"

She planted her elbows on the edge of the table and, with a sense of hesitation, gave a one-shouldered shrug. "Kinda."

"Hope...is there something else? Something that's pulling you a million miles away?"

Hope's chair squeaked as she stood, moving to collect another piece of pizza. The only reply she gave was to return to her seat, take a bite, and chew sluggishly.

I rubbed the bridge of my nose, resigned to remain locked out. I'd had enough to eat, so I took my plate over to the dishwasher, stopping for a moment to give her upper arm a gentle pat. "If you change your mind...if you want to talk to me, I'll be waiting."

Her blue eyes, often bright and startling, seemed almost colorless as she turned to meet my gaze. "Thanks," she replied. "But I'm okay. Nothing you can do anyway."

"Are you sure? Did you want me to stay home tonight? I was going to go—"

"No, no. Go see Soledad. She's nice. I won't be home anyway. Ava and I are going to see that new movie."

I wanted her to be a kid and spend time with her friends now her two weeks of being grounded had come to an end. It also meant I could go and have that drink with Soledad. But I also wanted her to ask me to stay, for both of us to cancel our plans so she could tell me everything on her mind and I could find some way to mitigate the swirling storm so clearly building momentum inside her. I didn't say any of that though. I sipped the remainder of my water, packed the glass away, and waited until she'd finished eating to say, "Have a great time. Say hi to Ava for me."

"Sure," she replied absently, heading toward the front

door. "See ya." As her hand reached for the knob, she stopped suddenly, turned. "Hey, Desi?"

I stepped into the entryway. "Mmhmm?"

"Your grandma, you said she was a civil rights activist, didn't you?"

Good old Grams. She was always on an adventure, and Hope still hadn't met her, but we'd of course mentioned her a few times. I wondered why she had chosen the moment she was about to leave to start this conversation, but perhaps something about having an escape route had made her feel comfortable enough to probe into the family history. She tended to shy away from asking personal questions, as though she wasn't always sure if she had a right to. I took it as another sign Hope was beginning to feel like she belonged with us. At least, that's what I wanted it to mean.

"That's right. She tried her best to be a white ally, anyway. She got started at Mel's Drive-in."

Hope cocked her head, her brow crinkling.

"There were a bunch of places in San Francisco, and the whole Bay area, that had ridiculously unfair hiring practices," I explained, dropping my shoulder to lean against the wall. "CORE was this incredible African American civil rights organization that worked with a group of people to protest at some of those places. Grams happened to work at one of them, Mel's Drive-in. They picketed together, this amazing group, pushing those companies to hire Black people, and to give those they did hire better opportunities to access training, so they weren't stuck at the lower levels of the organization forever. Grams was arrested, along with about a hundred other people, but she said that it was nothing compared to what her Black coworkers went through.

What they faced for standing up against the oppression they were subjected to. She took risks, but she always said they were nothing compared to the risks for Black friends had to take.

"In the end, most of those companies changed some of their rules, and stopped hiding all the Black workers in the back, which meant there was more career mobility. Not *nearly* as much as there should have been, but it was still a small victory. Something important."

Hope's eyes widened. "Wow. It sounds like all of them were pretty brave."

"Yeah," I said, pride welling within me, as it always did when I thought about my grandmother. "Grams was about twenty at the time. You know, I saw a picture of her in that picket line in a textbook at school once. She always tells us that she couldn't stand by and watch it happen anymore. She knew she could never understand what it means to be Black, but she definitely understood what it meant to be human. To be a friend. She didn't want them to feel alone, to feel unsupported in the burdens they were forced to carry.

"Grams says the people who marched in front of her, the people who'd been so badly treated by those employers, were the most inspiring individuals she'd ever met. She said everyone may remember names like King and Lewis and Parks, but, while those leaders were incredible, it was the ordinary people who risked their entire livelihood for local victories like the one at Mel's that moved her the most." I shook my head, unable to even imagine how difficult it must have been, but also how rich and deep the human spirit truly is to make such a strong stand against injustice. To stand up when hundreds of years of history and oppression kept trying to force you down.

"But, why do you ask? Something you're learning in school?"

"No real reason." She shifted her weight and adjusted the strap of her backpack. "Must be good to know your family were part of something like that. To look up to them."

Oh. This was about family history, not American history—about connection and family stories and life lessons passed on from one generation to another. A connection that must have been obviously and painfully missing from Hope's experience.

I moved slowly so she had the chance to stop me if she wanted, hugged her to me. "Your family made you. That's something we can all look up to. That's something good. You stay hopeful, and you *can* be happy." With her cheek pressed against my bicep, she nodded, then stepped away but didn't look at me. "See ya later." She slipped outside and, like she were laying down a sleeping child, closed the door with an unnecessary gentleness.

After she'd left, the house, small though it was, seemed thick with emptiness, the silence practically alive. I tousled my hair and stood there for a few moments, half expecting Hope might walk back through the door. But she didn't.

Hope wanted space, to be with her friends. There was no point sitting around here waiting if I couldn't be of any use. Not when I could see Sole.

CHAPTER SIXTEEN

SOLEDAD LIVED IN a secure brownstone apartment building about fifteen minutes' drive from my place. Despite the dark exterior and shuttered windows, the interior, with its spacious split-level lobby and elaborate, sprawling artworks, welcomed me the moment I stepped inside.

The unexpected, light-filled space would have been wonderful to photograph. Vaulted, timber ceilings and inviting armchairs completed the look and, somehow, even on that ground floor, this felt like the only place someone like Sole could have lived. As had been the case with Sole herself, the building's true nature bewildered me.

I made my way to the third floor where the decor was simpler but still cared for, the carpeted floors and pastel walls cleaner than you'd see in most places, the scent of fresh cut flowers drifting gently through the air. Whoever managed this building didn't only take pride in maintenance, they cared about the structure. Perhaps the property had been handed down through generations and represented more than only a multitude of rental incomes. Did such places still exist? I liked to think so.

I rounded the corner leading to Soledad's apartment, a surreal sense of anticipation grinding in my chest like the inner workings of a clock. I'd never been to her place before. She'd never been to mine, either.

In fact, I hadn't even seen her since our kiss in the escape room, and there was still so much we didn't know about each other, things I still worried made us incompatible, despite the insistent yearning that fermented within. Perhaps it was too soon to have such an intimate date. I should have suggested that we meet somewhere else, somewhere more public.

There it was: 3E. The door opened as I lifted my hand, preempting a ring of the bell and sucking the air right out of me. I wanted to laugh at my over-reaction to something so simple, but her easy charisma—thankfully—threw a blanket over the thought.

Soledad wore a pair of dark-blue jeans and a black tank top that showed off the definition of her arms. Her feet were bare, and her long, dark hair had been tied into a slick ponytail, neat and high. A hint of mascara emphasized her eyelashes but, otherwise, she wore little makeup.

I was glad I had decided on jeans and a button-up red blouse with a pair of ballet flats. If I'd dressed up, I would've looked ridiculous in contrast to her smart, casual approach to the evening.

"You found me," she said, gesturing her invitation to enter, the double meaning of her words obvious from the gentle smirk tugging at one side of her lips.

"Some things are hard to miss." I wriggled off my cardigan, and before I could ask where to set it, Soledad relieved me of my bag, the bottle of wine I'd brought, and the cardigan.

With her hands full, Soledad pressed her cheek against mine, turned her head slightly to graze the side of my face with her lips before withdrawing. Though nothing more than a friendly greeting, the kiss sent those clockworks in my chest ticking over yet again. "Thanks for inviting me over," I said as confidently as I could manage.

"Of course." After hanging my handbag and cardigan, she led the way to a modest kitchen that opened onto an eating area about the same size as the one at my house, though more rectangular in shape rather than square. Setting down the wine, she added, "I'm sorry it took so long for me to ask. I would've liked to see you sooner." She moved with a natural elegance that made it difficult to tear my eyes away. "At least cell phones make it easy to communicate in other ways."

"Don't be sorry. I'm glad you invited me over; it doesn't matter when. This whole being-an-adult thing, right? Your job is demanding. Family is important. Everyone gets busy."

"Very true," she sighed, her thoughts seeming to drift with her gaze for a few moments. I wondered how much she had to cope with every day in her job. Drug-drenched teenage raves were, no doubt, only the tip of the iceberg. Had she ever been hurt on duty? Had she been forced to hurt others? A night off for her probably came with a lot more emotional and physical baggage than it did for the rest of the population.

Sole indicated the modish glass dining table with her chin and, grateful for a distraction from my far-too-serious thoughts, I moved in that direction. "Make yourself comfortable. I'll pour." She tapped the screen of her phone a few times, and music played through Bluetooth speakers sitting atop the refrigerator. I didn't recognize the female singer, but her haunting voice seemed to caress the lyrics, to catch each syllable and soak the sounds in emotion.

"Who is this?" I asked.

"Her name is Amanda Ghost."

"Hmm. The name suits her, somehow."

Soledad drew two glasses from a cupboard and gave me a look I could only describe as quizzical.

"What is it?" I asked.

She shook her head gently, keeping her eyes on me. "It's just, that's what I've always thought too. She sounds like she came from some other place. Somewhere different to the rest of us."

Melting under her attention, I broke eye contact and pretended to wrangle an unruly cuticle on my finger.

As Sole arranged a platter of cheeses, crackers, and dips to complement the wine, I took an opportunity to look around the small, well-kept apartment from my seat.

On the wall to my left, a series of eight matching frames housed large photographs arranged in two neat rows. They seemed to move in chronological order. The first image, somewhat blurred, developed in sepia tones and stained by the passing of time, showed two young adults, a man and a woman dressed conservatively, his arm gently draped about her waist as she considered someone beyond the reach of the camera, a brittle smile on her face. I scanned the other images briefly, not wanting to intrude by studying the photographs too closely without invitation, until I reached the last.

The final image, crisp and high definition, featured a grown-up, albeit younger, Soledad posing with her mother, the pair holding a trophy. Sole wore all white and held a tennis racket in her free hand. Her mother appeared much the same as she did in the present, perhaps a bit taller now, as though some of life's challenges had eased since then, allowing her to expand her chest and release her shoulders.

"I was nineteen." Soledad set the cheese platter on the table, and I tracked her with my eyes as she sat adjacent to me, her knee gently brushing my own beneath the table. As she did, the music ticked over to the next song, a new artist.

"PJ Harvey?" I asked.

"Good taste," she replied, her index finger tracing the length of my jaw while I remained frozen, locked in place by the nerves firing throughout my body. She drew closer, the tip of her nose nudging my own. After a pause, she tilted her head and tentatively pressed her lips to mine. I stretched my neck, strengthening the kiss, inviting her closer. Her tongue lightly skimmed my own, and a forceful flush of heat convulsed through me, demanding more. The surge of desire, as pleasant as it was, also shocked me, and I touched my hand to her cheek, a silent request for us to slow down.

"Too much?" She moved to create a few inches of space between us, but not so far as to suggest offense on her part.

"No, no." I clasped her hands. The last thing I wanted was for her to believe I didn't want her. The problem was that I wanted her too much. And too soon. "I definitely want to do more of that." My cheeks flashed with warmth as she cocked her head suggestively. "But maybe after we talk some more?"

"That's fair," she said.

"You said you were nineteen?" I motioned toward the photograph.

"That's right."

"Is that your mother in those other pictures? She's so young. Young and beautiful...but in such a sad sort of way."

Soledad considered the pictures for a few long, silent seconds, a sadness that bore some resemblance to the woman in the picture surfacing as she did. "Yeah. My mamá stayed in Chile for as long as she could, but things became too difficult when she married my papá. And because of my uncle. She experienced a lot of trauma, stuff that she managed to protect me from."

"You don't have to tell me about this if you don't want to." I didn't want to push her into exploring family issues that may have been upsetting. I was painfully ignorant about Chile and its history, but I imagined that most people who left their homes to live elsewhere did so as a last resort. Aside from knowing Chile was a long, narrow country that ran alongside Argentina and Bolivia, with a largely Spanish-speaking population, I had limited knowledge of what may have prompted Soledad's mother and father to move to the States, to leave everything they'd ever known behind.

"Have you heard of the '73 coup?" Soledad asked.

"Ashamed to say I haven't. Though, in my own defense, I don't know a whole lot about the history of most places beyond what I learned in high school or from my family's stories. Is that terrible?"

Her lips pulled into a thin line, her eyes narrowing.

Oh crap. Had I diminished something? Been insensitive without realizing? Why was I so bad at this stuff?

"No." Her face relaxed and mine did too. She'd been teasing me. "Of course not. There are too many countries. Too many conflicts. No one can know about them all. I imagine you've not had much of a reason to look into this sort of thing."

I tightened my grip of her hand and mustered as much control as I could manage. I wanted her to see, to genuinely see, that I wanted to hear whatever she wanted to tell me. "I do now. You're my reason. Tell me about the coup."

Sole released a brief huff of laughter, her eyebrows shooting up. "Have you got ten hours?"

"That complex, huh?"

"Aren't most revolutions?"

"Good point."

She took a sip of her wine. I'd forgotten she had brought the glasses over and, following her lead, I tried the pinot grigio. My eyes almost rolled back as the delectable floral taste danced across my tongue, hints of honey and pear delivering a crisp yet light collection of flavors. The quiet lull between us was comfortable and, when Sole was ready, she started to tell me about her family's background.

"We-ell...I'll try to give you the short version." Soledad curled the fingers of one hand around the bowl of her glass and continued to tease my palm with the fingertips of the other. Her familiarity and closeness seemed so natural, as though we'd known each other much longer than we had. "To start with though, I should tell you that I know a lot about this stuff, but I didn't live through it. It's hard to explain. Like, I've seen the pain it inflicted on my relatives, and their pain caused me pain, but I've also had a degree of insulation and protection they never had. Does that make sense?"

I nodded, and she began.

"In the early '70s, Chile was under the leadership of a president named Salvadore Allende, a Marxist. He'd d been a sort of socialist Santa Clause, a visionary that gave lots of people hope. But things didn't quite work out. The country fell into disorder when he went on a campaign of rapid change.

"There were strikes, censorship, propaganda, and problematic property seizures, though less of the severe violence the world associated with other communist regimes." Soledad emphasized each change with a flourish of her hands, the frustration of what could have been versus what actually happened clear in her tone.

"But still," she continued, "the US cut diplomatic ties, supporting Allende's political enemies. Nixon wanted to force Allende to resign because they feared the creation of a socialist state that could forge an alliance with the Soviets or Cuba, but really, all he and his government did was fuel the unrest even further. At least, that's how it had seemed."

"Beyond belief," I said, cynicism dripping from my words. "Our leaders truly did interfere in everything, didn't they? That obsessive fear of socialism. God. I get protecting world peace and security; hell that's why the UN was born, right? We all want that."

I swallowed, my throat dry. Soledad stayed silent whilst I drank some wine and lubricated my throat, giving me space to think, to continue my response.

"But there's security, and then there's...I don't know? Hysteria? Is that what you could call it? Though, was Allende as bad as someone like Stalin? I know that a lot of socialist leaders don't exactly stay true to their beliefs once they take power. Do you think they had reasons to be genuinely worried about him?"

Soledad's grip of my fingers loosened. "Bad?" Soledad said, raising one well-sculpted eyebrow. "Not compared to Stalin—no way. I mean, Allende was obsessed with nationalizing things—big industries, land redistribution, and that sort of thing. But he was democratically *elected* to do those things. He had big dreams, you know? And I think plenty of people in Chile shared those dreams. When my mother talks about him, I can feel the admiration in her, see it, hear it."

Sole's tone changed as she continued, cracks in her veneer of calm, an emotive positivity shining through. "Employment improved; inflation was mostly under control at first. Heck, kids were given a ration of milk from the government every day. Some of what he tried to do was okay, depending on who you talk to. I can't pretend to understand all of it or how the changes impacted different groups, but there was plenty of interference from other countries.

"Allende wasn't perfect, no doubt about that. I've heard he was antisemitic, for example. And a few of the changes he made to the economy backfired. Still, some people see him as a hero. A martyr, even. As far as I know, he wanted to show the world that socialism could exist without the violence and suppression that happened in places like the Soviet Union or China. But who knows how it would have turned out? My aunty, for example, thinks that if the USA stayed out of it, left Allende alone, Chile could have developed into something amazing with him in power. Given enough time."

I moved my free arm onto the table as my hand lifted into the air, a questioning gesture. "A martyr to some, you said? So, he was assassinated?" It wouldn't surprise me. One person's hero was another's villain.

"He killed himself," she said, her eyes looking through me, as though she were imagining the possibilities, imagining how her life, and others' lives, would have been different if he hadn't died. She blinked and I thought I caught a glimpse of tears at the corner of her eyes, but they were gone almost immediately, dispelled by her eyelids. "There was a coup on his doorstep, spearheaded by Pinochet. The Chilean democracy had been pushed to a breaking point."

"And...and that's why your mom and dad had to leave?" I slid my hand along her wrist and arm, trying to offer some comfort as she dug into her family's history for my benefit. She didn't need to tell me any of this, but she'd chosen to do so, strengthening the connection between us with every word. Soledad didn't seem trapped within the walls that many other people I'd become close to lived behind. Her honesty and her openness were moving.

"There were...abuses." She swallowed, her gaze dropping to the table. "Human rights abuses, under Pinochet. But my father's brother...that's him in the picture my dad took." She pointed to the first photograph, the man with his arm about Sole's mother's waist. They must have all been such good friends. They seemed so comfortable together, Sole's uncle and mother. "They say he was tortured."

Instinctively, my hand flew to my mouth. A pointless

attempt to force the horror clawing up my throat from escaping. "Sole. My God, that's awful. I'm so sorry." It felt like the most useless thing in the world to say, but I couldn't seem to find any other words. Every sentence in the world seemed inefficient.

Soledad straightened her spine, steeling herself. Her tone was flat, monotonous, as she expanded on the details. I couldn't blame her. If I ever had to speak such words, I'd have to steel myself, too.

Her uncle on her father's side, Daniel, had been dragged to a place called Villa Grimaldi, an estate now infamous in Chile. There was no official record of his death, but he'd been taken to the Tower, and had never come home. That was one of the hardest things for their family, not knowing exactly what had happened, being left to guess.

The rumors of exactly what kinds of torture had been used at the Villa ferried me to the edge of my sensitivities. It took everything I had to stop myself from crying as she spoke. And maybe I didn't need to chain my emotions; I doubt she would have judged me. Yet it felt wrong to break down, as though my tears would be asking for her comfort, when it had been her family to go through such unthinkable trauma, not mine.

"What..." My throat clenched, stifling my voice. I waited a couple of seconds and tried again. "Why..." I shook my head, frustrated at my inability to form a sentence after everything Sole had laid out, everything she'd opened up about.

"Why did they target him?" she prompted.

My attention fell to the table as a twang of shame sounded inside me. Was it even my business to ask?

"It's okay," she said, wiping at her face. This time, the

tears were undeniable. "I wouldn't have told you these things if I didn't feel comfortable enough to do so. You're allowed to ask questions."

Soledad reached out, her thumb caressing my cheek, catching a stubborn teardrop of my own that hadn't stayed put like I'd told it to.

"They targeted all sorts of people, but Daniel was a trade union leader. He spent his whole adult life advocating for workers' rights. It's a dangerous business to be in when your country has been conquered by a dictator. Daniel wasn't a communist, but he may as well have been as far as Pinochet's government was concerned."

"Is that when your parents left? After he died?"

Soledad downed the rest of her wine, then topped up both of our glasses. She closed her eyes for a few moments, rubbing at them with the base of her palms and slightly smearing her mascara. Her back heaved as she inhaled deeply several times, each breath thick with inherited sorrow. When about a minute had passed, she opened them again, as though having prepared herself for the next part of the story.

"Not straight away. But after a while, yes. My mother wanted to stay close to her parents, even though they originally hadn't supported her relationship with my father. He was a Protestant and from a less affluent family. But somehow none of those things mattered as much by 1980, not to my grandparents anyway.

"Eventually, my grandparents persuaded my parents to migrate, to move somewhere that their children wouldn't be judged because of their father's background, where they wouldn't be tracked and stalked in case they adopted their subversive uncle's mantle. But it was too dangerous for them all to leave at once. It could have painted a target on the backs of everyone they knew, everyone they cared about, including my mother's relatives who were a little better off, socially speaking. So, my grandparents on both sides stayed behind while my parents and my mother's brother fled. About a year later, a few of their cousins managed to do the same, and they reconnected in California."

I tilted my head like I was trying to pour my thoughts onto the table. "I don't even know what to say. I should stop feeling sorry for myself when things get hard; that's for sure. Living with the shadows of those experiences must have been so incredibly difficult for all of you."

Both of her hands flew to my face, cradling my jaw and guiding my head to an upright position. "No, please. Don't think that way." She dropped her hands to mine, the warmth of her touch against my palms once more sending waves of affection through me. "Everyone has their own battles. Their own challenges to cope with. No one's resilience level is the same. I hope you won't keep your own experiences tucked away because you think they're not worth knowing after me telling you these things."

The muscles in my neck relaxed for the first time in about half an hour. "How are you so damned perfect? You just managed to turn a serious, heartbreaking conversation about your family into something... I don't know. Something kind and understanding."

"Desi, I've told that story to plenty of people. Not all of them melt into it the way you did. I could see the empathy burning through you. Not fake or rationed, but a total sense of concern. Even I can't truly understand the PTSD my mother and her cousins carry with them because they lived under a dictatorship and I didn't. I haven't experienced the hypervigilance that overwhelms them sometimes. The undercurrent of rage. You don't need to feel guilty for having a life less harrowing. That'd be unsustainable, for human beings to always try to out-do one another's pain. You understand, and you accept. That's all you need to do."

My chin dimpled as I drew in my lips, thinking. "I'm not sure I understand, not properly. But I can see some Chile-related Googling in my future."

She laughed softly. "You know, that's one of the things I liked about you when we first met."

"What do you mean? I don't remember mentioning my tendency to lose hours scrolling through things on my phone. Though that's not a special trait these days, is it?"

She ducked her head, staring into her wine. "No, I don't mean that. You were so direct."

I huffed, the sound ending with an ironic laugh. "Don't you mean abrasive?"

Sole's eyelids fluttered briefly, betraying a hint of frustration as she trawled through her thoughts. "Do you know how many people I know who tell me they're 'color blind'? That race doesn't matter? That culture doesn't matter, and they don't *see* color or race so they can't possibly be racist or misread a situation? A lot of people avoid talking about that stuff, avoid acknowledging all the things in a person's background that can have a huge impact on how they live or how they're treated. My last girlfriend told me I shouldn't think so hard about what happened in Chile, because, you know, I'm an American and my parents are now too. I think she even thought she was being supportive when she said that.

She was looking *through* my culture, pretending it wasn't there.

"I liked that you were so forthright at that restaurant. It shocked me, but I am so sick of this color-blind rhetoric I hear all the time. I'm Chilean. And I'm American. And I could tell that, eventually, you'd process that. Not pretend it wasn't there."

I couldn't help it. Though the edge of the glass tabletop dug into my stomach and my fingers knocked crackers from the food platter, I partially stood, catapulting across the space, and kissed her.

CHAPTER SEVENTEEN

WE DIDN'T EVEN make to the bedroom. Between hungry, feverish kisses, I managed to slide Soledad's tank top up her body and over her head, discarding the shirt along with my inhibitions. I pressed my hand to her chest, holding her for a moment so I could examine her. Soledad's bronze skin rippled over taut abdominal muscles; a simple black bra molded to her small breasts. As I stared, she reached, unclasped the bra, and let it slip tentatively from her body.

Seeing Sole half-naked disarmed me, as did the contradictory mixture of vulnerability and confidence in her eyes. She didn't flinch or shy away as I took her in, but there was no hiding the goose bumps trailing across her stomach.

"You're so beautiful," I whispered.

Wrapping her arms around my waist, she pulled me

close, pinning her chest to mine, assertive nipples teasing me through the fabric of my shirt. Pressing her mouth to the skin below my ear, she kissed her way along my neck with all the softness and sensory brilliance of a butterfly in motion. The subtle, tickling movements sent a wave along my spine, and I couldn't suppress the childlike giggle that escaped me. She drew back, her hands still planted firmly on my hips, and grinned.

"You did that on purpose."

She canted her head. "Perhaps."

In a swift movement, Soledad eliminated the distance between us, her mouth warm and wet against mine. Her kiss left me sinking into a blurred, whirling world of desire. Her insistent tongue parted my lips, and I greedily accepted her offering, the taste of wine rich in her mouth. Every hesitation, every doubt within me yielded to her touch.

With her mouth still against my own, Soledad knotted my shirt in her fists, tugging the fabric free of my jeans before unbuttoning the blouse at an agonizingly slow pace. I shivered as her fingertips grazed my skin, and she worked her way up until, finally, the blouse came free, and she lifted the fabric over my shoulders and away from my body.

I closed my eyes as Soledad dragged her fingers along my sides. A reactive ripple surged through my torso, like a cold wind caressing damp skin. Her kiss softened as she slid her hands to my ass. I gave in to her movements as she stepped into me. When the back of my knees found the edge of the sofa, she softly maneuvered me until I lay along the couch, and she gingerly lay down on top of me, her bare chest meeting mine for the first time. Like me, she was hot to the touch, despite the mild temperature of her apartment.

I gasped as she pushed her thigh between my legs, the pressure all at once unbearable and divine. I bit my lip to stifle the moan that threatened.

"You don't need to hold back, Des. You can let go. You don't need to hide anything."

For some reason, I believed her. No matter what she found beneath my clothes, whether it be the ugly scar on my outer thigh, or the stretch marks along the fuller parts of my belly, and no matter how I reacted to her touch, she wouldn't judge me. I could see it in her eyes, hear it in her voice. I was safe with Soledad Reyes.

All sense of reality melted into a kaleidoscope of color and sensation as she trailed her fingertips along my sternum whilst, at the same time, she covered one of my nipples with her mouth, teasing me with fleeting flicks of her tongue. Gradually, she increased the strength of her seal over my breast, drawing my nipple deeper into her mouth. A moan escaped from me at last. I slid my fingers into her hair and massaged her scalp. I ruined her ponytail, but I needed to respond somehow, to show her that she was doing exactly what I wanted her to do, that I felt every stroke of her tongue, that the suction of her mouth set me on fire.

It had been years since I'd been intimate with someone, and everything about her body, her movements, made me feel wanted. I hadn't realized how badly I'd needed her on top of me, how much I'd needed her hands, her mouth, her warmth against my skin. But everything about this felt right.

As her fingertips drew near to the top of my jeans, my back arched slightly as I clenched against a throng of pressure between my legs. She hadn't even unzipped my jeans yet, but my body knew what was coming, and the sheer anticipation had been enough to send a wave of pleasure through me.

I was disappointed when she moved, and my slippery, engorged nipple released from her lips. I dropped my chin to my chest to meet her eyes. "Can I take these off?" she asked, toying with the top edge of my jeans.

"I might implode if you don't," I replied. A suggestive grin crept across her face. "Yes. That means yes. Consent. Total consent."

"I'm glad," she said, keeping her eyes on my face as she dropped her chin and kissed the sensitive flesh of my belly. I shivered and, as though rewarding my reaction, she licked her way up my body, between my breasts, along my neck, across my chin, and, finally, to my lips. As we kissed, her hands kept themselves busy. Sole nudged open the button on my jeans, lowered the zipper, and separated the folds of material covering my boxer briefs. Tendrils of heat coursed through my body, melting any lingering sense of hesitation that remained.

Wordlessly begging Sole to take things further, I pulled her lower lip between my teeth, biting ever so slightly. Something inside me had been released, something unbridled and possessive, totally removed from the monochromatic, humdrum world that existed everywhere else in that moment, everywhere except in her arms. She knew exactly what I was asking, her lithe fingers tentatively sliding beneath my briefs as her mouth continued to explore my own.

My hands raked her back, short nails sinking into her muscled shoulders as I drew her against me, the hint of a moan swallowed by our kiss, as our nipples collided for a brief, delicious moment. I wasn't even sure who had made the sound but, regardless, the urgency between us manifested itself in that delectable note.

A demanding pressure continued to build in my center as she gently stroked the folds of my flesh, the promise of more behind each movement as she took her time, teasing the places around and near my clitoris, not quite fulfilling my need, yet fanning that need as sure as any fire. Keeping one arm wrapped about her shoulders, I reached down and tried to shimmy the rest of the way out of my jeans, guiding one side down over my hip and fumbling for the other.

"Jeans," she said as she broke away, her words accusatory. "They look so good. But not that great in terms of access."

"No," I whispered, still recovering from the breathlessness of our kisses. "I want yours gone too."

Soledad did something then that I hadn't expected. With her free hand, she cupped my cheek and, slowing the whole world down for a few seconds, stared into my eyes, her glow as warm as summer. Desire still churned insistently throughout my body, her other hand at rest beneath my briefs, but the look on her face floored me. It was a look that said much that couldn't be put into words, a look that foreshadowed so much more than the sexual connection we were about to share. We could be important to each other. I felt it, too, like a vision or a forecast.

The exchange cleared as Soledad blinked rapidly a few times, then leaned down and kissed me again, softly, tentatively. With her lips pressed against mine and my eyes closed, she took the opportunity to flick one of her fingertips across the top of my clit.

I gasped and a smile spread across her face. I tried to

trace her lips with my tongue, but she withdrew her hand and sat up, straddling me. Reaching, she pulled out her elastic and ran her hand through the thick, flowing hair that spilled over her shoulders. For the first time in what felt like forever, we were no longer touching, and disappointment shot down my spine as she stood.

The disappointment evaporated. Standing only a couple of feet away, where I could watch her, she unbuttoned her jeans and, swaying her hips from side to side, slithered out of them, kicking the Wranglers off to the side. She stood before me in nothing but a tight black pair of women's boxer briefs, much like my own, yet they looked so much hotter on her tennis-player's body. Her gaze fixed on me, she tucked her thumbs beneath the edges of the underwear, and slid them away, banishing them to the same corner as her jeans.

If I hadn't been lying down and assisted by gravity, I'm sure I would have been drooling. She was so damned beautiful. How could I be here, in this place, in this time, with a woman like Soledad? Surely a mistake had been made. Surely, she was meant for someone more interesting, more worldly, and more athletic than me?

Soledad held a finger up. "Stop that." She took up position at the end of the sofa. "No more doubts. I don't want to see anything on your face but pure..." She pulled off one shoe, then the other. "Unadulterated..." She leaned forward and tugged at my jeans, dragging them down my legs. "Pleasure." My face flushed with heat as she removed my briefs, leaving both of us naked.

Gracefully, like an agile cat, she crouched over me and climbed up my body once more. I spread my knees apart, creating space. She hovered over me, her petite breasts above my face, her thigh in my groin. I opened my mouth and arched, latching onto her nipple as I gripped her shoulders and guided her closer. She gasped as I massaged her butt with my hands, while continuing to suck at her breast, soft and delicious as it was.

She repositioned, forcing her breast from my mouth, but allowing her hand unfettered access to my labia. Using her middle and index fingers, she spread the folds of flesh ever so gently and, with her thumb, proceeded to drew soft circles atop my clitoris. Pressing her torso against mine again, she nibbled at my ear, then mapped the side of my neck with her tongue, settling into a soft suckling at the base of my neck near my collar bone. The teasing of her thumb against my clit quickened. Wild tremors fired along my nerves with every revolution, and I scratched at her back, searching for an outlet, some way to ground myself as she took me higher. I wrapped a leg about her waist and moaned, despite my usual tendency to try to keep as quiet as possible, to keep my composure. There was no staying composed with Soledad's wet tongue caressing, and her lithe fingers stroking.

With her lips still connected to my skin, she murmured, "You are magnificent." I shuddered as she slipped three of her fingers inside me, her thumb continuing to apply pressure to my clit. "I want to hear you make more of those noises."

My chest and stomach tightened as she thrust her fingers deeper, a long, low sound escaping from somewhere almost forgotten, somewhere deep within me, an inarticulate cry of pleasure. "Ahhhh."

"Yes," she whispered. "Exactly."

With one hand, I gripped her bicep as though holding on. With the other, I latched onto her ass, squeezing as hard as I could manage as she sped up, no longer tentative, no longer being gentle. I sucked my lower lip into my own mouth and bit down, my spine lifting off the sofa as ripples of sensation coursed through me. As though sensing how close I was to reaching a climax, she wrapped her free hand around my breast, pinching my nipple, tugging enough to excite me but not cause pain.

After a few seconds, she sat up, looking down at me as she slid a hand along my stomach, between my breasts, and to my lips. I flicked my head to the side, claiming one of her fingers. She happily allowed me to slide my mouth along her finger, drawing it in and sliding it back out again. And again. Soledad retracted her hand from my mouth and gave me a look as though she'd saved the best for last.

Her fingers were still inside me. She added strength to her movements by tucking her knees beneath her, pulling closer to my body and thrusting with her hips, her hand and her groin working in concert as my lower legs wrapped about her waist. I could feel the heat and the wetness of her flesh grazing against mine with each forward motion.

"Sole," I said, though the word was barely discernible, every part of me drunk on pleasure. "I...I'm...so close."

My muscles tensed and my heart pounded as she took me higher and higher, like riding a wave. A pleasurable, hot wave. The tingling in my body intensified, and everything seemed to contract and release as the building pressure unleashed. My hands flew to my face as I screeched, an inexplicable sound of ecstasy I'd never heard myself make before. I spasmed as the energy from her touch shot through me like a spring.

Soledad eased up, sliding her hand from me. I cupped her jaw, smoothing my thumb across her lips. She rotated her face to plant a ginger kiss against my palm. I sat up and knelt opposite her. Lifting her hand, she teased some of the short hair at the base of my neck, her eyes alert and hypnotic. I nudged closer, my hips and breasts pushing up against her, my arms holding her tightly. Kissing my way along her neck, I nibbled at her earlobe, relishing in the slight shiver I sensed along her spine. Taking my mouth closer to her ear, I whispered, "My turn."

CHAPTER EIGHTEEN

SOMETIME DURING THE night, we had made our way to her bedroom and, after three more *unbelievable* orgasms, I'd fallen asleep, exhausted and satiated. When I awoke, the sun had yet to fully rise, with thin streaks of pale-orange light peeking weakly through the slats across the window. I stretched out, my limbs heavy and stiff, as though I'd spent two hours at the gym rather than two hours wrapped up in Soledad's body. I rolled onto my side as I opened my eyes. Soledad wasn't there, though I could still smell her, and the state of the sheets and pillow looked slept in. At least I hadn't imagined the whole thing. Last night had happened and the simple truth of reality brought a cautious smile to my face, my heart full and practically bounding.

Finally admitting that it was morning and time to face

the day, I stretched out, a soft click in my shoulder reminding me I wasn't as young as I had been the last time I'd woken up in another woman's bed. Judging by the uninvited light bursting into the room through the window, it had to be at least 7:00 a.m., perhaps later.

I glanced about the room as I sat up, since I hadn't taken the time to look at much of it last night, except for Sole of course. Her bedroom, whilst still ordered for the most part, lacked the pristine regimentation of her open-plan living and dining area. The furniture in here didn't match, and books littered the top of her dresser, clumped together in haphazard and slanting piles. Aside from that, though, everything had its place. There were more framed photographs lining the windowsill, and all of her other possessions seemed to be neatly tucked away, the crimson comforter a rich splash of color within the otherwise muted room.

In the bathroom, I found a clean, empty glass, a toothbrush still in its packaging, and a small note resting atop a folded towel.

> *Gone to grab some breakfast for the both of us...be back soon.*
>
> *Help yourself to anything you like.*
>
> *Love, Sole.*
>
> *P.S: You're adorable when you sleep.*

I tucked my bottom lip beneath my top row of teeth, and my cheeks rose, the joy spreading not just across my face, but throughout my whole body. Lifting the note, I breathed it in, but the square smelled only like paper; there was nothing of her there. I set the note on the counter, then, after drinking a glass of water, brushed my teeth and hunted down the rest of my clothes. I'd woken up in nothing and, though I was alone, it felt strange to wander around someone else's apartment nude.

The pipes in the bathroom protested for a second as I turned the hot water faucet. The water was the perfect temperature without needing to turn on the cold, and I stepped into the shower.

The liquid soap and warm water were divine. As I lathered my body, washing away the remnants of a rather, I had to admit, sticky night, I found a faint bite mark on my left breast and, slightly amused, shook my head. I hadn't picked Soledad for a biter, but I also hadn't thought of myself as someone who'd enjoy that, either. Everything with Soledad became possible though. And safe too. Of course I'd been nervous as hell the moment we'd started yanking our clothes off, but not scared, not like I had been the first time with other women I'd slept with.

It wasn't great having to slip into the clothes I'd worn last night, but at least they'd been fresh before I'd come over. I towel-dried my hair, leaving it in a chaotic, but somehow effective, mess of short layers flicked across my ears and forehead, then wandered into the open-concept living and dining areas.

Even though I knew Sole wouldn't mind, I decided not to investigate anything not openly on display, including the fridge. Instead, I collapsed onto the couch and opened *Words with Friends* on my phone. Brenna had been waiting three days for me to make a move, and I knew she'd start to complain if I didn't plant some tiles on the board soon. Though, I wasn't sure why we continued to play these rolling games. I may have been a few years older than her, but my baby sister was much better with anagrams and words. The last time I had won a game was when she requested a lightning round after eight shots of tequila. Even though I was lying in bed at home, sober and alert, I had only managed to beat her by eight points.

Adding a couple of letters, I turned *pit* into *pithy*, rolling my eyes at the low point score, and closed the app. I sent a message to Hope, knowing that on a weekend there wasn't much chance she'd be awake for at least another hour.

Morning! Sorry, got caught up hanging out with Soledad. Let me know if you need anything.

Hope's reply came surprisingly fast. Clearly, I'd misjudged her dedication to sleeping in.

Hanging out?!!! Is that what people call it now!!

I swallowed and repressed an embarrassed laugh. This was new territory. How much information was too much information? Hope wasn't a kid. Heck, she'd be sixteen in about six weeks, so it would be insulting to treat her like a baby. But what was suitable to share with her? She liked Sole, so I didn't want to shut her out, but I also didn't want to disappoint her, or cross some kind of line regarding what was appropriate to discuss. Before I could answer, Hope sent another message.

P.S: I'm fine. There's enough food here for the zombie apocalypse.

That's a relief, I responded, adding a "phew" emoji. *I'll be home in time to make us both lunch.*

The text messages suggested Hope was feeling okay

today, communicative even; a genuine relief. Sometimes she exuded so much positive energy, her eyes bright and round and open to possibility. At other times, the brightness receded, and she collapsed into herself, like she'd trudged down a dark tunnel in search of something and didn't know how to find her way back.

The sound of a lock clicking in the front door made me jump, but Soledad called out as she opened the door to let me know she'd returned. Tousling my hair again, I stood and, not knowing what to do with my hands, crammed them into the tight front pockets of my jeans. The denim had felt good last night, but now, I wished I'd worn something with a looser fit.

Two soft thuds came, and I assumed Sole had kicked off her shoes. Her footsteps were quieter as she rounded the corner from her entryway, a canvas shopping bag in one hand and a cardboard tray in the other, two reusable coffee cups nestled on top. I crossed the room and relieved her of the cups as she set the canvas bag on the dining table. I placed the cardboard tray next to it, then finally acknowledged her properly.

"Hey," she said, reaching for my hand. *Hey*. Such a simple word, but with the inviting glint in her eyes and the gentle pull at the side of her mouth, she may as well have sprouted a sonnet.

I slid my fingers between hers and stepped closer. "You're back."

"An astute observation," she quipped.

I rolled my eyes ever so slightly, smiling so she knew I didn't mind her gentle teasing. "Sorry," I said. "Smooth, right? It's been a while since I've woken up in someone else's apartment."

Her free hand on my hip, Soledad drew me closer and kissed me, our lips not parting. "It's not like I started the conversation with a stellar opening line." She raised her eyebrows as though mocking herself, then her expression settled again. "But I'm glad to hear that."

"What? That it's been a while since I've slept at some-one else's place? Why?" I asked, scrunching up my face.

She shrugged. "I like the idea of having you to myself."

I hadn't expected her to say something so unbelievably sweet and also kind of terrifying, and I couldn't think of a reply.

After kissing me again, she broke away and took the bag to the kitchen bench and unpacked, letting me off the hook. It was then I noticed she was in gym gear, black three-quarter tights and a charcoal-gray tank top.

"How early did you wake up?" I passed her one of the coffees as I slid onto a kitchen stool. "Looks like you've been busy already."

"About five." She set two fresh bagels onto plates, retrieved a few condiments from the refrigerator. "I try to fit a run in on my days off. I'm not the fastest runner around, but my body definitely feels the difference when I don't go at least once a week."

The mention of her body made heat rise in my cheeks. The memory of her fingertips gently tracing the length of my sternum, the firmness of her muscles beneath my hands, and the intoxicating warmth of her mouth against my flesh.

"You okay?" she asked, handing me a plate.

I cleared my throat and took a sip of coffee. Even though I preferred tea as my first drink of the day, with coffee more of a midmorning indulgence, I needed that brief moment of respite from my embarrassment. Had she seen the thoughts sketched across my face? "Yeah," I muttered. "Just remembering something."

She rounded the kitchen bench and sat on the stool next to mine, smearing a generous lashing of cream cheese on her bagel with a knife. "Do you like any sports?"

I took the other knife she'd laid out and did the same, speaking as I cut the bagel into quarters. "I wouldn't go as far as saying I *like* sports, but I try to keep as healthy as I can. I spend way too many hours working at a computer not to."

As Soledad chewed, I couldn't help noticing—and not for the first time—the strength of her jawline, and the elegant length of her neck. Gorgeous as she was, even her bones seemed to warn the world not to mess with her, to assert her capacity to handle anything life could throw her way. It was an impression I'd formed of her that first time we'd met, her in her uniform, me a bumbling traffic-violator. It was hard to believe we'd come so far since that awkward blind date two weeks earlier. Soledad swallowed and asked, "What's your exercise of choice?"

"Hmm. Spin classes mostly. They seem to be the least likely to set off my chronic pain, and Clara will usually come with me. Though..." I touched my fingertip to my chin, wondering if it was a good idea to tell her this next part. "I used to play tennis in high school. Nothing like your achievements, though." I directed my attention to the photograph on the wall, the one with her holding the trophy and the tennis racket. She followed my gaze, her eyes widening when they settled on the picture.

"That was a long time ago. It was my first year of college and I'd worked so hard to get ready for that tournament. I'm not as good as you're assuming." Sole shook her head and reached out, her fingers draping over my wrist in a concerned gesture. I loved the ease with which she touched me, as though we'd woken up together twenty times before. "But hang on," she continued. "Back up. Chronic pain?"

I dropped the piece of food I'd been nibbling to the plate and brushed my hands together, discarding a few crumbs. "Yeah," I said, my tone apologetic, though it was more myself I was apologizing to. I'd explained this so many times. People always thought, when I said, "chronic pain," that I had some sort of debilitating illness. Something serious. Something they'd heard of and would empathize with. Whenever I explained that it was "just endometriosis," I'd be left with a stale taste in my mouth because it was always so clear on their faces that they thought I was weak or exaggerating, or perhaps even faking.

Soledad withdrew her hand slowly, but purposefully. "Sorry. You don't have to tell me about it if you don't want to."

I tugged her hand toward me. "No, no. It's fine. It's not life-threatening or anything. It's pretty common, really. Something like ten percent of women have it."

"Polycystic ovaries?" she guessed.

"Endometriosis," I countered. Her forehead furrowed. "You sure you wanna hear about my unexciting health issues?"

She leaned over, hovering a couple of inches from my face, our noses almost touching. Tilting her head, she kissed me gently and then settled on the stool. "Of course I do."

"Essentially, it has to do with the lining of the uterus not staying where it's meant to." As I explained the difficulties of reaching a diagnosis because of the limitations of ultra-sounds, coupled with the lack of research into the disease, Soledad watched me with rapt attention. I thought a clinical description of uterine linings wandering beyond the uterus, clutching to other organs and causing pain and bleeding, would be a sure-fire way to destroy the flow of conversation, but I couldn't have been more wrong. On the contrary, she seemed engaged, interested, and sympathetic, asking questions to clarify her understanding of the illness, as well as my personal experience of having lived with it.

"It sounds like everyone who has endo has a kind of different set of symptoms?" Sole said.

"Yep. That's why it took so long for my doctor to work out what it was. Most women get high levels of pain in their pelvis, like horrific period pain, I think. Most of mine emanated from my lower back, sometimes climbing as high as my shoulders, like it was sending out these tentacles that gripped my ribs and shoulder blades. For ages they thought I had back problems, even though I had all the bleeding too. I had my fair share of arguments with different doctors."

"How frustrating," she murmured, her tone expressing both compassion and irritation. "There are way too many times when women aren't listened to about their own bodies. So, what happens now?"

"I wait." I paused, reflecting on the months that had already passed. "My health insurance has finally agreed that I need laparoscopic surgery. That'll basically remove any tissue that is growing where it isn't supposed to, like a reset. Mine is probably in the Pouch of Douglas, given the symptoms. Then, the implant in my uterus should slow the re-growth down. I'll hopefully have much less pain in the years ahead."

Her mouth twisted, concern washing over her face. "The surgery isn't a permanent fix?"

I shook my head, tapping the side of my coffee cup with my fingers. "Nope. There isn't one, except for a hysterectomy, which is a much bigger surgery and they won't let me have one anyway."

Her eyebrows rose, questioningly. "I'm too young," I said, hints of a sigh surrounding my words. "Child-bearing age, as they say. Even though I keep telling them I don't feel the need to have any biological children, they're against doing that if you haven't had any babies yet. You live with it. But I'm a lot luckier than women even five or ten years ago. The operation is pretty minor—it's over fast, keyhole only, and it helps most people quite a lot. I won't even need to stay overnight."

"Well, when you have to go to the hospital, let me know. I can get you home and make sure Hope is okay if she needs to be anywhere, too."

I tilted my head pensively. "I haven't bored you or grossed you out? Too much information?"

Soledad pulled her lower lip between her teeth as though retrieving a thought she didn't yet want to share. "Definitely not," she replied after a moment, her countenance pensive and sincere. "There's nothing boring or otherwise about your life, or your body for that matter. I'm glad you told me." At that, she stood and began to clear away our empty plates. "Was the coffee nice?" she said as she packed the dishwasher.

"Absolutely. I must admit I usually drink coffee later in the morning, but it tasted great. Thank you."

"Tea drinker?" she asked. "I'll make sure I get some the next time I'm at the grocery store."

I couldn't withhold the happiness that bloomed. If that wasn't a clear indication that she wanted to spend more time with me, I didn't know what was. "That would be great. Thank you." I sank my chin into the palm of my hand. "You're not working today?"

"Nope. I'm on for the next six days, though."

My heart sank, realizing she'd be doing long shifts and wouldn't have time to see me. "How long have you been a cop?" I asked. I felt embarrassed almost immediately, remembering that she'd already told me she'd been an officer for about eleven years. If she'd noticed my momentary memory lapse, she pretended not to.

The skin around Soledad's eyes crinkled as she thought. "A while," she replied. "Long enough to recognize a good parent when I see one."

I directed a thumb at my chest. "Me?"

She chuckled as she wiped the counter with a cloth. "Of course, you. It doesn't take a genius to see how much you care about Hope. Although, that doesn't mean I'm not *also* a genius."

Laughing, I ran a thumb along my jawline. "And so modest, too."

"In all seriousness," Soledad said. "It takes a special kind of person to provide love, care, and safety for someone else's kid. I know that most foster carers don't want to take on teenagers. We see a fair few in that situation come through the station, one way or another." Her eyes turned stormy as she spoke, as though she'd gone adrift for a few moments, lost in memory. It was a sensation I could understand. It happened to me every time I thought about Brody, who'd come to represent all my failures as a parent. She must have noticed the change in my own face when she refocused, because she slid her hand atop my forearm and said, "What is it?"

Sighing, I covered her hand with my own, relishing the ease with which we seemed to be touching, expressing timid affection as we got to know each other better. "I think it's a story for another day. I don't want to ruin the mood or dump too much information on you all at once."

"Fair enough." She reached out, smoothing her thumb across my lip. "I'm glad you didn't write off the possibility of—" She hesitated, gesturing first at me, then herself. "—this. After that memorable first date of ours."

Heat rose in my face, and I laughed nervously. "Oh God." I swiveled gently on the stool, no longer looking at her. "Not my finest moments."

Soledad laughed too, a short yet sweet affirmation. "Well, you were right in some ways though. We do have a few philosophical differences that we'll need to deal with soon. I feel like we needed some more context, a better understanding of each other before we did that. We're almost there, I think."

Pulling my lips into a thin line, I silently nodded my agreement. Though my first impressions of Soledad had been, in large part, wrong, the fact remained that the behavior of some of this country's police officers terrified me. I remembered reading that an unarmed Black person in America is three and a half times more likely to be shot by a police officer than an unarmed white person. On top of that, those Black people are also less likely to be any kind of threat than their white counterparts, who rarely end up with a bullet in them. I was a white woman, someone who'll never be on the receiving end of a racially driven police report or bear the violent reprisals of police assumptions. I could never pretend to understand what it must be like to be a person of color, to live each day knowing that the statistics and politics of this world worked against me, and always had. Sadness and outrage still bubbled inside me every time I turned on the news because, like my grandmother said, we should all understand what it was like to be a *human*.

Sometimes, I felt such immense shame. Shame for every white person who had opposed the civil rights movement, shame for every police officer who pulled their weapon on a young person whose only crime was being black and being outdoors, shame for every moment of my life I'd failed to do something useful to stop any of it from happening.

Was it fair to put those atrocities onto every police officer I meet, however? Could I be an ally—as weak as I may be—to the Black community, who continued to be overrepresented in prisons and underrepresented in positions of authority, while dating a uniformed police officer? Soledad's own family had endured so much, including immense persecution. Surely she, and many other officers, would never draw conclusions, then draw a gun, based on the color of a person's skin. How complicated was the issue of race and authority for Sole, as a police officer of color? Maybe she strongly supported the proposed changes to legislation about when California police could shoot at a suspect. I hadn't thought to ask either of those questions when we'd first met—perhaps a sign of my own ignorance, my own limited lens.

I'd always liked to think I was on the right side of racism, that I was well informed and not prone to judgment or prejudice. But the fact that I had failed to consider Soledad's life more fully, the fact I hadn't even stopped to think about her culture, only proved that I have been kidding myself. No one in my position of privilege is without assumption or judgment, are they? I need to ask more questions. I need to better educate myself and never stop educating myself. Maybe the best I can do is own up to my own failings and do more to correct them, knowing that they'll never fully disappear.

Soledad was right. We needed more context, more understanding of even the basic elements of each other's lives.

Her voice sliced through the whirlwind of thoughts. "But," she said, "maybe we can save that philosophical discussion for later."

I exhaled, relieved. Neither of us were ready to explore those questions the day after we'd spent our first night together. I lifted her hand to my lips and kissed her palm. "There'll be time," I said.

"Yes. There will. Well, okay, tell me some more about yourself. Do you only photograph houses? Or do you have other work as a photographer?"

I laughed, nervous. "Uh. Not paid work, no."

"Meaning you don't only take pictures of real estate?"

"No, not only houses." I shifted my weight. "I've been teaching myself how to do portraits."

"Very cool," she said enthusiastically, her eyes widening

and her tone energetic. "Artistic ones? Or more of a glamor style?"

It felt silly to use the term "artistic," but the images I'd produced of my sisters and Hope were not glamor shots. "I suppose you could call them artistic. Though I don't know if anyone would find them all that creative or expressive."

She nudged me with her arm. "Well, how about you let me see some? Maybe I'll think they're artistic."

"Absolutely not. No way."

Soledad frowned but she didn't look genuinely hurt; it was more of a wounded puppy-dog kind of look. She was utterly adorable. "Someday," she began, staring off into the distance like an actor on a soap opera. "Someday, I might be able to process this denial and rejection." Returning her attention to me, she smiled gently. "I understand. It can be scary sharing your creative side with people. I hope you change your mind eventually."

I couldn't help but melt under her warmth. "Thanks. Maybe. Like I said before: there's time."

CHAPTER NINETEEN

DRIVING TO STINSON Beach would take us two hours, heading west on the I-80 with Sole in the driver's seat. Due to work commitments, we hadn't seen been together since our unforgettable night at her place. Seven very, very long days.

When she suggested a day trip, I didn't hesitate to say yes, and by 7:00 a.m. we were on our way with our towels, sunscreen, and hats.

Being a Wednesday, Hope was at school. I felt guilty for leaving the house before she was out of bed, but I planned to do my best to be home by six so we could still have dinner together.

I knew I was being overly anxious. Hope was nearly sixteen; she would hardly notice if I was home as she rushed off to the school bus. But it was hard not to worry about her, after the experiences she has had and the historically fragile nature of her family relationships.

At first, Gina had been annoyed that I'd asked to re-schedule a house shoot, but it turned out the family needed longer to clean the place up and were grateful when Gina requested the change. Things aligned and here we were, Sole and I, off to the coast for a few hours.

As we traveled, the cityscapes and roadside businesses occasionally gave way to meek and low-lying hills. Some ar-eas—particularly between the Cordelia Junction and Val-lejo—were more sunburnt than others, dark leafy bushes a stark contrast to the almost-yellow grass out of which they grew.

"I like the view here," Soledad said after we crossed the Napa River, driving alongside the San Pablo Bay. The road through here was only one or two lanes in each direction, where it had been four or five lanes when we had set out from Sacramento. The Bay hugged the edge of the road, only a few feet of plant life separating us from the shallow, glis-tening water that stretched along on both sides. Steady rip-ples moved across the surface, pushed along by a moderate wind.

I lowered the window, and air rushed through my hair, the rich smells of soil and water so different to the city. "Yes," I murmured. "It's nice to go for a drive. I haven't come out here for over a year."

"Really?" She gave me a surprised sideways glance be-fore redirecting her eyes to the road. "I love going to the beach. Even when it gets too cold to swim. I can always go running—"

"Running on the sand?" I looked at her, incredulous. "Ouch. No thanks."

She grinned. The fingers of her left hand curled around the steering wheel as we came up behind a slow-moving truck. "Or sit and read, listening to the waves."

"Now *that* I can get on board with. As long as it's a good book. I like reading, but I seem to get tired as soon as I try to focus my eyes on the page, so the writer needs to bring the suspense."

Soledad raised an eyebrow. "Suspense, huh? Do you read thrillers?"

"Mmm-hmm. Crime fiction type things. Maybe a good spy story."

"Wow," she mouthed. "I didn't picture you as the crime fiction and spy type at all."

I twisted my body and glared at her playfully. "Why not?"

"Aside from the whole anti-cop vibe?"

I cleared my throat, not sure what to say, but she kindly let me off the hook for my hypocrisy. "Figured you read sci-fi and fantasy. Dragons. Aliens. Maybe a spaceship or two."

I laughed and crossed one leg over the other. My butt needed the slight reposition. "You're not entirely wrong. I don't read sci-fi, but I do like to watch it. But more of the Earth-based things, not so much the outer space quirky aliens stuff. *The Abyss* is one of my favorite movies."

"Haven't seen it," she said. "I'll add it to the list. Right after *Mean Girls*."

"Oh God." My stupid Cady Heron joke at the restaurant. Sole gave me a teasing grin.

She drew my hand to her lips and kissed my palm. The

hairs on my forearm stood on end as she gently flicked her tongue against my skin, then released me. The truck we'd been traveling behind exited, and Sole was able to increase speed again, sitting a tick below the speed limit.

"What do you read?" My voice shook as I worked to mask the full effect of her touch and return the conversation to our previous topic.

She considered the question, her mouth adopting a cute, quirky shape. "When I have time? Everything. Weee-eell, everything except for crime fiction." She winked at me.

Damn, she was adorable.

"Understandable. Enough of that in real life, right?"

"Yep."

We chatted about more books and films for the next ten minutes, then drifted into a comfortable quietness. Though it couldn't last forever, everything seemed at peace—there on the road with Soledad Reyes.

AS WE APPROACHED our destination, an earthy, floral scent drifted from the roadside where wild lavender plants nestled against one of the narrow streets. I didn't recognize this road; Soledad had taken a different route to what I'd used in the past.

Sole slowed the car. She pointed to a house with a worn picket fence surrounding a squat house sitting vigilant next to a one-laned bridge. The wooden palings of the fence were covered in an array of stuck-on fish and birds, vibrant and colorful. "I always wonder about who lives there when I pass by," she said.

"That's a unique fence. I don't think I've come by here before."

"Yeah. I need to go the other way to get to the main beach and find parking, but thought I'd show you the sculptures. Or stickers. Actually, I'm not sure exactly what they are. My mother got us lost one time when we came across for the weekend, and we ended up driving around these residential streets for a while."

"I'm glad you showed me. This whole street is interesting. I've never lived close to the beach. There's a whole other vibe, isn't there? All seems quieter somehow."

"Yes. The coast has a special atmosphere."

Within minutes we'd found the main parking lot. On a weekend, finding a space can be difficult at Stinson, but being the middle of the week, we found one easily. We unpacked our beach chairs and bags and walked along a concrete track that soon yielded to sand, my shoes filling with it as we moved. The lapping waves grew louder, and salt caressed my lips and tongue.

Abruptly, the foliage enclosing us on both sides yielded to an expansive stretch of shoreline. Two older women had settled in low-lying chairs much like our own just ahead of the opening from the path, one of the women glancing up at us briefly before closing her eyes and settling into a restful state. A few other groups dotted the landscape, but it was not crowded, and we had our pick of spaces to set up.

We chose a spot about halfway between the waterline and the grassy dunes that marked the edge of the beach, and within a few minutes we had set up somewhere to sit. My skin always burned easily, and so I wore a wide-brimmed hat and sunglasses. I squeezed some lotion onto my legs and rubbed it in, working my way up until my arms, chest, and face had been covered.

"Want me to apply that to your back?" Sole asked.

"Er...sure. That would be great, thank you." I handed her the bottle and set a folded towel on the sand in front of her chair. I sat in a lotus position with my shoulders nudging her knees. The bottle made an awkward sound as she squeezed some of the sunscreen into her palm.

"That wasn't me, I swear."

"That's what they all say," I replied.

"Smart-ass," she said.

"I'm fairly sure that's your influence."

She silenced me with confident hands on my neck, gliding over my skin and gently rubbing the lotion in. I had to bite my lip to tamp down the moan wanting to escape my mouth as she worked her fingers into my shoulders. "Is this okay?" Sole asked.

"Mmm-hmm."

Her thumbs pushed into the ever-tense muscles between my spine and shoulder blades, and I gasped. "Ouch," I said.

She stopped immediately. "Sorry. Too much?"

"Absolutely not. It's a good ouch." I let my head fall to the side, grateful, as she resumed her magic. "Is this how you help all of your friends apply sunscreen?"

Sole laughed and, by way of an answer, slipped two fingers underneath the hem of my swimsuit. She fanned her index and middle fingers, brushing the swell of my breast. She leaned down, her mouth tickling my ear. "No," she whispered. She had to have known the reaction her fingers were causing; it must have been written all over my face, visible too in the heaviness of my breathing.

"Good…" I turned my head and kissed her, my tongue lightly nudging hers. She invited me in, an insistent hand in my hair pressing me closer. Salt on her lips. Heat in my belly. I could have lost myself in that kiss; I could have dissolved into an ether of ecstasy where only she and I existed. Remembering we were in public, I disconnected my lips from hers before I lost total control, mourning the loss of contact immediately. "Thanks for the help."

She pulled her bottom lip between her teeth, coy and delicious. "My pleasure."

As we settled into a tranquil time of wave-watching, Soledad took hold of my hand, maintaining our connection even when we weren't talking. My entire body relaxed as the unique calm that only existed at the edge of the ocean sank into my psyche.

I looked to the horizon, a meeting of sea and sky that stretched across the world like a seam. Along the shore, waves, frothy, silver and gray, leapt and darted like excited children. The soothing sound of each undulating crash of water reminded me of the week that Hope had moved in, when I'd brought her to the beach as a way to distract her from the discomfort of relocating yet again. We had been strangers, Hope unsure and uncomfortable, measuring all of her words like she was auditioning for something.

I needed to bring her back one day soon. Maybe the air and the openness could help her settle whatever had been bubbling inside her these last couple of months. We could come sometime around Thanksgiving, I thought.

After an hour or so of restorative beach-meditation, Soledad stood. "I'm going to dip my toes in," she said. "Want to come?"

I shook my head. "Soon. I'm enjoying doing nothing. I'll need to emotionally prepare myself to function."

"Totally understandable." She stifled a yawn; obviously Sole was as relaxed as I. She walked the short distance to the water's edge, her denim shorts tight on her ass. I followed her with my eyes, knowing I was ogling way too much, but unable to stop. She faced the ocean and stared out. Small waves broke against the sand and rushed toward her feet, lapping at her shins. With her arms across her chest, her ponytail lifting in the breeze, and her body outlined against the sky, she couldn't have been more perfect.

Was this it? Was this the beginning of something significant?

A shiver ran through me. My life was good the way it was, content. I didn't *need* a girlfriend, a partner. But I clearly wanted one more than I'd thought. Not just anyone though. Sole. I wanted her and she wanted me too.

Standing, I wrapped a towel around my shoulders and made for the waterline. I engulfed Soledad's waist with my arm, leaned into her. By way of a response, she kissed my temple. "Want to go and find lunch somewhere?" she asked.

I tightened my grip of her waist. "Yeah. That sounds nice. Somewhere local."

"Definitely. We can come back here."

"I'd like that." I kissed the top of her shoulder, and we broke apart, headed to our chairs to pack up.

"I don't want to be too pushy, but if you don't have dinner plans and want to turn this into a full day..."

I sighed, disappointed. "Sorry, I can't. I should be home in case Hope needs anything."

She gave me a look that seemed to communicate a mixture of understanding, disappointment, and expectation. Maybe she wanted me to invite her over, to have dinner with both Hope and me? Should I have invited her? I didn't know. I knew Sole and Hope had met already; they'd gotten along so well I'd been genuinely surprised. But having Soledad over for dinner at the house, Hope's and my home? It felt too soon. I didn't want to confuse Hope or have her think I wasn't going to be there for her because I was dating someone.

She lifted her backpack onto her shoulder. "That's okay. Well, you're still all mine for the next couple of hours, right?"

I dipped the toe of my shoe into the sand as my gaze dropped. Oh boy, I was in so much trouble with this woman. "Yes," I said, trying to suppress the embarrassed grin pulling at my lips.

"Good. Let's go grab some food. And..." Her voice hit a higher note on this last word.

"And?"

Sole stepped closer, set her hand on my hip. She leaned closer, and her mouth hovered over my neck, her breath warm and soothing against sensitive skin. I shivered again as her mouth, wet and attentive, bore down against my pulse point. She firmly worked her way along, finally pressing her lips to mine in a close-mouthed kiss. The sort of kiss that hid seductive secrets, that gave away nothing too soon. She withdrew. "Maybe we should skip the scenic stops on the return trip."

Too quickly I replied, "Yes."

She laughed. "Glad we're on the same page. Come on."

She led the way along the path but, if I was being honest with myself, I would have followed her just about anywhere. If, when we got to our destination, I got to kiss her again and again and again.

CHAPTER TWENTY

TWO DAYS AFTER the last time I'd last seen Soledad, I still felt like I had a fluorescent tattoo across my forehead that read: *Check me out! I have had mind-blowing sex!*

My cheeks hurt from smiling more often, and my phone had become a permanent fixture in my hand because I didn't want to make Sole wait more than eight seconds for a reply if she sent a message, which she did several times a day. I had turned into such a cliché, and I didn't even care. I was in a good mood; it would be silly to dampen that. So, instead of staying home by myself editing pictures and updating Gina's website in a silent, lonely corner of the world, I decided to go into the office, to be around people for a change.

Gina moved about her workplace with a determination that would leave most people feeling exhausted simply watching her. It was as though destiny knew she'd be in charge of a business one day and had made her chin ever-so-slightly pointed to help her carve through the air and get wherever she needed to be.

"And please, don't forget to send the Sullivans a *congratulations* card for their new purchase." With that final instruction to her baby-faced administrative assistant, Gina smiled weakly and flopped into the cushioned chair opposite mine. I didn't spend much time in the office, given I could do most of my work at home, but she'd made sure I had my own desk in case the urge to be around other people ever struck me. Which, for once, it had.

"That kind of day?" Using the balls of my feet, I swiveled gently in the office chair.

Gina huffed and shook her hand through her black curls as though trying to dispel the chaos of her afternoon. "We've had offers from four different people on the same house in the last three hours, and managing the negotiations became trickier than I thought. Some people take this whole house-buying business too seriously."

"Imagine that," I replied with a half grin. After all, no one took the house-buying business more seriously than she did.

Gina slapped her hands against her thighs. "Anyway. Enough of that. Were you able to get some decent shots of the Chandler home?"

I let loose a dramatic gust of air, and the choppy strands of hair above my eye dislodged. "That place is *not* easy to make look good, Gina. But yes. We have a couple of acceptable images for the listing. I'm tinkering with them now, so I think I can get them on the website by tomorrow morning."

Gina brought her hands together as though in prayer. "You're a gem. Thank you."

I lifted my cheek and gave an exaggerated wink. "All part of the service."

"Speaking of which," she said as she settled into the chair more comfortably. "Haven't seen you touching up pictures in the office for months. What changed your mind?"

I flicked my wrist in a questioning gesture. "I don't know… I guess I was feeling more social than usual. Wanted a change of scenery."

Gina gave me a look like she was accusing me of keeping a secret which, technically, I was. For some reason I hadn't told anyone that things between Sole and I had developed. Not even Clara, and I told her close to everything. I'd called her about ten seconds after leaving Rose's place after our first time together, and about that long after Rose had walked out my door, never to return, a couple of years after that. But this thing with Soledad seemed fragile and immense all at the same time—as though talking about it could somehow break the spell, and I didn't want to risk that happening. I wanted to keep her all to myself for a while longer.

"What?" I asked, a little defensive.

"There are surely better places than this to shake up the flavor of your days, Desi."

I waved her comment off.

"Have you thought any more about entering that contest I emailed you about?"

At first, I wasn't sure what she meant; then I remembered. "That community portraits thing?" Gina gave me an *of-course-that's-what-I-meant* look. "No, I didn't look at the site all that closely."

"Desi." She said my name almost like my mother would if I'd been caught up to no good.

Raising my hands in an act of surrender, I said, "Okay, okay. I'll take a look."

"Good."

"Maybe," I added. Before she could respond, my phone vibrated. "One sec." I held up a finger and, partially lifting my butt from the chair, retrieved the phone from my pocket. It was Hope. She rarely called—only texted. At least she was ringing from her own phone this time. Scrunching up my face, I accepted the call. "Heya. Everything okay?"

"Desi," she said, her voice thick with reluctance. "I'm in trouble again."

Feeling Gina's discerning eyes on me, I glanced at her and saw a small fraction of my own concern mirrored on her face. My mind stumbled over a thousand possibilities in the space of a moment. Had there been an intruder at school? Did someone have a weapon? Was Hope safe? Had someone been bullying her? Was she lost somewhere without any money?

So many scenarios. So many potential disasters. My hands vibrated with anxiety, my mouth becoming drier.

Just let her be safe.

"What is it? What's happened? Do you need me to come to get you?" I spoke so fast that the words all rolled together, but with my heart rate spiking, I couldn't help myself. What if Hope was going to end up like Brody, in trouble so often that she became bogged in a life characterized by suffering? No. That couldn't happen.

"Do you want to talk to her?" Hope said, her words directed at someone other than me, someone who must have been with her. With my spare hand, I rubbed at my forehead, hard. The pressure did nothing to still the shaking of my fingers, nor did it quell the tide of thoughts reaching a crescendo between my ears. "Here," Hope added. Rummaging noises and muted voices came down the line, the phone changing hands.

"Desi?" Sole asked. My heart swelled with both alarm and relief. If Soledad was with Hope, that meant my foster daughter had been tangled up with the police again. But it also meant there was someone there, someone vaguely familiar to Hope who would look out for her. And I had no shred of doubt that Sole would do her best by Hope, whatever the situation may have been. "Des, can you hear me? Did I lose you?"

I shook my head, untangling the web of thoughts locking me in silence. As I did, Gina stood, one hand on her hip, the other across her chest as she paced.

"Yeah," I croaked. "Sorry, Sole. I'm here. Is Hope okay?"

A moment passed. And another. Why was Soledad hesitating? Was it bad news?

"She's safe," Sole said at last. "But she's been picked up by patrol officers. My partner and I often get asked to help out with the juvenile cases when they turn up at the station; it's our unofficial specialty. She was caught shoplifting."

"Shoplifting!" My tone came out harsher than I'd expected, and Gina froze on the spot. My pulse drummed in my wrists as disappointment and anger flooded my body. It was that special kind of anger only experienced by parents, the kind fueled by fear.

"Yeah," Soledad replied. "She'd taken several items from at least two different stores. We're still discussing the finer details with the arresting officer, but I think you'd better come down here."

I clenched my fist, then released it again, forcing myself to be careful with my words, with my reactions. My toes tapped against the carpeted floor of Gina's office involuntarily. "Shoplifting," I repeated. This time, the word hung in the air as a question, an expression of disbelief rather than an accusation. What could Hope need that she would rather steal than discuss with me?

Almost as quickly as it had swamped my thoughts, the outrage subsided, swept away by the easing of my fears. At least this time, Hope hadn't been caught up in something as dangerous as handling money for a drug dealer. Or worse. Of course, I didn't want her stealing, but in that moment, with my temples still pounding and my hands unsteady, shoplifting suddenly didn't seem so bad.

"Mm-hmm," Soledad confirmed. "Her second offense. She's almost out of chances. But if you come in, we can discuss it properly."

I confirmed I'd be on my way shortly.

"Des?" Sole said, some of the professionalism fading from her voice. "Are you okay with me being attached to this? I know we are all still getting to know each other, but if it's awkward, I can have Washington discuss Hope's case with you. You met him last time. Or I can even—"

"No," I cut Soledad off, sensing her nervousness about the situation, a nervousness that seemed uncharacteristic for her. "It's okay. I'm glad that you're there." With that, I ended the call and set my phone down. For a few seconds, I stared mindlessly at the Star Fleet logo emblazoned across my phone case, unsure of exactly what to say.

"Geez, Desi." Gina handed me a glass of water that I hadn't seen her fetch and, though I wasn't thirsty, I accepted the offering with a grateful widening of my eyes. "Hope's at the police station?"

"Yes," I admitted quietly. "I don't get it, Gina. I mean, there are worse things she can do than shoplifting. But there's more to it than that. I don't understand why she's doing these things. Between the night with the cash at that rave, and this, it's like she needs money for something. Something she's not willing to tell me about."

Gina looked to the floor, her eyes unseeing as she pondered something. "Makes sense. But for what?"

I slid the glass of water along the desk next to me, thanking Gina as I returned it. "I wish I knew." I sucked in a deep breath, but it did nothing to settle the butterflies traversing my stomach. "She doesn't trust me, Gina."

She balked. "Why would you say that? You two seem to get on great. Given how old she was and how many families she'd already lived with before you, things seem pretty damned good from where I'm sitting."

"But she hasn't asked me for anything. She hasn't *told* me anything. I have no idea how to help her because I don't even know what the problem is. I feel so useless." For the first time, I'd given voice to the apprehensions about our relationship I'd carried around for months. Things were fragile when a new foster placement moved in, but that was nothing compared to the challenges of the ordinary, of the maintenance of a relationship that had been established but not yet thoroughly tested.

Gina leaned in, setting her hand gently on my knee. Like a true matriarch, she patted my leg gently and tucked her chin, willing me to look at her. When I did, she gave me an understanding, tight-lipped smile. "Because, Desi, she's a teenager. How much did you tell your mom when you were almost sixteen?"

The butterflies slowed their pace as I reflected on my own adolescence. Even though my mother had been about as good a parent as anyone could ask for, I'd still kept plenty of things to myself. Not necessarily because I didn't love Mom or want to share my life with her, but so I could have things that belonged to me and me alone. "I guess you're right," I conceded, sluggishly reaching for my car keys. "Are you ever wrong about anything, Gina?"

She chortled and rose from her seat, pretending to polish her nails against her pastel blue blouse before blowing on them. "Someday, perhaps. There's a first time for everything."

"True." I laughed for a moment; then the reality of driving to the station yet again set in. It was all feeling far too familiar. "Thanks for looking out for me."

Gina's face turned serious, and she extended her hand to help me up, a habit she'd developed when my endo pain had been at its height, before the IUD. "Always, Des. Despite what you seem to think sometimes, you're well and truly worth looking out for. Good luck."

After dragging myself out of the seat, I inhaled deeply and squared my shoulders. "Thanks," I replied. "I'll need it."

CHAPTER TWENTY-ONE

I FOUND MY way around the police station easily, which unsettled me. The first floor must have been cleaned in recent hours as the fruity scent of cleaning fluid almost overpowered me. Coffee still rode through the air in waves, and rushed footsteps echoed throughout the open-plan bull pen, the population of which seemed to have doubled since I'd been there last.

Sole waved from across the room, a manila folder fixed firmly beneath her arm as she spoke into a cell phone wedged between her ear and shoulder. Though she clearly had her hands full, Soledad still managed to glow with an aura of energy I didn't think I'd ever possessed—not even as a kid, back when the oft self-imposed expectations of adulthood had yet to dull my edges. As I moved closer, her voice came into focus, and I realized she was speaking Spanish, her language skills no doubt an asset to officers and clients alike in such a multicultural community.

I hadn't realized that Officer Washington, the man who had been so kind to us the last time Hope had been in trouble, was Soledad's partner. It occurred to me that Sole had mentioned him when she'd called earlier, but my mind had been in such a jumble that it hadn't fully registered until now. Officer Washington intercepted me as I approached Sole's desk, offering an assertive handshake. An uncooperative fluorescent light flickered and hissed directly above us, momentarily drawing my attention.

"Sorry to see you here again," he said, frowning. Washington glanced over his shoulder, and I followed his gaze to Hope, slumped in a chair nestled beneath the windows of the far wall. Her sunken eyes were downcast, her shoulders heavy. She'd drawn one knee toward her belly, her foot perched on the edge of the seat as she hugged her leg. She looked like she'd been crying not so long ago. Seeing her so defeated made something twist painfully inside my chest, a sense of taut anticipation at how this would play out dropping inside me like a rusty anchor.

"I don't understand why she'd try to steal anything," I said mournfully. "Can I talk to her?"

Officer Washington returned his attention to me and shook his head. "Best not just yet. Have a seat, and when Reyes is finished with her call, we can talk about a few things."

That didn't sound good. Shoplifting could see Hope end up in juvenile court, couldn't it? She could serve time, and that might ruin her. It would ruin me too. I couldn't stand to think about what her life would be like if she was locked away. Alternatively, even if she wasn't incarcerated, the state might see this as a reason to remove her from my care. Either way, I'd never forgive myself.

A choking fear rose within me, holding me in its grip as I studied Hope, both of us motionless. When Soledad returned the receiver of her phone to its console with a dull thud, I cleared my throat.

"Is she going to be kept here? Detained, I mean?" My voice came out as barely more than a whisper, as I did all I could to crush the shards of ice in my throat.

By way of reply, Washington put his hand on a chair near his desk, the same one I'd sat upon previously, gesturing me toward the seat. The wood felt cold against my skin, hard. He gave my shoulder a gentle squeeze, then took up position behind his desk. The chair and subsequent squeeze of my shoulder had been offered as reassurance, but all it did was stretch the moment until it felt like an explosive bubble. Why was he being so evasive?

At last, Soledad dropped the folder she'd been clutching, adding to a chaotic sprawl of similar folders of various colors perched precariously along the hutch of her desk. Her workspace nestled against Washington's and appeared as a stark contrast to his meticulously organized system of filing. She may have maintained the front area of her apartment impeccably, but she seemed to take a different approach to her workspace.

Sole pulled her chair around to form a close-knit semi-circle, her knees almost touching mine, but not quite. It surprised me how much I wanted to hug her at that moment, despite her professional demeanor and somewhat detached expression. I craved her arms around me. I wanted to be comforted and soothed. To have her ease my worries. But she was at work, in full uniform, and I was the carer of a perpetrator, so that was not about to happen.

"Thanks for coming in so fast," she said, her eyes unreadable.

"Of course," I replied, rubbing at my thighs with my palms. "How bad is it?"

Soledad and Officer Washington exchanged a brief but pointed glance, as though deciding who would be the one to respond. "Not as bad as you're thinking," Sole said. "But we need to explain a few things to you, the same as we have to Hope."

I nodded, and they began.

Hope had been confronted by a merchant at an electronics store, who'd been within his rights to detain her after he'd noticed her stalking through the more remote sections of the store, nervously eying the shelves. She'd burst into tears as soon as the manager had requested to search her bag, and not knowing quite what to do with her, he'd walked Hope to the staff's break room and called the police.

When the mall cops arrived, Hope had admitted to shoplifting before they'd even had to question her. She'd stolen seemingly random, unrelated items that added up to nearly four hundred dollars in worth. They'd told Hope that stealing was a serious crime that could land her in a lot of trouble, particularly if she did it again after she turned eighteen. She could also be charged with misdemeanor petty theft, leaving her with a hefty fine and even a few months of jail time.

At that, my stomach lurched and my eyes diverted to

Hope. I wasn't sure if she could hear our conversation over the bustling chatter that bounced about the station, but she looked straight at me. Her chin retreated and dimpled. Her eyelids seemed to quiver as fresh tears formed. I did my best to send her a silent message that could give her some measure of absolution: *It'll be okay.* Recognition bloomed in her eyes, and she dropped her head, hiding half of her face beneath her gray hoodie.

"You said that she *could* be in a lot of trouble," I probed when a pause presented itself in their explanation. "Does that mean she may not be...this time?"

"The juvenile court tends to look at this sort of situation with the goal of diverting young people from crime," Washington replied, massaging his brow as he spoke. "No one wants to punish someone so young, but we need to be careful things like this don't escalate, either."

I drew in a long, pensive breath. Everything he'd said seemed fair, though it still felt like something was coming; as though a heavy boulder hung over our heads, dangling, waiting for the perfect moment to fall, to flatten Hope and me. There was nowhere we could hide, and nothing I could do to keep her safe. And isn't that my job? To keep her safe? Perhaps I'd been negligent. Perhaps...perhaps this was all my fault.

"The merchants she stole from might send you civil demand letters. Basically, it's their right to seek damages through a civil suit," Washington said, his voice steady and flat. He'd obviously had to pass on all of this information many times before.

"But," Soledad interjected, "I got the impression from the store managers that they were satisfied Hope was genuinely sorry, so I don't think that'll happen."

"Not that we can promise anything," Washington added, his eyebrow arched at his partner as though sending her a pointed message.

"No," Sole conceded, her gaze dropping. "The court might put Hope on probation. That usually means she'll be instructed to stay in school for a certain amount of time, or maybe do some community service. They could also instruct her to attend a state counseling service."

That didn't sound so bad, I thought. Unless they also decided that her even needing to *be* on probation was down to my poor parenting, and then I could lose her. Maybe they'd be right, though. I'd been distracted recently. I hadn't been spending as much time with her as I should. Instead, I'd taken on more jobs for Gina, and I'd spent time with Soledad. I hadn't been there for Hope as much as I could have been. If I had, wouldn't she have talked to me about whatever it was she needed money for?

"She'll go to court?" My voice came out gravelly, like I'd swallowed a jar of sand and had lost the ability to fully form sounds.

"More than likely," Washington said, the hint of an apology in his tone. "But we aren't sure yet. For now, she'll go home with you. We'll make a recommendation to the OJJDP, and you'll receive a formal notice in writing of the outcome."

"Office of Juvenile Justice and Delinquency Prevention," Soledad clarified.

"Thanks," I said, turning my gaze to Hope. I hadn't yet told Soledad all of the details about Brody, about the fact I already knew who the OJJDP were and that they terrified me. I planted my elbow on the arm of the chair and sank my chin into my palm. "I wish she'd talk to me about all this."

Soledad folded forward, her hand gently nudging my thigh. To an unknowing onlooker, it would seem as though our touch were incidental, a simple error of proximity. The subtle fanning of her index finger against my leg, however, told me otherwise. "Hey," she asserted. "This is *not* your fault. Every parent who comes in here thinks the same things: What did I do wrong? How do I discipline my kid without pushing her away?

"Most parents think they've been selfish, but it isn't true. The ones who think that are the ones who are doing the best they can. You'd be surprised how many don't even turn up for their teenagers when we call. You're here. That's important, and eventually, she'll know that too."

There she goes again, I thought, *reading my mind*. I wished she weren't so good at seeing right into my soul. It was unnerving at best. At worst, it tempted me to let myself keep falling. But I couldn't. Hope needed all of my attention to get through whatever she was experiencing, and that meant I had to be home more and, when I was home, I needed to be present, instead of thinking about Sole, or wishing, selfishly, that I was with Sole. Disappearing overnight on a regular basis could very well be sending Hope all the wrong messages about what my priorities were. *I have the whole rest of my life to find a relationship, to build something with another adult. But Hope only has one shot at her youth. I only have one shot at making sure she knows she is safe—that she is loved.*

I shifted my weight, forcing Sole to retract her hand. The smallest glint of disappointment flickered in her eyes—

a disappointment that mirrored my own—but when she straightened, she was all business once more. Though we'd said nothing, I could see she understood that I needed to step away from what had been developing between us.

"Thank you," I said, looking at Washington. "You've both been patient, and I'm sure you've got a pretty full plate."

Washington huffed. "You could say that. But don't think anything of it. That's why we became cops. No one wants to see a good kid end up in a bad situation."

My knees groaned as I stood, as though I'd been sitting there for hours rather than a few minutes. The two police officers stood with me and, shaking my hand, wished Hope and me well. Soledad's hand, both strong and delicate at the same time, lingered a fraction longer than Washington's had, her smile listless. I'd upset her with my lukewarm responses. I wished I hadn't, but maybe it was for the best. I needed to pull back and, like the old saying went, there was no time like the present.

When Hope and I made to leave, her head still hanging low, her hands thrust deep in her pockets, Hope stopped. She pivoted, gazing at Washington and Reyes. Sensing her eyes on them, the officers paused their whispered conversation and looked at her. "Thank you," Hope mouthed. Though no sound came out, there was no doubting her sincerity. Whatever they'd said to her before I arrived, she truly, deeply appreciated their intervention.

A warmth glowed inside my belly. Any kid who thanked the cops that arrested them had to be special, had to care about people and care about herself too. And that meant there was still a chance to salvage our increasingly distant relationship. I could still reach her, because she was still *here*. The problem was working out exactly how to reach her and then to do whatever needed to be done.

Chapter Twenty-Two

HOPE STUDIED ME, her eyes narrowed and her forehead creased. "You've cooked me bacon?" She kept her attention on me though she avoided my eyes. Her posture seemed unsure as she slipped onto a dining chair, her fingers spread wide over the surface of the table.

Heaping crispy bacon atop a pair of poached eggs, I shrugged. "I've got to be honest, cooking this has not been my favorite experience this week, but just because I'm a vegetarian doesn't mean you shouldn't be able to eat things you enjoy." After setting the plate in front of Hope, I returned to the kitchen counter and collected my own breakfast, a serving of fruit salad with yogurt and coconut flakes, before sitting with her.

"Thanks," Hope muttered, her shoulders still slumped

as she picked up her cutlery.

"Why so serious?" I pointed at her meal with my spoon. "Don't tell me you're going off meat? Not that I'd be unhappy about that."

Hope prodded her food with the fork but didn't eat, her eyes remaining downcast. She still wore the same oversized hoodie I'd picked her up in last night, her cropped hair obscured and her torso all but swallowed. Had she showered? If she wasn't eating, and hadn't felt like cleaning herself up, I had even more to be concerned about that I'd thought. At least her jeans had been swapped for pajama bottoms.

When she didn't respond, I straightened my back and angled my head. "Hope?"

Her eyelids fluttered as though a sphere of thought had burst in her mind. "Yeah. Sorry, I heard you." She cut into an egg and, after letting the yoke spill onto the toast, collected a portion onto her fork and began to eat. My stomach unclenched and I, too, was able to eat.

After a few moments of silence, she set her cutlery on the plate. "Why did you make this?" Her voice was quiet, tentative.

Dabbing at the side of my mouth with a napkin, I tried my best to keep my face slack, to push down the disappointed parent, the hurt and angry mother who wanted to scream and rant and make Hope see reason. I forced a slow, contemplative inhalation into my chest, as though filling my sternum with clarity and patience.

"Because," I said, the word coming out too softly, too meekly. I cleared my throat and tried again, my voice stronger this time, but still calm. "Because I want you to feel safe."

Hope looked up, making meaningful, prolonged eye contact for this first time that morning, a silent question fixed upon her face.

"It terrifies me to think that you are out there"—I waved my arm, as though blanketing the world—"in unsafe situations. Holding money for a dealer. Stealing from stores. Anything could happen."

Hope dropped her head and her cheeks reddened. She said nothing, but made no move to leave either, her napkin pulled taut between her hands. And so I continued, "What makes it worse, though, is that you'd only be doing these things—making yourself *physically* unsafe—because you don't feel *emotionally* safe. Getting mad at you now...it wouldn't achieve anything. I know you're beating yourself up enough as it is."

I paused, taking a sip of water from a nearby glass. The cool drink did nothing to expel the sand that seemed to coat the inside of my mouth. Licking my lips, I forced myself to continue. I had to get this out. We needed to keep the channels of communication open if this foster placement was going to work. "You know you've done the wrong thing. And I know that you aren't someone who disregards laws, certainly not without a good reason. Please, Hope, know that I'm here. If you need money for something, you can talk to me about it. I may not be the richest person around, but I budget well, and I'll do what I can to help. If you need someone to talk to, or even to sit in silence with, I'm here for that too. You know that, right?"

Hope gave a slow nod. Though she'd glued her chin to her chest, casting most of her face in shadow, there was no missing the tears that rolled down her cheek. I wished she'd say something. I'd even have settled for her telling me to get lost, to shut up, to stay out of her life. Anything at all. But the quiet lingered, thick and menacing. The clock in the corridor ticked, louder than I remembered it having been before, but at a pace much slower than the beating of my heart.

At last, she spoke. "I know." She sniffed, perhaps trying to mask the extent of her tears. "I do. I just..." She shook her head as though disagreeing with herself, like she was about to tell me something but had thought better of it. "I know," she repeated, her tone leaving no room for further discussion.

I suppressed a sigh. Maybe that was the best I could ask for—that she was aware of another option to whatever choices she faced.

"I'm glad." I spooned some yogurt into my mouth, and Hope set about eating her own food. The new silence that descended wasn't an entirely uncomfortable one. Hope seemed relieved that I hadn't continued to push the issue, and she started swiping at the screen of her phone as she ate. Normally, I'd have discouraged her from playing with the cell phone during a meal, but I remembered what my own mom had always told me: you've gotta pick your battles.

After breakfast, Hope ambled to her room and gently closed the door. A few moments later, muted music sounded, marking a definite end to our interactions for a while. Having stacked the dishes and wiped the counter, I washed my hands under too-cold water. As I dried my hands, the old kitchen towel scratched my skin and I tossed it into the trash.

Gingey whined from the backyard. I appreciated the reminder of her presence, endlessly loving and unfailing.

Outside, cool, crisp air caressed my arms and neck as Ginger Snaps licked at my bare feet. Chuckling, I flopped onto a beach chair near the back door and let her leap into my lap. I roughed up her hair and scratched at her ears, ignoring the discomfort of her bulky frame as she moved about in circles until finally settling with the top of her head tucked beneath my chin. Warm and soft, a hug from Gingey never failed to bring comfort.

The day had not truly set in yet. Though the sky overhead was blue, my small backyard remained shrouded in shadow, the sun having not reached high enough to peek over the fences and trees. Through her open window, I could make out the music from Hope's room more clearly. As usual, I didn't know the name of the band, but I recognized some of the lyrics. Maybe I wasn't completely out of touch yet.

As Ginger Snaps and I sank deeper into our human-canine cuddle, my mind drifted.

I hadn't heard from Soledad since we'd left the police station, and I didn't know what to feel. It was likely she knew we needed space and didn't want to push, and she would've been right to think that way given the undeniable wall I'd erected between us without so much as a word. At the same time, I already missed her. Our steady stream of messages and voicemails had fast become a familiar and welcome feature of my days. I knew when her shifts started and ended, because I'd hear from her at each of those times. She knew what time of day I updated social media for Gina's company, as she'd often send me quirky comments, guessing at the type of people that lived in the houses we listed.

As though she'd sensed me thinking of her, my phone

vibrated, a message from Sole. Sometimes, it really did feel like the universe itself was pushing us together. But I couldn't think that way.

Sole asked if Hope and I were okay and if we needed anything. It took all of my willpower not to ring her and call out, "You! Come over, please. I just want you." As I sank my chin into the softness of Gingey's head, a sad sense of regret swam through me. I had been spending too much time away from home, both physically and emotionally. Hope may not have wanted or needed anything from me right at that moment, but that could quickly change.

Things seem alright, I replied. *Thanks for checking on us.*

I'd barely tapped the Send button when the screen flashed excitedly, an incoming call. It occurred to me to ignore the call, to let it go to voicemail, but given the speed at which Soledad had rung, she would know I couldn't have set the phone down. She would know I'd made the choice to dismiss her. As much as I needed to create some distance between us to be a better parent, such an obvious shut-down would hurt her, and I wasn't prepared to cause such upset, not when all she had done so far was care for us.

"Hi." The detachment in my voice surprised even me, and the moment of silence that followed told me Soledad detected it as well.

"You picked up," she said. "I thought that maybe you wouldn't."

"You need to stop reading my mind," I replied, sinking into the conversation, her ever-silky voice drawing me in.

"You wouldn't want to ruin all of my fun, would you?" Her suggestive tone left me frozen, unable to respond. After a beat she added, "It doesn't have to be finished, Desi."

The way she said my name always sent a sliver of pleasure through me. Though Soledad didn't have an accent like her mother's, there was a slightly uncommon inflection in how she said certain words. It wasn't just her pronunciation though; it was the mixture of sincerity and assertiveness that always framed her words.

"I think it does. Need to be finished, I mean." Guilt latched onto the inside my stomach, sharp claws pulling at the corners of my gut. "She's a good kid. I can't let her keep going down whatever path this is. If she ends up in juvenile detention, that would be it. Her life would be ruined."

"I do agree on that point. But you don't need to give up everything you want to be there for her. That is..." She inhaled deeply. "That is, if you do want me."

I rubbed the forefinger and thumb of my free hand together, then dropped my arm, embracing the sleeping pup still nestled into my torso. "You know the answer to that. I wanted to see where this could go, but I can't keep splitting my attention. New relationships are such a whirlwind; they're consuming."

And I had most definitely been consumed.

"Does this relate to the boy you cared for? Brody."

My eyelids were suddenly heavy and, as I spoke, I let them close.

"What happened with him?"

I felt like I owed Soledad an explanation. She deserved to know after I'd been so hot-and-cold with her. "It isn't an uncommon story. What with your job, it won't even seem all that bad."

"Try me," she challenged.

"Okay." As Sole did sometimes, I elasticized the vowel, drawing the word out. "He was almost twelve when he moved in. And such a charmer. You couldn't not like him. He loved reading. Loved mystery stories. And he had a decent singing voice." I laughed at the memory, "Gosh. He was so obsessed with Bruno Mars. Even though his classmates picked on him for it."

"Sounds like a good kid. What happened?"

I opened my eyes, the daylight greeted me, but I was in no mood for such a brilliant blue sky. "A few foster placements start off that way. Poor kids. They try so hard to make you like them because they want a family, but when it's a performance, like it was with him, then it exhausts them."

"It becomes unsustainable."

"Exactly. After about six months, the cracks started to show. I had a partner. Rose. We tried to set boundaries. We had rules like, if he wanted to go anywhere on the weekend, he needed to let us know by Thursday. The idea was to encourage him to be organized, to be mature. He was only thirteen, and we didn't want him running around without knowing where he was."

"Sounds fair," Sole replied.

I picked at a loose thread on my dog's collar, tugging until it broke. "I guess. He became so frustrated though. He'd miss the deadline and then tantrum when we said no. Rules are rules. And I mean tantrum. Picture a boy, taller than me, lying on the floor of his bedroom, flailing. Kicking his arms and legs. Screaming."

"Wow. That sounds intense, Desi."

"He started skipping school. We'd ground him. Take his phone away. Turn off the internet. Lecture him. Ban his

Xbox. It all made it worse. When we talked to a psychologist about all this later, she suggested Brody sounded like he had attachment disorder."

"I've heard of that," Sole said. "Is that when they didn't develop a healthy parental attachment as a baby?"

"Yeah. Their brains don't know how to build relationships because they never learned how during the most critical years of their development. If they start to love someone, or feel connected, they panic."

"He pushed you away. I'm sorry, Des. That must have been difficult."

"You could say that." I gulped, struggling to finish the story. "He went to another foster home for a few days. Just for respite, you know? To give everyone a break after he'd been suspended for acting up at school. During those few days, he ran off from the respite carer and came back to the house when we were out. Brought a bunch of his new *friends* with him. Teens he'd met wandering the streets when he was meant to be at school. They trashed the place. They drank most of our wine, smashing bottles against the walls and stomping the glass all through the carpet. The whole place stank of marijuana. We couldn't get the stench out of the curtains."

"Des..."

I turned to wipe my nose against my shoulder, given both my hands were busy, one cuddling Ginger Snaps, the other holding the phone. I sniffed. God, I wanted a cigarette.

"It's okay. It was a while ago now. He told his case worker he didn't want to come back. Rose didn't want him back, either. He'd wrecked the place. The last time I saw him, I told him that I wanted him to know we were not kicking him out. That he could stay, if he wanted."

"What did he say?"

I let out a short laugh, a sound characterized by disbelief rather than mirth. "Nothing. He said nothing. He didn't even look at me. Anyway. Long story short, he ended up in juvie about six months later. He was barely fourteen, and he served time for vandalism and assault."

"Oh." Her tone made it clear she knew exactly what that meant. Once a child that age ended up behind bars, the statistics were against him. "And he kept going back in?"

"Yeah. The sad thing is, he finally found a family, a group he seems to have stuck with. Only problem is...they're a gang."

"From what I've seen and what you've told me, Des, I don't think Hope will end up like that."

"You can't know that. Not for sure. I like you, Soledad. I like you a lot. But ultimately, it's not a risk I can take."

There was a long pause. "How about a compromise?"

I raised my eyebrows, surprised. "What kind of compromise?"

"Well, instead of cutting off the engine, why don't we gently press the brake pedal?"

"I'm not sure that would be enough. I don't even know if I *could* slow down." An embarrassing, but genuine admission. Continuing a relationship with Sole but limiting how much we saw each other sounded awful, given how many minutes of my day in recent weeks had been spent thinking about the next time I would see her and, more importantly, the next time I would touch her.

Soledad offered a suggestion. "A friendship, then?" When I didn't answer straight away, she added, "I like you.

And I like Hope and it could be good for her to broaden her support network. We could be friends, stay connected. We could take the pressure off ourselves and if, when the family situation settles, we still feel like we do now, then all the better. The possibility hasn't been cut off. We could keep things as they are or try this again."

Her idea tempted me more than I could say, though I still doubted my own self-control. She did seem to have a natural way of connecting with Hope though, and heaven knew both of us had room for meaningful friendships. Still, I wasn't sure. What if things didn't work out and Hope was hurt? Disappointed by another lost relationship. Maybe I could take this easy; have their spheres nudge, but not quite converge until I was sure things were working.

"Okay," I said, forcing a confidence I didn't feel, something I realized I did pretty often. A stab of guilt shot through my chest though. I couldn't quite articulate how or why, even in my own head, but I knew it felt selfish to go down this path.

Without missing a beat, Soledad chortled. "Good answer. Now that we're friends, how about you come over soon?"

I choked on my own breath for a second, letting loose an ugly-sounding cough.

"As in…"

"Both of you. Hope too. We could teach her how to play baseball on an Xbox. Or share the joys of Bruce Willis films or something."

Ginger Snaps yawned, a great, audible exhalation. My cheeks were warm with the embarrassment of my assumption. Gingey, not opening her eyes, nudged my chin with her nose before settling back to sleep. I took her puppy kiss as a sign. "Sure. Why the heck not?"

"Actually," she started, the pitch of her voice rising. "My family is having a party at my mother's house. A combined celebration—she's saying farewell to the old place, but it's also Chile's national day on the eighteenth. They celebrate almost all month in Chile, and we can't let September go by without a good house party. Will you both come? It won't be a date. It'll be friends and families being together and enjoying each other's company."

"Are you sure? Would we not be intruding?"

She laughed. "Oh, Des. Wait until you come. You'll see that no one could be intruding. People bring their partners, kids, friends, maybe even a neighbor they've spoken to twice if they feel like it. The perfect distraction for Hope. I should warn you though: it'll be *loud*."

The joy in her voice was more than inviting. This sounded like something Hope and I could both enjoy, and a generally positive experience. Hope respected Soledad, which was a small miracle given she'd had two run-ins with the police. We could all do with a nice party, couldn't we? "Okay," I said assertively. "We're in."

As the call ended, the sweet sense of elation I felt whilst talking to Soledad broke apart like fragile leaves in the wind. I'd kept her in my life, and perhaps even secured a kind of mentor for Hope, someone who could be a positive influence, but at what cost? I had never believed in that insta-love stuff. And I wasn't in love with Soledad, but I still had no doubt that, given enough time, I absolutely would fall in love with her. Being around her enough to keep a connection alive, but not enough to truly satisfy the emotional and physical longings inside me was going to be hard. But so was finding a way forward with Hope.

"Good thing you're a puppy, Ginger Snaps. Being a grown-up is way too damned hard."

CHAPTER TWENTY-THREE

SOLEDAD WASN'T KIDDING when she said the party would be loud. The last time I had seen Claudia Reyes's house, it had stood as an impeccable lone soldier, neatly dressed and at full attention. Now, teeming with bodies and pulsating with music, the property had transformed entirely.

Blue and white decorations adorned nearly every window and doorway, and over the front door hung a Chilean flag, a long and flat strip of red along the bottom, the top half split into blue and white and a five-point star at the center of the patch of blue. The silky material slid along my face and chest as Hope and I passed beneath it, led into the building by an older man who had answered the door. At least six foot three, the man had fleshy arms that strained against the sleeves of his tight shirt, arms that waved and gesticulated as he shouldered his way through the energetic crowd, carving a path for us to the kitchen, talking to people as he went.

"Llegaron las gringas!" he announced as we entered the room, his deep voice booming over the music wafting through the open window. A group of seven or eight women, ranging from a girl slightly younger than Hope who sliced cabbage through to a woman so well aged that blue veins popped in her hands and wrist as she peeled vegetables, continued to chat despite the boisterous declaration of our arrival. The man swatted the air and huffed, as though dismissing the group for the tenth time today. "Good luck, *chicas nuevas*." He grinned at us as he turned, ambling back the way he'd come. When he'd disappeared, the women broke out into a triumphant, joyous laughter that startled me. Hope gave me a questioning look, and I shrugged, a silent instruction to *go with it*.

"You're here!" I heard Sole but couldn't see her. A moment later she edged past the older woman, seeming to emerge from nowhere. She wore one of her signature tank tops and a pair of washed-out, torn jeans, her hair flowing down over her shoulders. "Don't mind us. That was my uncle Lucas. He offended one of the girls this morning, so now he's in the doghouse, so to speak." She greeted first Hope, and then me, with light kiss to the cheek.

"Really?" I looked over my shoulder, but Lucas was long gone.

"Nothing too exciting," she replied. "But they'll tease him for a few hours. There's always some drama or another around here. All part of the fun, right?" Her cheeks lifted as a grin reached for her eyes. "I'm glad you're both here."

I bit my lower lip and dropped my gaze, readjusting my internal settings to *just friends* before making eye contact again. "So are we. Seems like a very lively event."

Sole laughed, and my stomach clenched at the easy beauty of her luminous eyes. "That it is. And you haven't even seen half of it yet." She looked to Hope. "How are you? Staying out of trouble?"

"I'm fine, thanks."

Sole lifted her chin in an expression of mock indignation. "Fine? That's all I get from my baseball groupie?"

Hope's smile seemed more genuine now, her eyes rolling gently as though giving in. "I'm good. School. Home. More school. It's all okay."

"Excellent." Sole clapped her hands together. "I better show you around. Introduce you to a few people."

We met the group of women who'd been pretending not to watch us, each one a cousin or an aunt, except for the youngest who was the daughter of Claudia's neighbor. Each of them welcomed us in turn. They all managed to move about the medium-sized kitchen with ease, swapping plates, chopping boards, and utensils, changing position and accommodating each other's movements as though they'd done it all a hundred times before. It was incredible. If I had been in a kitchen with Brenna and Clara trying to prepare an elaborate meal, the three of us would've ended up in a vortex of cranky slurs that resulted in someone ordering pizza.

"Hope," Sole said, directing her attention to the youngest of the women. "Did you want to help Carla with the ensalada?"

"Ahh..."

"It's easy. But you don't have to if you'd prefer not. You're more than welcome to come outside. But if you'd rather have something to sink your hands into—"

"Sure," Hope said, her eyes more excited than her tone. It was a good idea. Give Hope something to do, and someone around her own age to do it with, to help her ease into the new social setting.

"Great." Soledad ushered Hope over to Carla, and almost immediately the girl began directing Hope, placing a large bowl of cilantro in front of her. Hope nodded in response to Carla's instructions, and my core warmed, seeing her sink into the interaction, the two of them chatting straight away.

When Soledad appeared at my side, once again at the periphery of the busy kitchen, I silently thanked her with a look. "Hopefully my *tias* don't interrogate her too deeply," Sole said. "The aunties love meeting new people. Oh! Do you want to see the asado? And meet the grill-master?"

"Absolutely."

Just as women had dominated the space within the house, men largely populated the outdoor area. Red, white, and blue lanterns hung from a line of wire suspended between the house and the back fence. Beneath them, about twenty men and a couple of women dotted the fence line, mingling in groups, their faces turned toward the asado as they tapped their feet and swayed their hips in time to music that filled the space with a positive energy.

A large grate rested atop a firepit that had been covered when I'd photographed the house, hot coals bright against the dark edges of the asado. Skewers tightly lined the grate, each covered in diced pieces of meat with either potato or bread on each end.

Soledad noticed me inspecting the food. "Anticuchos," she explained. "They're so good! We marinate the meat in spices, things like cumin, garlic, or ají pepper. I love them. Oh!" Her hand flew to her mouth, her face scrunching up in a look of subdued horror. "I am so sorry. I forgot you're a vegetarian."

I chuckled and scratched my thumbnail against my eyebrow. "It's fine. It seemed like there were loads of salads inside. I always find something I can eat. But I bet you're right about the taste; it does smell incredible out here."

She dropped her hand to her side. "Sorry," she said, like she was apologizing for giving me a present and taking it away again.

I grasped her forearm. "It's fine. Don't worry!"

Scanning the area again, I saw Austin and his new girlfriend, Lena, engaged in conversation with a man in his late fifties or early sixties across the other side of the yard. I should have realized he'd be there.

"Is it all right? That he's here?" Sole asked, following my gaze.

I nodded, though not convincingly, because she gave me an apologetic look.

"Family's family," she said. "Have you met Lena?"

"Yeah. Clara and I ran into them. Can't say I found much about her to be all that impressive."

Soledad let out a surprised chuckle. "You are definitely no good at first impressions."

"What do you mean?"

"Lena." Sole flicked her chin toward the chatting trio. "She's not only studying to be a human rights attorney, but she not long ago won a community award for her work in a local shelter that mostly helps homeless LGBT teenagers."

"Seriously?" My tone did nothing to mask the extent of my surprise.

"Why are you shocked?" Her question contained no malice; her questions never did. But she was curious, and I had to admit, I wasn't entirely sure myself.

"I guess…" I sighed. "I guess because I was making assumptions. She's young, and she—"

"Scooped up your sister's boyfriend?"

"Yeah," I muttered. "Geez. I am a bit of an asshole sometimes."

"Aren't we all?

"You are way too accommodating. I was being a jerk. I try so hard not to judge people. I even get snippy when I see other people do it. But then end up doing it myself anyway. It's hypocritical."

"Don't worry so much. No one can stop themselves from making judgments. Not really. It's more important to recognize them, accept them, and hopefully be open to repairing them than to act like they don't exist."

I didn't know what to say. In a few words she'd given me one of the best pieces of advice I'd ever received in my entire life. The universe, doing me another solid, sent a distraction so I didn't need to find a way to hide how amazing I found this woman to be.

"There's our favorite *paca*!" A young man with a voice as bright as his demeanor threw his arms around Soledad's shoulders and planted a dramatic kiss on her cheek. "Where have you been hiding?"

Soledad jabbed him in the stomach with her elbow and

wiped at her face. "Inside, where do you think? I was help-ing. ¿Y *tú*??"

He scoffed and moved alongside her. "Oh, nothing im-portant, just feeding everyone."

Soledad sighed, though there was no malice in the ges-ture. "Desi, this is Daniel, our grill-master for today. Though he thinks that makes him lord of the universe."

Daniel held out his arm and I shook his hand, his grip firm. "She left out the part where I'm also her brother. Her younger, much better-looking brother."

Her eyes crinkled with amusement. "Oh, please. You're fifteen months younger than me."

"You have a brother?" I asked.

"Tres, actually," Daniel answered for her. "Though it's all downhill after meeting me. Max and Tom are around here somewhere if you insist on seeing for yourself."

"He's quite modest, as I'm sure you can tell," Soledad quipped. "Vamos, vamos." She shooed him with her hands. "Don't ruin the food." He raised his palms in mock surren-der, kissed Sole again, then took up position by the asado. Another man handed him a glass containing an amber-col-ored liquid, and they fell into a boisterous conversation that couldn't be heard over the distance and the music.

I tried a tentative "Sole?"

"Mmhmm?" She watched Daniel as he sipped at his drink and, using the most impressive tongs I'd ever seen, tenderly kept watch over the cooking food.

"Why do they call you *paca*? I remember your mom say-ing that when I was last here."

The music had grown louder, and she drew a circle in the air near her ear, indicating that she hadn't heard me.

After two more failed attempts to communicate, she took hold of my hand and led me around the side of the house, along a narrow path which took us to the front lawn.

The music, still distinct, had been muted enough to let us hear each other, and we settled on the porch, kicking our shoes off to sit with bare feet on the grass. We were alone out there, and suddenly the emotional wedge I'd driven between us became sharper, more invasive and palpable. I wanted so badly to edge closer, to press the outside of my thigh against hers, to intertwine our fingers, to... *Stop it. Hope is inside and you're here for her as much as for yourself. To help her unwind. To build friendships. Keep it together.*

"Wait one sec." Sole bounded to her feet and, before I could respond, disappeared inside, the screen door flapping closed on its own a few moments later. Whilst she was gone, I brushed my feet along the lawn, scrunching up my toes to caress the grass and enjoy its soft, ticklish texture.

Within a minute or two, Soledad reemerged, two drinks in hand. She passed me one as she sank onto the porch once more.

"Pisco punch," she explained. "A drink from home with a Californian twist."

"Alcoholic?"

"Yes. But if you stay for a while and only have one, you should be fine to drive."

"Well"—I practically hummed the word—"if a police officer says it'll be okay..."

She gave me a lopsided grin, watching as I tried the punch. Smoother than it smelled, the drink tasted of grapes, pineapple, and another more artificial sweetness I couldn't identify. As I swallowed, it took on an exciting kind of bite, akin to an underripe apple. Too strong to do more than sip, it was still palatable. Conscious of Sole's eyes on my mouth, I turned my body slightly and gazed down at the liquid in my glass. "That's delicious."

"I'm glad you like it. You know, pisco is something of a matter of national tension. Peruvians say they made it first. But us Chileans know the truth." She raised one eyebrow, mischievous.

"Good to know. I'll be sure not to step into that particular debate if it ever comes up."

"It's for the best," she said, her tone deadpan but her expression still rascally.

We passed the next few moments in quiet contemplation, each of us working our way through the pisco punch. "So," I finally said. "Why *paca*? What does that mean?"

"You caught that, did you?" She gave a one-shouldered shrug. "I've had the nickname for years now. Ever since I became a cop. It means, sort of, boss lady. It's not always a nice word in Chile, depending on how people use it. Cops, especially lady cops, aren't always well liked." She leaned back, pressing one palm against the porch behind her, lifting the glass to her lips with her other hand. After swallowing, she continued. "The family means it with nothing but love, though."

The screen door swung open and Claudia Reyes, dressed in a flowing dress that flared out from her waist, sauntered onto the porch. Soledad shuffled over, making space so Claudia could sink into the space between us. Mother and daughter, side by side, seemed so strong. Fierce and determined, somehow, like the world couldn't touch them as long as they stayed together. I wondered if the two of them would ever let me photograph some portraits, the two of them together.

"Desiree! Wonderful to have you back. That lovely Hope of yours is getting on so well with our baby Carla. We might need to adopt her."

"Thank you so much for having us here, Mrs. Reyes. And inviting Hope right into the fray. I'll come in and check on her soon."

Claudia patted the back of my hand like a true matriarch and looked to her daughter. Her eyes narrowed as though she'd read something between us. "This is *Fiestas Patrias*. You two are being too serious. We may not have ramadas here, but we can still celebrate in the space we have. Come. Eat. Dance." She flared her arms, her elbows gently brushing against both of us, encouragement to stand.

"We'll be there soon, Mamá. Give us a few minutes."

Claudia tilted her head and her face creased. "Okay," she said, the same resignation in her eyes creeping into her voice. "Oh, I should warn you though, your Tia Martina is looking for you. Perhaps avoid the dining room. She says she has some fantastic new man she wants you to meet."

Soledad pulled her lips into a thin, tight line. "Right. Thanks. One of these days she'll work out that I have no interest in marrying one of her friend's sons and will stop asking. We'll be in soon, truly."

I hadn't considered that Soledad's family may have mixed emotions about her sexuality, but why wouldn't they? Many families often did. She didn't seem to be at all insecure or concerned about her own identity, but I shouldn't have subconsciously assumed that her confidence meant she'd never encountered any sort of opposition or disapproval.

Claudia patted my hand, and Soledad's, one more time and, with a fair amount of effort and creaky knees, stood, then returned to the house. Once the door had settled back into place, I found a sense of curiosity pinching at my sternum. "You said lady cops aren't very well liked in Chile?"

"Depends who you ask and what they've experienced. But yes, that's generally true from what I know. I've only spent a few months of my life, in total, in Chile. But they're very serious people, Chilean police. They wear army green, the women always have their hair slicked back, identical makeup even. Stern as hell. You don't mess with them." She set her empty glass on the porch and leaned forward, pressing her forearms against her thighs.

"Does that mean..." I hesitated. Was it my place to ask questions like this?

"Go ahead," she prompted, her head turned to look at me. I loved her openness. She never seemed reluctant to share of herself.

"Does that mean people in your family, your community, would have been angry you became an officer? Is that a job they'd disapprove of?"

She dropped her head, then lifted it again, staring off into the distance as she interlaced her fingers. I twisted, to meet her both physically and emotionally. "You could say that. There can be a lot of tension when you're a woman, a lesbian, a cop, and Latina. A few of my friends and relatives found it hard to reconcile that I could be all of those things at the same time. And in my family, where police back in Chile have been the source of so much fear and pain, I can't blame them for feeling that way. Even I find it difficult sometimes to remember the reasons I've chosen to become part of a force that, in a time and place removed from my own experiences, has hurt people I love. I know that I don't fully understand the trauma and the experiences of my parents' generation. I'm impacted by it, but in a way that's more removed, that's less visceral. I guess I can only hope I've made good decisions for the right reasons."

"Why? Is that okay? To ask why you took all that on to be a cop?"

Soledad hitched up a leg, tucking it beneath her as she also twisted her body to face me more directly. "Of course."

She tousled her hair; I think mostly to give herself a moment. The tightness of her features told me a great deal about how difficult this reconciliation of identities had been for her, or perhaps, remained. Still, I was beginning to realize that Soledad, as open as she was, had a tendency to rope in her emotions. The challenging emotions, anyway. She seemed to adopt a sort of stoic façade whenever she delved into something deep about herself. I wondered if she ever let herself be truly vulnerable, let her heartbreaks show on the outside.

"It may sound cliché, but I wanted to be a vehicle for change. I imagine you already know how underrepresented people of color are in the police force. Combine that with Stop and Frisk, or Terry Stops and..." She trailed off, her index fingers lifting to punctuate the implications of her comment.

"And there's constant distrust between people of color and cops," I clarified. This was something I'd learned about that day with Jason. "*Your* community, and cops."

"Exactly. I know our police system is unjust in so many

ways. I do, I know that. Everything you said to me that first night we met, properly met, was true. But I don't want to be part of that; I want to push back against the systemic racism. Maybe if there are enough cops who push back, who build trust on the street, even a little each day, who show people of color that some cops are there to *protect* them, not oppress them, things could change. Institutions of power need to be challenged, and what better way to challenge them then from the inside? That's not possible in every country, but I think that things could get better here. I don't want an environment where people feel scared of the authorities that are meant to protect them."

"God," I said, the word almost swallowed by the grit in my throat. "You are incredible. You know that?"

"Ha," she retorted, the syllable mirthless. She leaned forward, scooping up a smooth stone that had rested near her foot. She turned it over, staring into it like a crystal ball. "I'm not exactly breaking down the whole system. But I'm trying to shake it. If enough of us shake, maybe it'll look different one day. Be different."

An uneasy weight settled in my chest. "I'm so sorry, Sole, for how I spoke to you on that blind date. We would've been entirely on the same page if I hadn't made so many assumptions, if I'd asked this question."

She tilted her head, a gentleness settling within her eyes. She discarded the stone with a flick of her wrist. "It's all right. I could have spoken up and, to be honest, it's still a surprise to me that I didn't. I hadn't expected that kind of conversation and...and sometimes I forget how people see us. Cops, I mean. But I shouldn't forget. That's the whole point, right? To confront those things. To confront racial profiling and police brutality and the school-to-prison pipeline. That's why I joined. To be one more person in the way of that system, knocking square on the front door and announcing that it's had its day."

I reached forward and squeezed her hand, once, before pulling back. I couldn't let the contact linger. If I did, I'd never be able to let go. "You said some people found it hard to accept? That you'd joined the force."

"Yeah. Especially the older women," she said wistfully. "Some of my cousins and one of my aunts didn't let me hear the end of it for years. There's still a lot of gender-related expectation in our community, so that was one problem. Mostly they've moved past that now. When I hit the five-year-mark in my career, they seemed to accept I wouldn't change my mind."

"And?" I sensed there was more to the story, that it had hurt her more than her exterior suggested.

"My uncle's family struggled the most. I did too, really. Police had tortured him, and then I'd become one. I think about that a lot, and I can't pretend not to carry around doubts because of it." She paused. "A few cops had something to say about it too. Stupid stuff. Comments here and there. Asking where my loyalties lie, with the force or the crims. Like all Latinxs are criminals."

I balled my hand into a fist, channeling the sudden surge of anger in my body. "God, people are such assholes."

"Yes," she laughed flatly. "That's true."

"Do you ever confront them? Or report it or anything?"

"No. Not really. That would likely put an even larger target on my back."

I gave her forearm a gentle squeeze. "Sole, is that a

reason you haven't gone for a promotion?"

"Hmm. Caught me. Yeah. I... Well, I do love what I'm doing now. But I also know if I tried to move up the ranks, I'd have to deal with a lot more racist and sexist garbage. I'd have to use a lot of energy proving myself in ways other people wouldn't have to. Men, white people, straight people. I'm not sure I could do it. Or that it would be worth it."

"You'd be so good in a leadership role. You'd be even more of a positive role model than you are now. I'm not sure, but...it kind of feels like that's something you might *want* to do?"

"Maybe." Sole slid her hands over her knees, gripping them. Since we'd met, I had assumed Soledad was confident in just about every part of her life. She always seemed self-assured. I guess even people like her could be scared about their own limits, even if the signs of that fear were subtle. "I keep working. I have things I care about, things connected to the job, but not wholly the job, if you know what I mean."

"Like looking out for the juveniles?"

"Yes. And some other things. One day I'll have to tell you about the CCWP. California Coalition for Women Prisoners. They're amazing, and I do volunteer work with them when I can."

"One day?"

She grinned. "Yes, but not today. Don't you hear that?"

I remained silent for a few seconds. Muffled voices engaged in chatter. Music. Stomping of feet. "What? What is it?"

"That," she said, a touch of the dramatic in her tone, "is *la cueca.*"

CHAPTER TWENTY-FOUR

CUECA STRUCK ME as one of the most beautiful displays of joy and heritage I had ever seen. We missed the first few moments but the intoxicating melody, carried by guitar and accordion, drew me in the moment we reemerged into the backyard. Scattered chairs had disappeared, replaced by three couples who moved in time to the music, energetic on-lookers keeping time with the clapping of hands and tapping of spoons.

Hope leaned against a post near the back door, Carla at her side, guiding the rhythm of Hope's clapping. Her limbs were loose, and my spirit soared to see her so relaxed and involved. Confident in her comfort, I turned my attention back to the performance.

Men and women danced in pairs, moving back and

forth in semicircles, opening and closing the space between them, yet never touching. The movements, fluid, sensual, and too fast for me to follow, seemed like a sort of seduction. But there was also a kind of defiance too. Each dancer gripped a handkerchief, either white or red, raising and lowering the fabric as they stamped, twirled, and pivoted.

The connection between dancers burned like the promise of something yet to come, something communicated through the ferocity of their shoes tapping against a wooden deck, reinforced by the strength of their eye contact.

Something in the song, the energy of the space, drew my gaze to Soledad. She stood so close I could feel the heat of her body along the length of my arm, her glow as warm as summer. She seemed to sense me looking at her and turned to meet my stare, but only for a moment, flashing me a grin, her bottom lip catching between her teeth before falling into that same beat with her hands. After a few seconds, she nudged me with her hip, urging me to join. I've never been one to fall into the pulsating movements of a crowd. I'd happily sit to the side as my friends cut loose on a dance floor, content to sway and sip quietly on a drink. But not this time. Not only did I join in with the clapping, I lifted my left foot, reinforcing the beat with yet another limb, my hips eventually coming into the equation too.

"No, no, no." Hope's protestations were a mixture of embarrassment and excitement. A young man, perhaps seventeen or eighteen, gently held one of her hands, his other outstretched toward the unofficial dance floor. Her cheeks flushed pink as he coaxed her forward, buoyed by the encouragement of the crowd, Sole and I included. Though she shook her head in reluctance, she followed the young man, interest flashing in her eyes. In the boy, or the dancing, I wasn't sure. But I could tell she was pleased to have been asked.

The young man showed Hope where to stand and handed her a white handkerchief produced from the back pocket of his jeans, along with one for himself. I could see him better now and, with that aquiline nose, deep-brown eyes, and strong chin, there was no doubt in my mind this had to be the youngest of Soledad's brothers. Hope stifled a laugh with her hand as he twisted his body to the left, guiding her to mirror his actions. One of the women, who'd been with her own partner moments earlier, approached Hope and, from what I could tell, asked if she could help her. Hope agreed, the positivity radiating from her more genuine than I'd seen in months. The small trio worked together, teaching her a few basics of *la cueca*.

Though Hope's movements were stiff and mechanical compared to our hosts, it was obvious she loved every second. At one point, she caught me watching her and ducked her head, sheepish. I made a point of straightening my spine and lifting my chin, indicating that she had nothing to be embarrassed about, that she was doing a great job. She grinned and returned her focus to her dancing partner.

My family spent time together, we had dinner parties, went to baseball games, wandered through market stalls at the weekend, but nothing so lively and energetic as the asado. Hope could lose herself in the revelry, let her worries melt under the heat of the guitar strings, channel her thoughts into the persistent pounding of her feet.

We'd come here together, Hope and I. This could have been a date, an introduction of Soledad's new girlfriend to her family, but instead it was an open show of friendship that hadn't left Hope out of the equation. This was exactly what she needed.

As the recorded music slowed, the crowd quieted somewhat, though the backyard still hummed with conversation and laughter. Most of the dancers dissolved into the small crowd, one of the men heading straight for the grill to scoop up a skewer.

"Your brother?" I said to Sole when the volume of the music had lowered enough.

She nodded. "Tomas. He's seventeen, but an old soul."

"That was so nice. To get her involved."

Sole chuckled. "Sure, he's nice. But he's also still seventeen. I make no promises he won't ask for her number."

"Wow. So that was..."

"Uh-huh." She crossed her arms over her chest, rocking on her heels for a moment. "I'm sure he recognizes a sweetheart when he sees one."

"Smooth. Both of you: so very, very smooth."

The music started up again, though it was more of the background ambience type of sound that had permeated the space earlier. It seemed the dancing was over, for a while at least. Most people seemed to be taking the opportunity to grab some salad from inside the house or retrieve meat from the asado.

Hope appeared, her face flushed, her forehead shiny with a thin slick of sweat. "I can't believe I did that," she said, puffing as though she'd climbed a few sets of stairs.

I gave her bicep a squeeze and dropped my hand again. "That was freaking amazing!" She beamed at my compliment and relief bloomed in my chest. You could never be quite sure how a teenager might take a compliment, especially one from their immediate carer.

"You're a natural," Sole added. Hope gave a modest scoff. "No, really! It's a complex dance and you were already getting it. A few more tries, and you'll have it."

Hope's eyes dropped and she ground the tip of her shoe into the wood. "Thanks," she replied, not looking up.

"Are you hungry?" Sole dropped her hand onto Hope's shoulder. She lifted her head at that. "I thought so," Sole added. "Come on inside. You should eat some of the ensalada you helped to make! And, you've got to try the anticuchos."

"Yes, please," Hope said. And I could tell she wasn't only grateful for the food.

CHAPTER TWENTY-FIVE

CLARA'S FACE AND neck were as red as an overripe apple, and mine must have been, too, if the heat pulsating across my skin was any indication.

"Don't you slow down, Desi! I'm watching you!"

Michelle, our spin instructor, always seemed to look straight at me any time I let up for even a second. If I slacked off for five seconds in a period of ten minutes, you could bet your ass that'd be the exact moment she glanced up from her handlebars to check on our progress. I glanced at Clara, who flashed me an evil *you-got-caught* grin.

With Michelle's fierce attention boring into me, I pumped my legs harder, forcing the pedals to move, focusing on the upward pull, and letting the momentum propel my feet through the bottom half of the arc. My hands clutched at the top of the handlebars as Michelle ordered us out of our seats. My quads burned as we attacked the rise we created with the gear lever. My torso dipped subtly from side to side as I fought back against the load beneath my feet.

"Come the fuck on," Clara said through gritted teeth, arguing with her own legs.

I chuckled. At least it wasn't only me who felt like she was about to have a cardiac episode.

Michelle held her palm in front of her body. "Take a walk." She slowed her pace and I did the same, grateful for the reprieve. Standing, I stretched first one calf, and then the other, sucking down the air as my heart rate gradually settled. "One more round," the instructor announced. I groaned. "Enough of that, Desi! Don't you let that sister of yours out-race you."

She had a point. Glancing at the screen on Clara's bike, I saw that she and I had both completed nine miles. Screw that, I was going to get past her. I made eye contact with Michelle, silently letting her know: *challenge accepted.* We all planted our butts on the seats, the tempo of the music picking up speed. I tucked my elbows closer to my body, squared my shoulders, dipped my toes, and surged. Clenching my eyes shut, I lost myself in the beat, absorbed in the rhythmic sound of a room full of whirling pedals and rotating flywheels. Nothing but me and the music—I flew.

"Damn," Clara huffed. The music petered out and the instructor gave the order to slow our legs. "Someone had their vitamin intake today," my sister added, puffing.

Sitting up, I planted my hands on my hips. My chest heaved and my lungs burned as I took in as much oxygen as possible. I adopted a steady recovery pace and peered at

Clara. "Healthy competition is all," I teased. She waved me off like she was swatting a fly, then took a chug of water from her sports bottle.

After a quick shower, we found a quiet spot in a cafe near the gym and ordered a couple of protein smoothies. It had still been dark when we had arrived, but now, over an hour later, the sun had risen and there were a few more cars on the roads, more pedestrians on the sidewalks. It was as though the city had gradually opened its eyes to greet the day, one lazy lid at a time.

I loved these mornings when, once a week, my sister and I would slam ourselves on the bikes, catching up on whatever had been happening in each other's lives.

"How's Evie?"

Clara rolled her eyes, but her coy expression told me she was glad I'd asked. "Spoke to her last night."

"And?" I rolled my hand through the air, urging her to continue. "It's been months since you met in South Australia. It seems you're still chatting regularly."

Someone called out my name and, before I had a chance to react, Clara made her way to the counter to collect our smoothies, then returned a few seconds later, a paper straw between her lips. I narrowed my eyes. She was making me wait on purpose, dragging out whatever story she had to tell for dramatic effect. For someone who claimed to avoid social interactions as much as possible, Clara was pretty good at drawing them out when she wanted to.

Finally, she came up for air and set the drink down. "I've booked a flight."

"Far out!" My hands, apparently having a mind of their own, smacked the top of the table, my fingers sprawled.

"You're going back to Australia?"

Clara crossed her arms in front of her chest. "Why the hell not? I found a cheap flight direct to Adelaide, and I still have some vacation time. Apparently, I haven't had much of a life for the last couple of years. I have to wait three months though, because the boss likes notice for extended leave."

"Extended leave?" I smirked, both amused and impressed. "Look at you, traversing the planet to see a woman who works outdoors and wears jeans every day of the week."

"Don't forget stunning. You've seen her, right?" Clara made for her phone as though about to show me pictures of Evie. Again.

"Yeah, yeah," I mumbled. "Surely it's not all physical, or you wouldn't be going back. But...how's this going to work? I mean, you said there's no way she could ever move here."

Clara's fingertips traced the edges of the circular table as she spoke. "No. It's not only her family and friends, but Evie is strongly connected to her Aboriginal culture, Des. There's this beautiful kinship she feels to the land she lives on—like it's inside her, and she has a responsibility to care for the landscape. The way she talks about places, it's more like they're people, people that she relies on and who rely on her. I'm sure she'd love to travel around a bit, but...forever? She hasn't said she'd never leave permanently, but I worry that it would break her heart if I ever asked her to."

My throat clenched as I tried to get my next words out. "You...you're thinking about going there...long-term? Relocating?"

The idea of either one of my sisters living on the other side of the state made my chest hurt, let alone the other side of the planet. I wanted Clara to be happy, to be with someone who made her embrace life the way Evie did, despite the distance. But I'm also selfish, and hated the idea of not seeing Clara at least twice a week, of not experiencing her loving taunts on a regular basis.

Clara dragged her hair over her shoulder and toyed with the end of a few strands, "Not yet."

"Yet?"

She inched forward, as though sharing a secret. "It's not beyond the realm of possibility."

"Wow," I mouthed silently. "Clara the romantic. Who knew?"

"Okay," she said, her tone assertive. "Your turn. It's been a few days since that incident with Hope. Things settled yet?"

"Sort of. She's at school, seems to be doing her homework. She's quiet at home, but that's not surprising."

"I take it she hasn't given you any idea of why she needed to steal all of that stuff?"

I shook my head.

"Hmm. Frustrating."

"Yep," I replied. "She did lighten up around Sole and her family the other day, though. It was nice to see her relax. Even if only for an hour or two."

"And Sole? How are things with you and her?"

I sighed. There was no way Clara wasn't going to push me on this again, but I'd still hoped that I might have been wrong. "It's not a good time for a relationship right now. We're trying out the whole friendship thing. It won't drain quite as much of my time or energy that way."

"Oh come on, Des. That's total bullshit and you know it."

"No," I rebuked. "It's not. Brody ended up in juvenile detention and now look at him. He's part of a gang, people he met in there, constantly in and out of jail. I keep thinking I'm going to see his face on the news. Another dead drug dealer."

"And don't forget, big sister, you spent a lot of time with Brody. He had your undivided attention. Didn't stop him from getting into trouble."

"Yeah," I admitted reluctantly. "But like you guys have said before. Hope isn't Brody. I think I smothered him. Tried too hard. So, then I went the other way with Hope; I've not been attentive enough. I need to find the space in the middle, and I can't do that at the same time as cultivating something so intense with Soledad. As much as I may want to."

Clara leaned forward again, this time taking my hands in hers, demanding my full attention. "Listen, okay. You listening?"

"Yeah, yeah. I'm listening."

"You're the one who told me to go for it with Evie. You said that life is too short to avoid people and things that feel right. Who's to say that you being happy isn't exactly the thing that will help you find that parenting balance you're so worried about? Think about Grams. Fearless, remember?"

"This isn't about fear." I drew my hands away, tucking them into my lap, Clara's stare unforgiving as I did. "Okay, maybe it's about fear. But not just fear of seeing where things go with Sole. And you know that."

"True." Clara glanced at her watch, then stood. "Walk back to the car with me?"

I picked up my smoothie, which I hadn't touched yet, and joined her. For the first minute or so, we strolled in silence. Several people walked past us, dressed in business suits, clutching coffee cups in one hand and cases or bags in the other. A few seemed to be talking to themselves, engaging in hands-free conversations via their phones.

"Thanks," I said as we drew closer to Clara's car. She gave me a questioning look. "For reminding me of my own pearls of wisdom. I'm sure it'll all work out."

"Of course it will. Remember what Grams always says?"

In unison we said, "It all works out in the end. Because if it hasn't worked out, it's not the end." We both laughed, hugging as we said goodbye.

"Rose was an idiot. She had no idea what a good person you are, or how lucky she was. Trust me when I tell you that Soledad is a fucking genius in comparison. If she likes you as much as you like her, I'm damned sure that she'll wait."

My shoulders climbed as I inhaled deeply. It was a question that had burned inside me, but I'd been too scared to ask. Would Sole wait? It could be months, or even longer, before I could give her the full focus of my energies, give her the affection and time someone as fascinating and daring as her deserved. But, still, might there be a chance she would still be single, still be interested, by then? It was an unrealistic, and entirely unfair, thought for me to have. Yet, there it was.

"Listen," Clara said, her body language more hesitant than her tone. "Can I tell you something about Sole?"

"Of course."

"She'll kill me for this."

"What?" I jabbed her lightly with the side of my arm. "You can't not tell me now."

"You know how, when she pulled you over, she

disappeared behind the car to check your plates?"

"How—"

Clara held her hands up. "She told me. Anyway. Sole did that because she needed to hide the fact she was desperate to laugh."

I scrunched up my face, unimpressed. "She wanted to laugh at a woman she was giving a ticket to?"

"No. She wanted to laugh because she recognized your last name. When she heard you pronounce it and thought about my description of you, she knew for sure you were my sister, that she'd be seeing you that night."

My mouth fell open. "Soledad knew? She didn't say anything. Why didn't she cancel?"

"Well, there is the fact that she is kind of a smart-ass sometimes, so that's why she wanted to surprise you at the restaurant. But..."

"But what?"

"Des, she thought you were adorable."

Now I clamped my jaw shut, giving Clara one of my trademark *you're-full-of-shit* looks.

"I'm serious. You were in a rush, you were stumbling over your words, a total mess." I huffed, but I knew she was right. "She wanted to meet you even more after that. Meet you properly. That woman liked you from the first moment, even when you were making an ass of yourself."

I had no idea how to respond. Soledad needing time to retreat behind my car to collect herself certainly explained the weirdness of that whole moment. She'd toyed with me a little, getting to the restaurant early, waiting and knowing how shocked I would likely be. Yet, she hadn't told me any of this, meaning she felt embarrassed about it now. Or maybe she wasn't as honest as I had thought. But somehow, still, the whole thing was sort of adorable.

"Thanks, Clara. I don't know what to do with that information right now, but Sole's sense of humor is definitely even cheekier than I had thought. I'll see you at Mom's on Sunday night?"

"Naturally. Try to stop taking yourself so seriously, okay?" She hugged me one more time before disappearing into the driver's seat.

Though she couldn't hear me through the glass, I whispered, "I'll try."

CHAPTER TWENTY-SIX

HOPE AND I drifted from one stall to another, investigating the local farmer's market, reusable bags in hand. Boisterous conversation, an acoustic guitar being played off in the distance, and a general sense of festivity had lulled us both into a comfortable silence, enjoying each other's company and the ambience of the event.

"Hey, Des?"

"Mmm," I replied absently, turning over a few apples to pick the ones I wanted.

"What did you think of what the governor said? About Columbus Day?"

This was the last market in our suburb before what we'd long referred to as Columbus Day. Recently, the governor of California had declared that right across the state we would recognize Indigenous Peoples Day this year, celebrating resilience rather than conquest.

"I was glad he made that announcement. It's a change long overdue in my opinion." I passed four apples to the man behind the table who set them on a scale and told me the price.

"I always get a bit nervous at this time of year," I added as I reached for the cash in my back pocket. "There are still the inevitably difficult conversations surrounding Thanksgiving ahead, but really, most of the stuff I've heard people saying about Columbus Day has been pretty positive."

I thanked the fruit seller and slipped the apples into my shoulder bag, and we began walking again as we continued to talk. "Not that I don't love talking to you about stuff like this. But what prompted the question?"

Hope walked with her hands jammed into the pockets of her zip-up hoodie. "My history teacher brought it up on Friday. It was kinda interesting, and sad."

"What specifically did you find sad?"

"I hadn't thought of it, but two boys in my class are from Italian families. They said Italian Americans were upset they wanted to change the day."

I nodded, practically able to picture the discussion that may have happened in Hope's classroom. "I can't pretend to understand everyone's perspectives, but yeah, that does make sense doesn't it? Columbus Day was also about celebrating Italian contributions to society, not only the arrival of Columbus himself. It's always hard when the origins of an event don't necessarily match up with the positive values and messages the event collects along the way.

"Right now, though, on the back of that apology from

the state to Indigenous peoples, the change felt right somehow."

"A guy from my class, Javier, tried to bring the topic back up in English the next period."

"How did that go?"

She raised her eyebrows and cringed. "Not great. Mr. Crawley said he didn't intend to waste class time talking about 'political correctness' or debating semantics."

"That's a shame." I adjusted the bag on my shoulder, now heavier with the apples. "I suppose some teachers might be worried they won't handle controversial topics well?"

Hope gave a noncommittal shrug, casting her attention to a row of hand-sewn goods lining a nearby table. Her pensive moment was over for now. She often started up a conversation about something serious, be it philosophical or political, but there always came a clear end point where she'd absorbed enough information and wanted to marinate that information on her own for a while.

Hope's comment about the Italian boys in her class was an interesting one. I was pained to admit that was a perspective I had failed to consider. Gosh, the world was a complicated place. No wonder relationships could be hard to navigate. Even relationships between the different parts of ourselves, our own identities, and perceptions. I'd felt myself, especially in the last few months, becoming more aware of my own assumptions, more aware of my quickness to judgement, judgments based on a lack of experience or understanding about myself or about others.

I'd never be without those judgments because that's how human beings operate. But maybe I could do better at admitting they were there and acknowledging other angles a situation could be looked at. That in mind, I truly do hope our state can find a way to honor both groups, Italian Americans and Native Americans in the future, without linking our holidays to the atrocities of murder and terror.

Diversity might be complicated and messy to talk about, but it's also one of the best parts of our world and the least people like me can do with our privileges is use them to openly discuss and explore what's happened in the past and how we can move forward. So many people had taught me that. Jason, Grams, Mom, Gina, Soledad...

"Hey, Des?" Hope and I had stopped walking again, and I had barely noticed, so caught up in my usual contemplative circles. She held up an avocado. "Can we get a couple of these?"

"Far out," I said, moving closer. "You're *asking* to buy fresh vegetables? What is the world coming to?"

Hope rolled her eyes ever so slightly. "Don't gloat too much, alright? But yes, you have converted me. Avocado on toast is a good breakfast."

I nudged her gently with my arm. "Good plan. But don't squeeze them, okay? That's a horrific sin against the old alligator pear." The woman operating the stall, an older lady with light-brown skin, a wide smile and knowing eyes, nodded in agreement, as though she'd already told people that same thing twenty times today.

"Desi?" The unnervingly familiar voice came from behind me, close enough to be crisp and clear amidst the symphony of haggling and conversation. My ribs contracted, tightening the protective cage around my heart.

"You okay?" Hope asked. I opened my eyes.

I gave her shoulder a reassuring squeeze. I withdrew a twenty-dollar bill from my back pocket and handed it to her. "You buy some things and I'll catch up with you. You've got your phone?"

"Yeah." She held the cell phone up for me to see.

"Good. I'll see you soon."

Confusion awash on her face, Hope looked from me to the woman behind me. Resigned to leave her questions unasked, she turned away.

I tightened my stomach muscles, preparing for the inevitable flood of emotion, and turned to face Rose. Her hair, longer than I remembered, curled about her shoulders in thick, black curls, contrasting her pale skin. She'd gained a few pounds and the extra weight suited her, softening once narrow features. Holding a take-away coffee cup in one hand, she wore a pair of black jeans torn at the knees and a free-flowing white peasant top. Rose had never been short on natural beauty and, even after more than a year since we'd last seen each other, she still made my heart do a little jump. I was pleasantly surprised to realize it was a much smaller jump than it had been the last time.

"Hi," she said, her tone unsure.

"Hi." I took a few steps and she followed, leading us to a quieter spot away from the stalls, beneath the shade of a tall, broad tree. For a few seconds we stood there, the silence far less comfortable than it had been minutes earlier with my foster daughter.

She spoke first. "You look good."

"Thanks. You too. How's things?"

Rose pointed at nothing in particular with her index finger, her attention off in the distance somewhere as she spoke. "Pretty good. I got promoted about six months ago and finally have an office rather than a cubicle." She brought her focus to me, and the familiarity of her eyes sent a dull thump through my chest. It wasn't a reaction that told me I still wanted her. No, it was something else. More of a longing for a dream I once had, but no longer genuinely believed in.

"That's awesome. I know how hard you worked to manage your own team at the firm. I'm happy for you." I looked back to the line of fruit sellers a few feet away. Hope had only moved about three stalls along the line. She held up an apple, inspecting it, then set it back down.

"And you? You're still fostering by the look of things?" Rose said.

"Yeah." This was a sore point between us, after what had happened with Brody. "She's almost sixteen. A great kid. She has a kind soul."

"That's... That's great."

I suppressed a groan at the insincerity of her voice, an unwelcome change that reminded me of far too many arguments. "It is. Things aren't always perfect, but they're still worth doing."

She nodded as a pensive look crossed her face. "Yeah. That's fair. I do hope you find what you're looking for if you haven't already." Her tone had softened, and I believed she meant what she said, even if I was confused.

"What...what do you mean by that, exactly?"

Rose took a sip of her coffee and looked to the ground before returning her attention to me. She sighed, sadness in the sound. "I don't want to be mean. We did that to each other enough in those last few weeks."

"Yeah," I murmured, remembering. "We did." I stood

straighter. "But I don't think you're going to be mean. I'd like to know what it is you thought I was looking for, what I could have understood better about where you were coming from."

Her forehead furrowed. "You want to hear my perspective? Like, really hear it?"

"I do."

She smiled, the kind of easy, thoughtful smile that relaxed tension in both the giver and the recipient. "Okay." She sank back against the tree, more comfortable than moments before. "I guess it felt like you were so fixated on the destination that you didn't see things right in front of you. Didn't enjoy the journey. I know how cliché that sounds."

I moved closer, joining her against the tree. "Clichés are a thing because they're sometimes true, right?"

"True." Rose tried for more coffee and, finding the cup empty, let her hands fall in front of her body. "You seemed so fixated on a happy ending for Brody, and those brief placements we had before him. Like all that mattered was some kind of tick-a-box successful outcome for them. Somewhere in there it seemed, to me at least, that you forgot to live your own life. To be yourself. To be...with me."

Her thoughts on this weren't entirely new, I was sure she'd told me similar things somewhere amidst the tears and the fights, but I'd been so focused on her ultimatum—*me or foster caring*—that I had failed to take in the reasons for her posing that choice. I'd been too hurt, too angry, and if I was honest with myself, too indignant to have truly, properly, sincerely listened.

"You're right," I whispered.

Rose adjusted her position, facing me more directly, her

arm pressed against the tree rather than her back. "I...I... Thank you, Desi. I don't want to be right in the way that you're wrong, though, if that makes sense."

"I think it does. We're both right, and we're both wrong."

She leaned closer, hugged me briefly before stepping back. "Yeah."

I wiped at my cheek, realizing a few tears had brimmed over my lower lids. I hadn't expected to see Rose when I'd come here today, and I didn't know what I had expected when I sent Hope on her way so Rose and I could talk, but it wasn't this. It wasn't mutual understanding. It wasn't healing.

When the hug broke and we saw we'd both let loose a few tears, we both laughed. "Wow," I said.

"Wow, indeed." She touched my shoulder. "I'm glad we ran into each other."

"Yeah, me too."

Looking around, Rose spotted a trash can, closed the gap in three steps, tossed the coffee cup, then returned. The brief reprieve from our conversation had a strong impact, breaking the seriousness and giving us each a moment to rein in whatever thoughts or feelings we'd each experienced. For me, it felt like a hovering rain cloud had changed shape somehow. Not disappeared, but lightened, letting a few rays of light through.

I had hated being mad at her after the love we'd shared. And I had been mad at her, despite desperately wishing I wasn't the kind of person to stay hurt or to hold a grudge. But now, with only a few words, something shifted. I had assumed she blamed everything on me, maybe even that I'd blamed everything on her, but neither of those scenarios were true. We were two people who had lost sight of each other. Who had stopped being open to learning, to trying, and now we were okay with it all.

"You truly do look good," she said, a touch of mischief in her voice. "The haircut works."

"Thanks. It didn't sit right when I first did it but seems to have settled over time."

"You looked nice with long hair, but this suits you. Like, this is what you always looked like but didn't know it yet."

Laughing, I ran a self-conscious hand through the longer portion of the hair in question.

"Are you seeing anyone?" Rose asked.

My cheeks warmed and she flashed me a knowing grin.

"I'll take that as a yes."

I scrunched up my face. "Not technically, no. I sort of was seeing someone. Almost. But not really."

"That clears it up," Rose said, her expression softly incredulous. "What's her name?"

I pinched the bridge of my nose, trying to decide if I should avoid the topic altogether, given Sole and I had decided to keep things at friendship level for a while. When I opened my eyes and saw the look on Rose's face, I knew that wouldn't work. "Soledad. She's... I'm... We're going slow for a while."

"Can't hurt to take things slow."

"I hope so. I need time to work some things out. Settle a few things in my life and see where things all fit."

"Does she deserve you?"

My eyes widened. In four words Rose had given me one of the best compliments a person could give: to suggest I was someone special. To place a high value on my company in life.

"You okay?" I hadn't answered and the quiet had become a lull.

"Yeah. I... Yeah, I'm okay." I stood straighter, reconnecting with the conversation. "Sole is amazing. As cheesy as that might sound. She's a cop."

Rose's eyebrows rose as high as they could go.

"I know," I laughed. "Surprised me too, that I could get over some of my assumptions. But she isn't like those cops we hear about in the news. She wants to do better than all of that. She's funny, she's fit, she's..."

"Special," Rose added. My cheeks warmed with embarrassment. "Des, look at you. This woman has gotten to you. That's so good to see."

"Yes, I suppose she has. But I'll have to wait and see if it can all iron out. If the kinks in the story don't get in the way."

Rose reached out, took hold of both of my hands, and held them between hers. The gesture felt reassuring, calming in the way a friend might be. "I'm glad you've maybe found someone. I hope she can distract from all those tickboxes you worry about so much, though. You don't need to be perfect, Des. Sometimes those kinks you're talking about can be the best part."

"Yeah." I pulled my lips together into a tight line. "Thanks for the support, Rose. I didn't remember you being so damned wise, though."

"All in a day's work." She pretended to dust off her shoulders and I laughed. "I have to admit, I've had some time to myself to think."

"What do you mean? I hope things are going well for you too?"

She dipped her head from side to side for a second, like a thought in her mind was being used as ping-pong ball. "More or less. My career has become more consuming than I'd expected, but I'm sure I'll learn to balance it all out. I've been too tired to think about relationships."

"As long as you're happy." I gave her hands one last squeeze before withdrawing. "I should go and find Hope. She might begin to think I've gotten lost in a field somewhere."

Rose laughed. "Fair enough. Hey. You know how you said Soledad is a cop?"

"Yeah?" My tone was suspicious. I thought we'd managed to dodge going too in depth on that point, and I'd been glad. Rose knew all-too-well my outlook on most things political.

"She's not..."

"Not what?" I urged. I felt a touch of annoyance lapping at the base of my skull. I hoped she wasn't about to say anything mean, not when we'd been having such an honest and palatable conversation so far.

Rose bit her lower lip for a second. "A Republican?"

I laughed, as awkward as that may have been at that moment. It was an instinctive reaction that I couldn't hold in. Then, the reaction settled. "Shit," I said.

"You haven't asked her?"

"I... Well, no. I mean, you don't go around asking people that these days. Do you?"

Her mouth tightened, a flash of sympathy in her eyes. "Maybe not. But I can see how much you like her, and it's great that you've softened on the whole police officer thing. I don't want you to get too far in before you realize something that would be even harder for you to reconcile."

I couldn't think what to say. Soledad and I weren't dating and, even if we were, I didn't think that was something I had the courage to ask her. Did I even need to know? How would I react if I didn't get the answer I wanted?

"I'm not sure if that's something I should talk to her about. I'll have to think about it."

"I want you to be happy."

"So many clichés today," I teased. In a more serious tone I added, "Thank you. That means something. It does. I want that for you too."

Rose leaned forward and pressed her cheek to mine, kissing the air near my ear. "Look after yourself," she whispered.

I closed my eyes. "You too."

As quickly as she'd appeared, Rose was gone, swallowed by the crowd of market shoppers. I took a few moments to gather my thoughts and collect some composure after the unexpected development of not only seeing my ex-girlfriend but having what felt like an important conversation with her.

It only took a couple of minutes to track down Hope, who'd sat on a bench beneath a shady tree at the end of the aisle we'd been strolling along together. She played with her phone, a few pieces of fruit resting in the bag on her lap.

"Thanks for waiting for me."

She looked up at the sound of my voice. "Everything okay?"

"Yeah, all okay."

"Who was that lady?" She stood, shouldering the bag.

Thinking for a moment about how to best respond, I settled on simply, "She's an old friend."

CHAPTER TWENTY-SEVEN

THIS WAS OFFICIALLY the most ridiculous outing I'd ever been on with a friend. Though it hadn't been that long of a drive, I'd spent the entire time fighting the urge to crawl through the window at every red light and escape into the distance. I could grab some sushi, put on an oversized shirt, climb into bed, and binge-watch old episodes of *Jane the Virgin*. Though even starting a training schedule to complete the New York Marathon sounded preferable to what we were about to do. What was I thinking? I am not an adventurous person, and this was not going to be my kind of place.

As Soledad's car rolled into the spacious parking lot, I groaned, purposely sounding like a kid being dragged to the dentist. "Are you sure about this? Maybe it's a bad idea. I'm going to be Judgey McJudgeface in there. I'll end up offending someone. You, probably."

Shifting the car into Park, Soledad set her head against the headrest and considered me, a look of mock sympathy playing on her face. "Judgey McJudgeface?"

I laughed. "Okay, fair enough. Not that funny. But you know what I mean. This is not an activity I pictured myself doing."

Soledad pointed to the building. "Hey, you made it this far. I promise that this is usually a safe environment. I mean that physically and emotionally. If the whole thing upsets you, we can absolutely leave. But I truly think you'll be surprised by how cathartic shooting can be. In a controlled, sensible environment, that is. I'll look after you every step of the way. Don't forget though, you *did* agree to come!" She nudged me gently with her elbow.

I exhaled audibly and tousled my hair as I examined the building more closely. A huge sign sat atop the main entrance, imposing red letters on a white background: *Gun Range*. The font had been, it seemed, specially designed, with the *R* pierced by a bullet hole and a barrel acting as the middle portion of the *G*. When Soledad had, after about two weeks of fragile silence passed between us since the house party, offered to help me unwind, this was the farthest thing from my mind when I'd considered all the possibilities of what she'd meant. "How did you even get me here?"

"Like it was hard?"

I gently smacked the back of my hand against her thigh. "Smart-ass."

"Always." She reached for my hand, stopped, drew back. "Sorry. For a second there, I forgot. Friends, right?"

My eyelids were heavy with disappointment. "Yeah," I murmured. "That's right." After a loaded pause, I added, "We're here. I guess I better go inside and let you try to convince me that shooting inanimate targets can apparently be an effective stress relief."

The smile on her face certainly melted me as easily as boiling water melted ice. "Fabulous, let's go."

Inside, I tried my best to ignore the sour taste rising in my throat. The whole place felt disconcerting, from its gun shop covered in wall-to-wall weapons to the boisterous and diverse clientele. There were more people here than I'd anticipated. Why did so many people come to a place like this? Though, hadn't I myself admitted to Sole it could be a decent weekend activity?

I was mostly quiet as Soledad sorted out the lane hire. When they asked what sort of weapons we wanted to rent, my mind went blank, I couldn't even name one type. Sole, thankfully, answered quickly, requesting Glock 22s. We didn't need an instructor because Soledad had more than enough experience to guide me through the process. After finding our lane, she took me through the basic features of the weapon.

"The magazine, that's this here, holds fifteen rounds. They've preloaded the ammunition, but we should still check that the bullets point forward. The trigger, here, needs at least five pounds of pressure before it'll do anything, so it's unlikely that it will go off by accident." As she continued talking, I homed in on each word, fixing my attention to the details in an attempt to ignore the slight sheen of her lip gloss and the unusual floral cocktail of her perfume. Sexy and warm all at once, the scent of her threatened to send me spiraling. I blinked rapidly a few times, forcing myself to concentrate on the explanation she so professionally offered, going through a few more safety details.

"Here." She offered me hearing and eye protection. I unhooked the eyewear from her wrist and slipped it on, the plastic harsh and uncomfortable. Soledad stepped closer and fitted protection over my ears, the palm of her left hand grazing my cheek as she withdrew. I swallowed, ordering my desire back into my core where it could be more easily controlled.

"Thank you."

Her eyes held me in place as she replied, "You're welcome." We looked at each other for a moment too long and, when I realized how close we stood, I cleared my throat and twisted so my body was front-on to the target. This was a bad idea. Being friends with Soledad was an altogether stupid notion. I doubted that I could make this work, this whole supportive, platonic friend thing. All I wanted to do was drag her to me, envelop her completely, and fall back into that cavernous realm of pleasure we'd experienced before. But I couldn't. That is, I shouldn't. We were already pushing the terms of what a normal adult friendship might entail. How many of my other friends did I catch-up with two weekends in a row? Zero. That's how many.

"Well, now for the technical bit," Soledad announced.

"Wait. You're saying all of that other stuff *wasn't* the technical bit?"

"Not for the actual shooting. Now be quiet and pay attention," she said, her tone less serious than the words themselves.

"Yes, ma'am." My facial expression flattened into a

deadpan, deferential façade, but my cheerful tone kept the atmosphere light.

Sole passed me the Glock, still empty of the magazine and I reluctantly accepted the gun, the metal cold and uninviting. "We'll talk about your stance soon, but for now, let's focus on the weapon itself. You need to wrap your fingers around the grip. The idea is to have your middle finger touching your thumb. Keep your index finger away from the trigger until it's time to shoot. Keep it all tight. The tighter you hold the gun, the more accurate and consistent your aim is going to be."

I followed her instructions more intuitively than I'd anticipated, my hand nestling against the grip.

She inspected the position of my fingers and nodded. "Good. Next, you'd need to load a round into the firing chamber. You do that by releasing the slide. Just go slowly; there's no rush. When you're ready to go, raise the barrel and point at the middle of the target. Do you see that window? Position the target so you can see it through there."

"I don't see it."

"Here." She gently positioned her wrist below my forearm, nudging my arm and the barrel of the Glock higher. My horrible fingernails arrested my attention for a second, reminding me of the promise to myself I'd broken, to stop biting them. Soledad, her wrist still supporting my arm, leaned closer. "See it now?"

I blinked in acknowledgment, my voice suddenly gone, incapable of speech. *Get it together, Desi! It was just your arm.* At least the fact I couldn't stop fixating on every touch between us meant I'd barely registered the fact I was about to engage in something I'd never believed I would engage in.

I'd never considered trying this out as some kind of leisure activity.

"Great," Sole said, pulling away. "After that, you'd be nearly ready to pull the trigger. You wrap the first knuckle around and gently squeeze or press. The more jerky your trigger squeeze is, the more likely your arm will twitch and send the shot off target."

Soledad showed me how to adopt a fighter's stance, with one foot forward and the other back, shoulder-width apart. She told me it was important to have the foot correlating to my dominant hand be the one at the back to ensure maximum stability. If someone were to try to push or knock me whilst holding a gun, it would be less likely to go off if I were in a strong pose. It hadn't occurred to me that Soledad had to, on a daily basis, be hypervigilant about such things. Well, it had, but I hadn't let it completely sink in. One wrong move and she could seriously hurt herself, or be hurt by someone else.

"You've got it." She clapped, bringing her index fingers to her lips as she inspected my stance one last time. Her eyes roaming my body, as clinical as her scrutiny may have been, made my pulse quicken. The temperature in the room rose. "Ready to give it a try?"

"Do I really need to shoot the gun? I mean, you've taught me some great stuff, but do I need to put the bullet into the target?"

She frowned. "Of course not. I wouldn't make you do anything you truly don't want to do, Des. But I think it might help you blow off some steam, open a valve so to speak. I'm sorry. I thought you wanted to come. I definitely wouldn't want to be that insensitive."

"No. No, you're right, I did agree when you suggested it. Now I'm here, I guess I don't see how shooting this thing would help me relax."

Soledad's eyes widened as she searched the ceiling for what she wanted to say, one hand rubbing at the base of her neck. "It's hard to explain." After a couple of seconds, having collected her thoughts, she returned her attention to me. "Part of it is the pure pleasure of mastering a new skill. There's a measurable sense of achievement when you fire at a target like this. An instant rush of adrenaline when you get it right and hit your mark. And yeah, there is this sense of power, a sense of control that we don't always experience from day to day. But it doesn't always have to be a bad kind of power. You're doing this as a sport, as recreation, not for any other reason. But if you want to leave, or only want me to shoot, that's fine. This was my idea, and I could have been wrong about it being a good one."

Her copper-brown eyes were a little wild, perhaps worried that she'd upset me. Truth be told though, I wasn't upset. Everything she'd said was logical, and I wasn't about to lose my identity or my ideologies by giving it a go. More than anything I wanted to dissipate her worry, to show her I understood what she was trying to do, that I wasn't upset. I'd needed a reminder of what we were doing and why we were doing it, sure, but I wasn't upset.

"No," I asserted. "Try anything once, right?"

Her posture relaxed. "Exactly."

Giving me space to move, Soledad took up a position that allowed her to watch and guide me but wouldn't cause any dangerous distractions.

I took a few moments to breathe through my feelings

and adjust my stance.

"Are you all right?" Soledad sounded concerned. "You can change your mind. It's only a game, really, what we're having a go at here. And there's no need to make yourself feel awful for the sake of trying something new."

I closed my eyes for a couple of seconds and said, "I'm all right. Okay. Here we go..." I squared my shoulders, lifted the barrel, found the sight window, and lined it up with the target. It was difficult to hold the target in the sight, and Soledad reminded me to hold tight to the grip. I curled the first knuckle of my index finger over the trigger and applied some pressure. I yelped as my hands and wrist surged, my forearms vibrating as the empty casing flew out of the top of the gun, clanging against the floor. "Holy shit."

"I'm coming closer," Soledad warned. I made sure my finger was nowhere near the trigger and gently laid the weapon on the counter in front of me, the barrel facing down the lane. An unusual scent wafted through the air, acrid yet not overwhelming. "How did that feel?"

I laughed nervously as I removed the ear protection. "Umm. Strange. It was so fast. I didn't expect it to be so..."

"Strong?"

"Yes. If I didn't have my feet planted, it would have sent me flying."

"Do you want to empty the magazine?"

"Yeah, actually. I think I do."

Soledad rocked on the balls of her feet. "Go ahead. But, ah, maybe keep your eyes open when you squeeze."

"Oh God, did I seriously close my eyes?"

"Well, I can only assume that's why you missed the target so miserably."

"Ha. Ha. Ha," I said, each syllable dripping with sarcasm. "I'll also try to keep my hands still this time."

We spent the next hour or so taking turns on the lane. I even hit the target a few times, the subsequent sense of elation undeniable. Soledad was right; it did feel good when your aim was true. The real joy, however, was watching Soledad. Her whole body, from her feet to the top of her head and along the length of her arms, was strong and assertive. Her shots were unfailingly accurate, her shoulders barely shifting with the recoil.

"You're so good at this."

Sole tipped her head, mock modesty in her expression. "I've had a lot of practice. Carrying one of these around is a big responsibility."

"No doubt." I chewed my bottom lip as I remembered our interactions the first time we'd met, properly met, at Lucca restaurant. When she had actively chosen to meet up with me, despite my bedraggled appearance and inarticulate babbling, to give me another chance and find out who I was—something I wouldn't have done for her had the situation been reversed.

We'd already come to understand each other in so many ways, but maybe Rose's pointed question from the other day had some merit; perhaps it *was* one more elephant that had to be acknowledged.

As I watched her take up position to shoot her last round, I registered an unpleasant buzzing in my stomach. I didn't know if I should ask Soledad about her political stance. Was that inappropriate? Did I even need to know?

Not every Republican or Democrat has identical views, so it's not as though her supporting a party I had always disagreed with was a fair indication that all of our philosophies were incompatible. Plenty of Republicans supported *Roe vs. Wade*. Plenty of Democrats didn't. Just as some Democrats had fought against marriage equality, and some Republicans had whole-heartedly supported it. I'd spent a lot of years fixating on the red versus blue distinction, and Rose wasn't wrong to worry political ideology could be an issue for me, given it had been in the past. Watching Sole though, witnessing her resilience, experiencing her patience, the labels didn't seem as important anymore.

Soledad released an empty magazine from her Glock, removed her safety gear, and turned her attention to me as she continued gathering up what we needed to return. "I can practically hear the cogs turning in your head. You okay?"

The buzzing in my stomach came to an abrupt stop, replaced by a pooling warmth that seemed to happen almost every time she looked at me with those knowing eyes. "You know, your mind-reader trick can be kind of annoying."

"I think you mean endearing."

"You wish."

With her tongue pinched between her teeth, she gifted me a delightfully adorable grin, the kind that told me she wouldn't argue the point anymore because she knew she was right. "But really, you okay?"

We turned our backs to the lane, leaning against the counter we'd stood behind to fire. "I was thinking about some things. But nothing you need to worry about."

"Are you sure? I don't want you to feel like you can't talk to me openly."

"It's not that. I do feel that way."

She raised an eyebrow and my heart sped up.

"I mean, I feel I can talk you openly. But the stuff I was thinking about... It actually isn't all that important.

"Oh, boy." Soledad handed me a few things, and we started toward the service desk. "I'm now unbelievably curious. Will you tell me what it is?"

I hesitated, staying quiet while Sole interacted with the man at the desk and returned out gear. As we walked in the direction of the car, I asked, "Are you sure? I don't want you to feel like you actually need to answer the question I had in my head. Or think that it's something I'll hold against you."

The automatic doors hissed open and we stepped into the fresh air. "I'm sure. Like I said, curious." She pointed at her chest to emphasize the point.

"I guess... I was thinking about your political views. If you supported a specific party."

"Are you asking who I voted for?" Soledad withdrew her car keys from a shoulder bag, slowing as we approached the car. "Because we can talk about that."

CHAPTER TWENTY-EIGHT

WE SETTLED INTO her car and I peered through the windshield. The wind swept through nearby treetops and lifted dead leaves from the pavement, sending them rocketing through the air.

"Okay." Sole put her key in the ignition and turned. The engine whirred to life and the car filled with low-volume music that lessened the sense of suffocation within the vehicle. "I know you're not making me answer; I pushed you to tell me what you were thinking. But after some of our conversations, this is something I've been reflecting on a lot. So, here goes. I haven't supported either major party and I've never voted. I'm not registered."

"Are you kidding?" My head snapped around, disbelief burning in my eyes. "You didn't vote?"

"No," she confirmed, her tone neither apologetic nor proud, only flat.

"You realize that some elections come down to a few hundred votes? I don't know what's worse—voting for him or not voting at all."

I didn't mean for it to come out so harshly. I'd been determined not to be judgmental, but the words seemed to escape my body without my permission. I forced my muscles to relax. "God, I'm sorry, Sole. That wasn't fair at all. I told you I wouldn't hold your views against you and I shouldn't."

Sole tapped the side of her thumb against the steering wheel. "It's complicated, Des. There's this feeling of frustration in some families, you know? It wasn't easy for my parents to get their citizenship and, even when they did, they never felt entirely American, never felt like their views mattered much to anyone. People stare at my mamá and me if we speak Spanish in public. Strangers told my parents to go back where they came from countless times, sometimes even in front of me, when I was a girl. People assumed my brother, Daniel, was going to be a failure as a kid because his skin is so much browner than mine. And that's not even the half of it.

"My father didn't truly believe that voting could change things; the whole system is so complicated and confusing, especially for people born in another country. It's also a tricky thing for police officers, because of the sorts of attitudes we can face on the job, from other cops even, if we are seen to take sides."

The music petered out, replaced by the voice of a man with newscaster speech patterns providing the title and artist of the preceding song. The way he varied the melody of his voice commanded my attention, despite the fact I wanted to give Sole my full consideration. "Mind if we turn that down?"

"Of course." She tapped the volume until the announcer's words sounded like the distant chattering of a child.

"Thanks." I twisted my torso so we were facing each other, crossing one leg over the other. Some hair had slipped from her ponytail and fell about the side of her face. I wanted so badly to reach out with my fingertips, follow the line of hair along her cheek. All of that energy looking for rivers we'd need to cross to get along, when in actual fact, Soledad had become part of my bridge.

"I'm sorry," I murmured. "I shouldn't have reacted that way. I need to be better at filtering things like that.

"You're right. It *is* complicated, and that's something I'm realizing more and more that I need to be mindful of. I don't know what it's like to experience the things your family has experienced. All my life I've tried so hard to be a good person. To interrupt racism when I see it. Not to shy away from difficult conversations or situations."

Forgetting what we'd agreed, I slipped my hand onto her knee, locking my gaze onto hers. "But I'm also a hypocrite. Until spending time with you, I forgot no one can fully rise above prejudice, especially someone with all of the privileges I have. I spend so much time trying to be good that I forget to be human, to be open. To admit my mistakes and learn to do better.

"I shouldn't keep carrying around so many assumptions, including assumptions about voting. I apologize for what I said. I didn't want to ask you because I want to not let the answer diminish all the things I know about you. The really, really great things. And it doesn't."

She gave me a tight-lipped smiled. "It's okay. You weren't entirely wrong, either. I wish I had voted. At the time, I assumed my vote wasn't all that important. You're not the only one who could benefit from reexamining some things." She rubbed at the back of her neck and closed her eyes, seeming to find a tightness in the muscle. I wished I could loosen the knot, press my palms and fingers against her flesh, and help ease the tension that lived there. She opened her lids. "We're all guilty of making generalizations. Hindsight. What an amazing teacher it is."

"Very true. Much like morally upright police officers who remind you not everyone can be painted with the same brush. But...hang on a minute. Did we just escape a who-did-you-vote-for argument?"

Her eyes fluttered in an adorable show of mock pondering. "I think we did. But."

"But?"

"Well. Des, why do you think you asked me? I know I pushed, but you could have said no... Did you want to pick a fight?"

I swallowed. Rose had put the idea in my head, that's true, but I'd been the one to let it fester to the point Soledad could sense how hard I was thinking. "I—I don't think so." She gave me a loaded look. "Maybe. I guess that could be true."

"You seem determined to find reasons to keep me at arm's length. Not all walls come from political rhetoric, you know."

Though her tone remained gentle, it felt as though each

word had been hurled like a stone. It was never easy when someone threw a truth bomb. Dipping my head ever so slightly, I said, "Wow. You don't hold back, do you?"

Sole squinted. "Never."

I chuckled.

"But..."

I crinkled my forehead. "But, what?"

"My turn. I think it's safe to say I've satiated your curiosity about all the big stuff. The things about me that made you wonder if we were compatible."

My eyebrows seemed to rise of their own accord. It felt like we were drifting into dangerous territory here, deciding whether this relationship was destined to be more than the friendship we'd agreed upon. Though I knew the answer deep down, this was happening sooner than I wanted. Sooner than was good for my relationship with Hope.

"As friends," she clarified. "Compatible as friends."

Gosh, she was good at knowing the right thing to say. "Yeah. That's true. Safe to say you've helped me understand a heck of a lot. You've been patient with me and I'm grateful. So, go ahead. What do you want to ask?"

Sole pulled on her earlobe before brushing the edge of her nose with the tip of her index finger. "I'm curious. I understand why, morally, you're so passionate about Black Lives Matter, why you worry so much about police officers, especially in this state of all places. But is there more to it? Is there something specific that sparked that passion?"

The question ached like a bruise, a torrent of memory sweeping through me, an inundation of guilt.

"Yes," I said, my voice low and barely audible. I cleared my throat, swallowing the gritty lump lodged there. When I spoke again, I sounded more myself. "I feel so stupid, some-times, when I think about this. It wasn't even me they mis-treated. I was the lucky one in the situation. No." I caught myself. "Not lucky. *Privileged.*"

Sole gingerly set her hand on my forearm. "What hap-pened?"

I pinched the bridge of my nose. "I was sixteen years old. I'd been at a party, nothing too unruly, a bunch of us playing board games and eating too much sugar. Talking rubbish, that sort of thing.

"It got late, though. And my mom was working so she couldn't pick me up. Three of us decided to walk home to-gether, since we lived in the same area and it would only take about thirty minutes."

Sole nodded, her eyes serious. She didn't interrupt, or prompt me when I paused, only waited, patiently, until I'd finished explaining.

"About ten minutes down the road, we were confronted by two police officers. It was dark, and we were loud I guess, but we weren't doing anything more than making too much noise. One of the cops yelled at us to stop, and we almost jumped right out of our skins. They didn't ask us to stop; they told us to stop. *Ordered* it. The guy's tone was terrify-ing, and we'd been off in our own world. None of us had ever been spoken to by police like that before."

Soledad's brow furrowed, her jaw taut. "That's unnec-essary," she lamented softly.

"Yeah." I wiped at the wetness on my cheek, a few way-ward tears leaving tracks as I followed the memory along its trajectory. "We all stopped straight away. We went silent and stood there like animals caught in headlights. Next thing we know, the cops are right up in front of us, scream-ing. What were we doing out on the street at night? Were we selling drugs? Were we carrying weapons? Where did we live? Where were we going? None of us managed to answer."

"Of course not," Sole said. "You were kids. Scared to the bone. Was...was one of your friends Black? Is that how this is connected to my question?"

As I rubbed at one of my eyes. "Jason."

"They targeted him. When none of you responded?" Soledad's face was grim as she considered me with brooding and watchful eyes.

I scoffed and my tears slowed as anger dislodged the sadness. "Oh yeah, they targeted him. The officer who'd yelled at us first, the one leading the whole thing, got right up in Jason's face, puffing his chest out, you know? His part-ner stood shoulder to shoulder, so they made this kind of wall. Vincent—that's the other friend I was with—and I were somehow shoved aside, though I can't remember exactly how that happened. What I do remember is Jason crying. His lips trembling. He couldn't get his words out. They kept asking what he had in his jacket, what he had in his jeans. But he was too scared to reply; he tried, I know he did, but he couldn't.

"Vincent and I were scared, too. We were looking at each other not knowing what to do. I rocked on the balls of my feet, like I might run and launch through the closest win-dow to escape the whole thing."

"It was a Terry Stop," Soledad said, a statement mixed with a question.

"That's what they said later, yes. That we gave them 'reasonable suspicion,' though I don't see how yelling about who'd won a game of Clue was a sign of criminal activity."

Sole shook her head. "Bastards," she murmured. "There are way too many cops that use that law to do whatever the hell they want, especially if their partner backs them up in whatever story they concoct later on. What happened to your friend? To Jason?"

I sank into the car seat a further, my chin dropping to my chest as a jagged, weighty stone formed in my gut. Jason Brooks. What happened to him was nothing short of a direct and tragic consequence of the racism that permeated so many of society's institutions, that underpinned so many people's actions.

"He..." I tried to speak, but my tongue felt like concrete all of a sudden and I had to wait a few moments before trying again. "He wrapped his arms around himself. You know, like a kid might do when they're afraid, a self-hug type of thing."

Soledad's head dropped as though she knew where this was going. "He tucked his hands under his armpits?"

"Yes," I croaked. "The next thing I knew, one of them reached for his gun, the quieter cop of the two, while the other grabbed at Jason's arm. Jason's arm flew up and, I don't know if he'd meant to do it or if it was a reflex, but he backhanded the cop trying to grab him. At least, I think that's what happened. It's hard to remember all the exact details."

"The one with the gun...did they..."

I shook my head again. "No, thank heavens. No one fired. Jason seemed as shocked as anyone that his hand slapped the loud one's face. He went rigid, paralyzed, and it was easy for the two officers to pin him and put cuffs on. They were so rough. One kept pointing the gun, and the other had my friend on the ground, his knees in Jason's back.

"Sole...I...I didn't do anything. I stood there. Vincent and I both stood there and did absolutely nothing. I actually covered my mouth and my eyes when they slammed him to the ground, didn't even give him the dignity of having his pain been seen, properly *seen*."

I felt my sentences speed up, my heart struggling to keep pace. "I could have defended Jason somehow. I could have called out for help, for witnesses. No one was going to listen to us; we were teenagers and Jason's friends, so we had no real credibility. If I'd found someone to be present, to *see* it, then maybe he wouldn't have been charged with resisting an executive order. He wouldn't have served time. He—"

"Wait. He was put away?"

"Life can be so shit, you know. He'd turned eighteen only three days before. If he'd had better friends, braver friends who weren't glued to the spot like silent statues..."

Sole cupped my chin, forcing me to look at her, to see the sincerity in her eyes, to see how deep her concern burrowed. "You were sixteen, Des. They had all the power and you had none. That's what abuse does, when authority is used to intimidate." She dropped her hand to my lap, enclosing my fingers within her palm.

"He never came out of prison, Sole. Jason was a complete nerd. He wasn't tough enough for that place. He did what he had to so he could survive and ended up charged with more crimes." A sharp, icy sensation stabbed at my sternum as I thought of the last time I'd visited him, when he'd told me that the kid I'd known was gone forever, that I shouldn't bother turning up anymore. The deadness of his eyes confirmed every word that came out of his mouth. "I swore I'd never be silent again. That I'd never, *never* look away. And I sure as heck wouldn't vote for anyone who refused to take a stand, either."

Soledad drew gentle circles on the back of my hand with her thumb, each revolution gradually slowing my thunderous heartbeat, the silence stretching out as my tears dried. "I'm sorry for what happened to your friend. To his life. To his family."

"Yeah," I whispered. "So am I." I looked at her, speaking more confidently. "I wanted to do better. I still want to do better."

Then, she kissed me. Sudden. Feverish. Impassioned.

And I couldn't stop myself from kissing her back.

CHAPTER TWENTY-NINE

SOLEDAD HELD ME with her whole body. The soft, rhythmic thud of her heart pressed against the naked skin of my back lulled me into a tranquil state, a place where everything seemed calm and warm. Her arms enveloped my torso, and her leg draped over my own as she stroked the skin along my bicep.

"That's one way to spend an afternoon." She nuzzled the back of my neck with her nose before pressing a whisper-like kiss to the top of my shoulder.

Biting my lip, I grinned. "Are you always such a smart-ass?" I teased.

"Only when inspiration strikes."

Twisting around so I could see her face, I tucked my knee against her thighs and brought my hand atop her hip.

"Inspirational is an appropriate word for today's events," I replied. As though sharing the same thought, we both moved in for a languorous, absorbing kiss, her lips gliding over mine as she twirled her fingers through the longer strands of hair above my ears. Unrestrained yet timeless, it was the kind of kiss that made promises.

After an indeterminate amount of time, I drew back, dropped my forehead against hers. "You know, I was so determined that I wouldn't end up back in this bed."

Soledad brought two fingers to the side of my face, feathering a touch along my cheek, following the line of my jaw before lifting my chin to kiss me chastely. "For a minute there you'd almost convinced me you wouldn't."

"Only a minute?"

She grinned and twisted her expression into one of mock-contemplation. "Weeeell... Ninety seconds tops." Her face softened as she brought her attention back to my face. "You're not as good at pushing people away as you seem to think. Something I'm grateful for, by the way."

I traced her bottom lip with my thumb, my gaze floating from one part of her face to another. The gorgeous ridge of her aquiline nose, her distinct cheekbones, her generous lips. "You are unbelievably beautiful, Sole."

Her skin pinked. "You are," I pressed. "I think a lot of things in my life have been monochrome for a while now. You've turned everything to color."

She laughed, her eyes bright with amusement.

"What?" I asked, my tone playful. "What's so funny?"

"I just pictured you stepping through the front door of a farmhouse into the land of Oz, surrounded by gallivanting munchkins."

Now it was my turn to laugh. "Wow. That's a distinct image. I was trying to say something nice, you know."

Sole's smile melted into a calm, contented expression. "I know. And it was the sweetest thing anyone has ever said to me. I know you have been scared of this, of us, but I'm glad you're here. You're worth the wait, Desi, but I'm relieved I didn't have to wait long." She slipped her arm beneath mine, drawing me closer until I nestled my head beneath her chin. She drew soft, lazy circles on my back with the tips of her fingernails, sending waves of goose bumps across my skin. I could feel the warmth of her along the entire length of my body.

After a few moments of quiet thought, I said, "I didn't realize it was fear."

"Hmm?"

"What you said before, about me being scared, of this, of us. I didn't believe that about myself. I thought I was content the way things were, that I didn't need to be in a romantic relationship to have a good life, to be a good parent."

"And you don't," she said, stilling her hand between my shoulder blades. "You don't need anyone to be a good parent."

"I think I know that, that I believe it. But not needing something doesn't mean not wanting it. Maybe I could be a better parent if I had someone, if I had *you*, in my life. You've already helped me be a better person, with everything you've shared with me. The experiences, the stories, the affection. All of those things have crawled inside me, led me to moments I've treasured.

"I could be fine on my own. But I can be better, my life can be better, if I let you in."

"And have you?" she asked, her voice low.

"I want to. I'm almost there. I'll need to have a conversation with Hope, I think. Make sure she's okay with me splitting my attention."

Sole's hand slid upward, and she sank her fingers into my hair. "Sounds like a good idea. But I want you to know I'd never expect you to put Hope's needs anywhere but first. Yours too, for that matter. Clara explained to me before I even met you that your priorities lie with the foster kids you care for. With your family. It was one of the reasons I agreed to meet you."

I drew back, tilted my head to look at her. "Really?"

"Definitely," she confirmed. "Who knows? Maybe, if things go well, I'll be part of your family someday too."

How I wish I had something clever, smooth, or charming to say in response. Soledad had made it clear she was in this if I wanted her to be. And I did want her to be. The words wouldn't come though. All I managed to do was reset my body against hers, once again cuddling into her chest. She didn't push for a reply though. She never did when it came to the big questions surrounding our relationship. Oh, she pushed me to be honest with myself, to open my mind and see the world more clearly, to de-mist my rose-colored lenses, but she never pushed me to take a step with her I wasn't ready to take.

And I was beginning to love her for it.

SOLEDAD POPPED A grape into her mouth and chewed. We had barely stopped looking at each other the entire time she'd been preparing an evening platter of fruits, cheeses, and small portions of various types of bread. Neither of us spoke for a time, enjoying the comfortable quiet as she sipped on coffee, and I worked my way through an English Breakfast tea.

I needed to get going soon, though. The day had all but disappeared and, although Hope was more than old enough to sort out her own dinner, I wanted to be home early enough to be around for a while before we both went to bed. In case she needed to chat. To simply to make sure a full day didn't pass without the two of us connecting in some way.

"You need to go?"

"Far out, Sole. How do you *do* that?" I reached for a section of Turkish bread topped with goat's cheese and gave her an incredulous look. "Your ability to read my mind is still scary."

"You tend to wear your thoughts on your face and your heart on your sleeve. It's one of your best qualities."

I dipped my head, my cheeks flushing. I mumbled an embarrassed "thanks," then nibbled on the bread. I gave a gentle moan. "Wow. That is delicious."

"I'm glad." Sole looked at her wristwatch. "How long before you head off?"

I sighed, resigned. "Maybe twenty minutes?"

"That works for me. I have to work tonight anyway, but not for another hour. More tea?"

I glanced at my empty teacup. "That would be great. I have time for one more. It's not like the caffeine will be a problem. I doubt I'll be going to sleep all that early."

She raised an eyebrow as she moved toward the kitchen with my cup. "Why is that?"

I bit my lower lip and tilted my head. "Let's call it adrenaline mixed with a healthy dose of emotional turmoil."

Her hand flew to her heart, gripping her chest. "Turmoil? Ouch."

I chuckled. "Not the bad kind of turmoil. More the can't-sleep-because-I'm-replaying-my-afternoon type."

"I see," she replied, her tone knowing and suggestive. She returned to the table and set the teacup in front of me. I wrapped my hands around the warm ceramic.

"Thank you."

"Any time."

I lifted the cup and blew over the top, sending soft ripples across the hot water. "I feel like I owe you somehow."

Her features scrunched, confused. "How so?"

"You've told me a lot about your family. About you. And you've invited me into parts of your life, like the asado, and even today at the gun range you shared a skill you've spent years perfecting."

"True. I've loved the time we've spent together. Though, I think I've been too pushy and it's definitely your turn to pick where we have our next date."

"Next date. I like the sound of that." I took an experimental sip of my tea and, finding it had cooled, invited a longer gulp into my mouth. "But I would love to spoil you, take you somewhere nice. Though it might be light on the crime-solving and physical exertion."

"Excellent," she said, spreading her fingers on the tabletop. "I can't wait. Really."

"That was a good way to change the topic, but I still want to share something with you."

She reached out, interlacing her fingers with mine.

"Okay. Anything. I'm interested, whatever it is."

"Can I borrow your laptop? Or maybe an iPad? Something with the internet and a screen larger than my phone."

"Of course." Bounding from her seat, she disappeared into the bedroom and re-emerged with a sleek laptop. Nothing fancy, but something lightweight yet sturdy. "Feel free to sign me out of whatever accounts I'm logged into if you need to access anything."

"You don't want to do that? In case your emails pop up or anything?" I pressed the power button and crossed my arms while the system started.

"There's nothing much exciting on there. Besides, you can see whatever might be on there. I don't mind."

Suddenly shy, I gave her a subdued smile. Her trust in me, her willingness to let me dive right into her life, continued to warm my heart. "Thanks."

After a few seconds, the operating system loaded, and I opened a browser. Switching the Google account over to my own, I opened a folder, clicked on the first file, and gestured for Sole to join me. She switched chairs, cuddling in close to me, her arm pressed up against mine, her hand pleasantly resting on my thigh.

"Wow."

"Do you like it?"

She let out a short whistle to reinforce her original response. "Absolutely. This is a beautiful photograph!"

On the screen, I'd brought up a picture I'd taken of my younger sister, Brenna, about a year and a half ago. A head-and-shoulders shot, we'd set this one up in a makeshift studio at my place, hanging a dark curtain across the living room wall. It was the first time I'd experimented with portraits and, soon after that, I'd become addicted.

"What kind of lighting is this? It makes her look so... Well, mature and thoughtful. Not that she doesn't seem that way, but your sister looks kind of at peace and confident here."

My cheeks flushed as Soledad examined the finer details of the picture. "It's a standard kind of portrait lighting. Butterfly light is when you light them from ahead, and just above. See it creates this shadow here below the nose? Hence the name."

"Whatever it is, you've done a great job."

"Brenna has amazing cheekbones, so this one makes them stand out."

Sole leaned closer. "Oh, you're right. They really do. I bet she loves this. Do you have any others?"

"Mmm-hmm." I switched over to a photograph of Hope. Different, this was from an outdoor shoot in a local park. Hope, in focus, sat cross-legged, looking off into the distance, a blurred footpath and green lawn in the background. She looked so beautiful. Not because of anything special in the photography, but because that was just Hope. Her long red hair curled about her shoulders, framing the soft features of her face and highlighting the smattering of freckles across her cheeks and nose.

"Oh, Desi. This. This one is stunning."

"This is a soft off-camera flash. I didn't want anything too powerful or obvious."

"No, this seems perfect. It's Hope. As she is, lost in her own thoughts. Natural and comfortable. That's the kind of picture that people should see, Des. Have you sent this into magazines or for contests?"

I laughed. "Far out. It's not *that* good!" I took another sip of my tea. "Thanks for the encouragement though."

Sole fixed me with an *I'm-not-kidding* expression. "You haven't shared these with anyone, have you?"

I shook my head. "Hope, of course, since it's her picture. And my family."

"And now me." She grinned.

"And now you."

Moving gently and slow, Sole closed the small gap between us and kissed me. Leaning her forehead against mine, the tips of our noses still touching, she said, "Thank you. These are amazing. I can see you in them as much as I can see your subjects." She moved away and I missed the heat of her skin straight away.

"I haven't wanted to share them with people before now."

"I'm glad you did. You should think about sending them out into the world, though. Even online, you could make a kind of portfolio or blog or something. Nothing too serious."

I tapped my chin with my index finger in mock contemplation. "We'll see."

"Don't think I won't remind you about this."

"Oh, I'm sure you will. But not everything about you is irresistible, you know."

"Lies!" Grinning, she kissed me again, longer, deeper than the last. A small moan escaped my mouth, swallowed by hers.

Her phone started to bleep, and she groaned, resigned, as she withdrew from me. "Damn. I better get ready for work."

"And I should head home."

We both sighed in unison, then laughed at our mutual disappointment. "Adulting," she said.

"Yeah. Will I see you soon?" I teased the end of her ponytail, letting the smooth strands of hair slide over my fingers.

"Tomorrow?" She turned her head, kissed my palm with feather-soft lips.

"Tomorrow," I confirmed, too enthusiastically. "And the day after."

CHAPTER THIRTY

WHEN SOMETHING SIGNIFICANT happened, particularly something heartbreaking, it seemed as though there should be a kind of atmospheric recognition. Drums beating. A bugle sounding. Perhaps rain should pour from the sky. None of those things happened when Hope disappeared. It was exactly the opposite. The sun kept shining. The gentle swish of cars passing by my front window continued. Ginger Snaps sat expectantly on the back step, her tongue lolling, and her tail wagging.

The house adopted an obstinate silence; not even the clock in the hall seemed to understand the magnitude of what was unfolding. But the rushed scrawl left on a note in the kitchen left little room for doubt:

Sorry, Desi. You've been great, but I have to go. Please

don't look for me.

I caught my own reflection in the surface of the microwave, gave myself a withering glare. "You idiot," I whispered hoarsely. I collapsed onto the floor, my rear end slamming against the tiles, my legs incapable of holding me up. I clutched the note in my hand, staring at it with disbelief.

What did she mean, she had to go? Go where? Why? For how long?

My consciousness receded.

The earth beneath me fell away.

My eyes stung as salted sweat dripped from my forehead.

I couldn't think of what to do. I had to do something though, right? I was the carer, the adult, a person with responsibility. I was meant to know what to do.

White noise reverberated through my skull and slithered down my spine. Tension and confusion made my mouth taste like chalk. *Think, Desi! Think!* I retrieved my phone from the pocket of my jeans, my hands shaking as I thumbed through the contacts list. Not one number for any of Hope's friends. I swore, realizing I hadn't even tried calling Hope herself yet. It took a few tries because my hands were slick with sweat, but I finally managed to initiate a call. Brrrrring. Brrrrring. Brrrrring. *Come on! Pick it up!* Brrrrring. Brrrrring.

Fear flared inside me, sticky and corrosive as the phone continued to ring. "Hey. You've called Hope. I don't actually check my voice mail, but you can leave me a message anyway if you like talking to yourself."

"Hope! Wh... Where are you?" My voice cracked midway through the sentence as my thoughts scattered. "Please let me know you're safe," I pleaded. "Even if you don't want to tell me what's going on, tell me that much. Please?" The last word was almost drowned out by the deluge of tears that pushed their way past my last and best attempt to hold my emotions in check. The phone fell from my hand, clanging against the hard floor as my grip, much like my legs moments earlier, faltered. The phone beeped, the impact having cut off the call.

For what felt like an eternity, I stayed there on the floor, curled up like a frightened hedgehog. I'd never been more alone.

Anything could be happening to Hope right at that moment. She could have been at a train station, isolated and vulnerable, with some creep watching her, ready to take advantage. She might have been wandering a dangerous alleyway, trailing behind a drug dealer who didn't give a shit about her, about to be shot by a rival gangster. She could have been lost and afraid and too proud to ask for help.

Dammit. I had *no* idea where she could be. What kind of a carer had no clue where to even look when their teenager went missing? If I knew her better, if I'd connected with her friends more directly, I'd have a starting place. But how many people asked their teenager's friends for their numbers? I didn't even know if that was something a parent did. Because I was not a parent. I was a useless stand-in. A failure who couldn't keep her safe.

I sobbed so hard my chest hurt and my eyelids swelled. It felt as though an ever-tightening chain wound about my sternum.

After a time, I wasn't sure how long, tiredness swept through my limbs and my eyes dried. No tears left. I wiped at my cheeks with the back of my hand, disgusted by what came away. Standing, I washed my hands and face with splashes of cold water, then blew into a tissue, rubbing too hard against tender nostrils. With my head bent over the sink, I lengthened my arms and stretched, fighting against a stubborn tightness in my upper back. Upon straightening, a fraction of the fog in my head had lifted. My stomach ached and my mind raced, but the frothy thoughts began to take form, to adopt meaning.

Thankfully, my phone had not broken when I'd dropped it. I flicked through my recent call list to locate my mother's phone number. It didn't matter how many years passed, how I matured; she'd always be the first person I turned to.

"Mom?"

"Desi!" I heard my own turmoil reflected back at me. It only took one word, and she knew I needed her.

"I don't know where Hope is." My voice sounded wrong somehow, like it belonged to a person miles away.

"Don't move a muscle. I'll be right there." Then, nothing. She'd disconnected.

I made my way to the sofa and curled up, facing into the seat rather than toward the television. With my arms pinned close to my body, I opened every application I could think of, searching for some sign of Hope's whereabouts. I may not have had any of her friends' phone numbers, but I knew a few of their names, and I had social media. As I searched, I started to grind my teeth. Hope had made her Instagram account private. Her Facebook profile hadn't been updated in three months and, as far as I knew, she had never set up a Twitter account.

"Where are you?" I whispered, my voice as fragile as my

nerves.

My body twitched involuntarily when the doorbell sounded. I'd become so involved in my online wanderings I hadn't noticed the last fifteen minutes go by. My mother had arrived. I wanted so badly to collapse into her, and so I ran for the door and wrenched it open. Her eyes locked onto mine and I crumbled again. She caught me and held me up, hooking her elbows under my armpits to lead me back to the couch.

Smoothing my hair, she looked at me, her eyes full of sympathy and her mouth downcast. "Did she run away?"

Silently, I recovered the now-creased note from my pocket and handed it to her.

"I see." Mom dropped the note onto the coffee table, then massaged her temples for a moment. "Do you think it was planned?"

I sniffled, cringed as mucous slid down the back of my throat. Standing, I found a box of tissues then rejoined my mother. "It must have been at least partially planned. That's why she needed money. The note looks like she wrote it in a hurry though, so maybe she had to change her plans."

Mom covered my knee with both of her hands, a small yet warming gesture. "Have you called the police?"

I rolled my eyes but closed my lids so she couldn't see the full extent of my frustration, which wasn't directed at her but at the situation. "She's sixteen soon, and technically she's only been missing since this afternoon. They won't do anything. Not yet. By the time I can report her missing, she'll be long gone." Sole's face flashed in my mind, and I suddenly wished, with all my heart, that she were there with me too.

"What about your new girlfriend? Isn't she a police

officer?"

"Yeah," I said, barely audible. "I'm not sure if she'd be allowed to do much. Not officially."

Mom tucked her index and middle finger beneath my chin and lifted my head, encouraging me to look at her properly. "It can't hurt to ask, can it? Clara told me Soledad works with young offenders quite a lot; maybe she has some ideas about where to look."

My mother had a point, and yet I didn't want to call Soledad. Not only did the idea of confessing my failure to her make my throat constrict, but the situation felt like a family matter, something I should be able to solve within my immediate circle.

In my panic I'd also forgotten that Sole was someone other patrol officers handed their juvenile cases over to whenever they could. She worked with teens every single day, and she was good at it. Maybe I should have brought her and Hope closer, rather than trying to keep my relationships with each of them so separate. I'd created a sort of Venn diagram, with the two of them on either side and only a slither of opportunity to tie them together in the middle.

I was angry at myself for not drawing Soledad closer to both Hope and me, denying Hope the chance for another support person, a positive and approachable role model who had more experience helping youth-at-risk than I ever would. Yet, I was also incensed that I'd let Soledad get so close my mother was suggesting I bring her into this situation. She wouldn't have said that if I hadn't sent signals about the increasing depth of my feelings. I'd been too distracted, I'd even admitted that I had been, yet I kept giving in to my own selfish desires. And now Hope was gone. I'd been with Soledad all afternoon and Hope had disappeared.

Another thought struck me with all the ferocity of an electric charge aimed right at my spine. "Oh, shit." My words were harsh, but my tone hollow.

"What is it?" She clenched my knee tighter, trying to re-focus my attention.

"Her caseworker. Hope's caseworker. We hardly ever hear from her because, really, she has a heck of a lot of kids on her case load. But when I report her missing, officially, they'll notify her and, even if they find Hope, they might not let her come back here."

"That's ridiculous." Mom sank into the chair, her hands slipping away from me, leaving a cold void in their wake. "You haven't done anything wrong. Surely they wouldn't move her to another carer. Kids run away. It happens all the time—they can't blame you for everything."

I laughed mirthlessly. "Of course they could." I dropped my head into my hands and, when I spoke, it sounded al-most as though I were under water. "Who the hell knows what influences their decisions? God. Maybe they'd be right to send her somewhere else if—"

"*When*," Mom asserted.

I sighed and sat upright. "Okay. *When* they find her."

She held out her arms and invited me to her. Without hesitation, I hugged her, my upper body collapsing into her, her perfume a sweet mix of white iris and subtle musk. Mom drew sluggish circles on my back with her palm and hummed a gentle tune into my ear. As she did, my heart rate began to settle, the heat in my face subsiding. "Call your girl-friend," she said, calm but commanding. "You won't be able to sit around tonight and do nothing. We can do the age-old parent thing and drive to the interstate bus depot, see if Hope is there, and while we do, you can ring Soledad and see if she can help at all."

"Okay." I roughed up my hair to dispel some of the stickiness. "Yes. Let's do that."

"First..." Mom rose to her feet and offered her hand. I took it and stood. "Have a glass of water. Change your shirt. Brush your teeth. Do whatever you need to do to feel more human again."

I planted my hand on my hip and, with the other, rubbed at my jawline.

"No, I know that look," she said sternly. "It's not a crime to take two minutes for yourself. It won't make a huge difference in the grand scheme of things, Desiree Adler." Desiree Adler? She meant business. "Go on."

As I shuffled toward my bedroom, my legs were lead, and my eyes throbbed from the strain of my own crying. I closed the door and dropped my head gently against the mirror. After a moment, I stepped back and took myself in. Mom was right. Disheveled was the word that came to mind. I needed to tidy up. Tilting forward from my pelvis, I inspected my face more closely, the gray circles under my eyes, the criss-cross of red lines within them. I felt like cracked pottery poorly repaired, unable to keep my doubts and my flaws inside where they belonged.

In the quiet, I had to be honest with myself. My intense emotive reaction had been most certainly about Hope—undiluted fear for her safety. But, and I needed to confront this about myself, there was also a hint of something selfish behind it too. When Hope had come to live here, I'd been convinced that this time I would get it right, that this time I'd help someone truly feel like they were part of the family, that as much as I hated the word, I'd help *rescue* someone.

How foolish. How arrogant. And how simplistic.

People didn't *rescue*. They supported. They challenged. They nurtured. My expectations had been, somewhere deep down, misdirected. That said, I didn't doubt that I had supported her. Challenged her. Nurtured her. And she'd done the same for me. I didn't need to rescue Hope because that concept diminished her autonomy and her resilience. It also undermined the love I'd genuinely come to feel for her.

We were family now. She needed to know that. I needed to tell her.

CHAPTER THIRTY-ONE

AFTER A STERN talking-to by my mother, I swallowed my chaotic inner dialogue and rang Sole. At first, I couldn't form the words. They became lodged behind a vacuum in my chest and refused to emerge. She was patient though, coaxing the information out of me gently.

"Des, I'm so sorry. I honestly didn't think, after meeting Hope, that she'd run away."

"It's not your fault. I'm the one who should have seen it coming. But I don't know what to do."

Though I couldn't see her, I could sense Sole's concern in her voice. "Well, I think you need to start with a missing person report. If you call the California Missing Children Clearinghouse, they'll take all the details and get her into the system."

"Don't I need to wait twenty-four hours?" I sensed Mom's eyes on me and turned my head to make eye contact. She looked as surprised as I. Turned out we were carrying around a bunch of misinformation in our heads.

"No, definitely not," Sole said assertively. "Something of an urban myth. You can report her missing as soon as you feel worried for her welfare."

"Okay. Yeah. Okay, that's good." I cleared my throat. "I want to look for her too."

A moment of silence.

"Parents rarely find runaway teens through their own investigations, Desi."

My mouth was dry, my throat constricted. I couldn't reply. I couldn't explain to her how important it was for us to try anyway. After a few seconds passed, she spoke again, her tone less matter-of-fact and more sympathetic. "All right. Well, given she left a note, it's not likely she's been hurt. Save calling hospitals until more time has passed. Focus on bus and train terminals. I wish I could help you. But...I'm so sorry but I have another two hours left on my shift." Her last few words were strained, but part of me was relieved. It still seemed strange to bring in someone other than my mother or sisters. To let someone know how broken I felt, how badly I'd let Hope down.

"That's okay," I replied, finally forcing my voice to work. "Thanks for the advice."

"I'll be here, Desi. If you need anything at all."

"Thanks," I said, my voice a hoarse whisper. I disconnected the call and let the phone drop unceremoniously to my lap.

"It sounds like she cares about both of you," Mom

observed.

"Yeah." It wasn't the right time to reflect on Soledad's intrinsic empathy. I couldn't process any more information. There'd be opportunity later. I already had my phone's browser open and was searching for information on the CMCC. I soon wished I hadn't. "Jesus," I whispered as the reality of what I'd read sank in.

"What is it?" Mom flicked on her indicator, changing lanes so she could take the next turn, which would lead us to the bus station on Richards Boulevard.

"Seventy-five thousand, mom. There are at least seventy-five thousand runaways reported every year in this state alone. There's no way they'll be able to do much to help. Some of these kids are as young as ten." I didn't tell her another statistic that came up in my search. Eighty percent of runaway girls reported being assaulted in some way. My ribs shrank and my tongue seemed as thick as wet concrete.

"You should call them anyway, hon. Worry about the foster system later. But you never know who might spot her and if you haven't made a report—"

"I will. I'll do it now. I don't know why I didn't ring before."

"It's the worry, Des. Panic doesn't make sense. Everything is thrown into a blender. Deal with things as you can."

Dismissing the browser, I opened a message from Soledad that had come through. She'd sent the number in case I hadn't caught it when we were talking. Tapping the text, I instigated a call. Following the prompts, I reached a human voice on the other end at the same time the bright lights of the bus station came into view. The car slowed and Mom directed us into a space. She shifted into Park, but left the engine on, the low humming and soft vibrations preferable to the silence that would have otherwise seemed overwhelming.

I'd thought that talking to another authority figure about Hope, verbalizing the danger she could be in, would be difficult, that I'd have to force the words out as I did with Sole, like trying to squeeze a square peg into a round hole. But that didn't happen. Instead, I adopted a professional style of speech, outlining everything I could think of about Hope's recent behavior, recounting our benign interactions that morning before she went to school, and providing the names of Hope's foster care agency, school, and closest friends, Ava and Imogen.

"We'll provide an email address so you can send through a recent photograph," the CMCC worker said, his voice deep and stoic. "However, I'll need a physical description in the meantime."

I scratched at my forehead as I imagined Hope's form and thought about the most useful descriptors I could provide. "She has red hair that's very short because she shaved it and it's starting to grow back. Her eyes are pale blue, her chin smooth and her nose narrow."

"And her height and weight?"

"Um. I'm not sure, but I'd guess she's around a hundred and forty-five pounds and about five foot four."

In the driver's seat, my mother gave me a thumbs-up, agreeing with my estimates.

"Thank you, ma'am. Call us immediately if you think of anything else that might help locate your foster daughter, or if she turns up."

Oh Lord did I want her to turn up. Maybe she'd change

her mind and call me, ask me to pick her up from somewhere, to take her home. "Yes. Of course. Thank you." I dropped the cell phone into my lap and looked to my mom. Her eyebrows slanted inward, creasing the skin above her nose. "Okay. That's done. Let's check inside."

"Okay," she agreed, unbuckling her seat belt.

The air and noise inside the terminal made my stomach turn. A mixture of body odor, disinfectant, and stale food, the miasma of scents was too much for my already fragile senses. Similarly, a cacophony of voices and hurried footsteps left me disoriented for a few moments and I had to put my hand on Mom's shoulder to center myself, to reconnect with the speed at which the real world seemed to be moving.

"Are you all right?"

I breathed out unevenly, normalizing somewhat with each shuddery exhalation. "Felt weird for a second there. Should we split up?"

She shook her head, her long, diamond-shaped earrings swaying as she did. "I don't think so."

Even though we could cover more ground separately, I was glad to stay with her. Arms linked, we moved about the area, scanning each face as we went. A few people reacted poorly to our stares, one or two sneering and a couple of others purposely changing direction to escape our scrutiny. I couldn't blame them; I wouldn't like two strangers analyzing my face either.

As we started our second lap, my heart dropped lower in my chest, heavy and tired. The same people, perhaps moving in different directions, perhaps having settled on a seat somewhere, occupied the spaces. The area seemed expansive and claustrophobic at the same time. The air didn't taste right. "She's not here." The resignation in my voice clear, Mom wrapped an arm about my shoulder.

"We haven't checked outside. Don't give up."

Inclining my head, I let her lead. I wanted to stay positive, but Soledad was right about the chances of finding Hope this way.

Doubt caressed the base of my skull with cold, skeletal fingers and the throbbing in my head sped up. It only became worse when, twenty minutes later, we hadn't spotted her. "Mom." I grabbed at her forearm, compelling her to stop walking.

"What is it?"

Shifting my weight from one foot to the other, I started mindlessly at the floor. "This won't work."

"Des, we should—"

"No, Mom. It isn't giving up. It's being realistic. This isn't a movie. We won't come across her in some obvious and convenient location. There are over half a million people in this city. If she's even still in the city. It's more likely that she'll come home on her own and, if she does, I'm not there. I *need* to be where she can find me." A tear slid over my cheek and I wiped it away.

My mother's features changed, her eyes widening and her jaw relaxing. She agreed with me. For now, we had to wait.

CHAPTER THIRTY-TWO

MY HEART BUZZED like a pneumatic drill. Arms and legs thrusting. Propelling me forward. My sneakers slid and squeaked against the polished tiles of the hospital floor.

"Hey!" someone yelled. I thought I knocked into them, but I wasn't sure. I had to get to the third floor. I had to.

Taking the stairs two at a time, I burst through the final door and bounded toward the information desk, harsh fluorescent lights guiding my way. My limbs ached.

"H...Ho..." Words wouldn't come. My lungs were full of sand. My chest heaved and I coughed.

A gentle hand slid along my shoulder. "Desi."

I turned and, the moment Soledad's large eyes came into view, I burst into tears. She embraced me, pressing her chest against mine and tucking my head into the crook of her neck. "Shhh," she cooed as she teased the short hair at the base of my neck. "Take a second. Get your breath back." As I opened my eyes, the blue fabric of her uniform dominated my vision. Soledad kept one arm firmly around my waist as I stood to full height. "Where is she?"

Sole's eyes moved to the right as she looked over my head. "Bed seven." Taking hold of my hand, she guided me to the room where I'd find Hope. The door-less entry seemed wrong. Too dull. Too benign. Surely the opening that led people to their injured family members, to their ill friends, needed to be more imposing.

"Desi." Soledad squeezed my hand, compelling me to turn, to stand toe to toe with her. The expression on her face, solemn and apologetic, scared me. "I want to warn you. She's going to look worse than you might expect."

My fingers vibrated, like the tiny bones in my hand wanted to escape my body. "What do you mean?"

"She's been shot, Des. I know they told you that, but people don't often realize what a toll even the least dangerous bullet wounds can have. Her body is working hard to deal with the damage inside her. The bullet hit her femur, so they'll be taking her into surgery as soon as they have an OR free, to get the fragments out. As long as the surgery goes well, she should be okay. I thank God that it didn't hit her femoral artery. But there's still a lot of healing ahead."

My temples thundered as though someone were playing drums inside my skull. I planted my palm along the top of Sole's chest near her collarbone in an attempt to anchor myself to the real world. She covered my hand with her own, tucking her fingers beneath mine.

How could this have happened! Hope was such a kind

person. She was funny and bright. She had Anne Shirley freckles and thoughtful eyes. She wanted to be a veterinarian one day.

Someone out there had lifted the barrel of a handgun, aimed at my girl, and squeezed the trigger. They'd *squeezed*. Even though she was so young. They didn't care. They'd hurt her and they didn't fucking care.

"Is she awake?" I asked, barely managing more than a whisper.

"No. They've given her some rather strong medication for the pain, and she's asleep. She's stable, and it won't be long before they can operate."

The next few steps, the steps that took me into the hospital room, were the hardest and most necessary steps I'd ever taken. When I moved beyond the privacy curtain and her ghostly white face came into view, I surged forward, gripping her hand. "Hope. I'm here. We're here. You're not by yourself."

Hope's hair was stringy and wet, plastered to her forehead by sweat. Her breathing came in sharp, shallow waves, and her eyes rushed about beneath their lids. As I watched her, a violent sob tried to claw its way out of my diaphragm, but I wouldn't let her hear it. Wouldn't let sadness invade the space, a space of healing. And so I swallowed, my saliva tasting like rust.

Soledad appeared beside me, bringing a chair with her. With tight, tired legs, I eased into the seat's sterile embrace, tucking it as close to the bed as physically possible. Hope's hand, clammy and cold, remained limp. If she could feel me, or hear me, there was no indication. I wished I could reach into her mind somehow, let her know that I'd be right by her side no matter what came next.

"Desiree Adler?" A masculine voice sent ripples through the air, and I jumped about an inch off the chair. "Sorry. I didn't mean to sneak up on you." A serious-looking man in his mid-twenties with dark-blond hair stood at the edge of the curtain around Hope's bed, clutching a clipboard beneath his arm. He wore a perfectly ironed, lily-white business shirt, black pants, and polished black shoes. "I'm Grant Barry. Hope's case worker."

I blinked against confusion that cast spots into my field of vision. "I don't understand. Her case worker's name is Prudence."

Grant Barry pushed at the bridge of his glasses and, for a moment, reminded me of Clark Kent, meek yet intelligent, arriving for his first day at the *Daily Planet*. An idiotic thought to have at such a time, but there it was. "I've taken over most of Prudence Carey's caseload. Sorry we didn't meet earlier, but the placement seemed fairly stable and, well, I imagine you understand that stable placements are less of a priority."

I cleared my throat. Given Hope lay before us, white as porcelain, feverish, and badly wounded, stable was unlikely to be a descriptor in his next report. Was he here to strip me of my guardianship? To expel me from Hope's life?

After a silence that lingered a second too long, I answered him. "Yes. I understand." It wasn't surprising that Prudence had left the job. Grant would be Hope's fourth case manager in twelve months. The turnover rate had been high with every child I'd met. Clearly, being a social worker was a stressful job.

He came closer and, in a manner that felt protective,

Soledad stood behind me and pressed her hands to my shoulders. "Are you the officer that made the arrest?"

My attention snapped to Soledad. She slid one hand to the hollow at the base of my neck in response, as though asking me to wait to question her.

Arrest? Was Hope being charged with something? No. No. That couldn't be true.

"I was there," Sole responded. "My partner, Officer Washington, stayed with the shooter, and I accompanied the victim here. Hope's birth mother was also apprehended. She'll be charged with drug possession and child endangerment."

Scenarios whipped up a frenzy in my mind, like debris caught in a tornado, flung from one place to another. I didn't even know where to start. When Soledad had called me, all I'd heard was that Hope was hurt.

Gunshot.

Hope.

Hospital.

None of the details had mattered at that point. But now, amongst the glowing monitors and the beeping machines and sanitized linens, a need to know those details, to process them, as they threatened to overwhelm my sensibilities. My spine pulsed with impatience. My toe tapped wildly against the floor.

"And you—" Grant. Mr. Barry. Whatever I was meant to call him...his gaze fell to the place where Soledad caressed my neck, the caring strokes of her thumb the only thing that stopped me from floating into space. "—know the family?"

His use of the word "family" had a strangely curative effect. He'd referred to Hope and me collectively, a splinter of light in the darkness.

"Yes." Soledad responded assertively and without hesitation. "Desiree and I are together."

Together. Shit. Should I clarify that?

But she wasn't wrong. We had decided we would give this another shot, after all. So, there wasn't anything to clarify. Except my own scattered thoughts.

As though sensing my moment of hesitation, Mr. Barry looked to me. "Together?"

I had to stop denying Soledad full entry into my life. If she was here by my side at the worst of times, then I had no reason not to let her world converge with Hope's. She wouldn't run away when things were hard. She wouldn't expect me to choose between her and Hope. She wouldn't let me keep drifting.

"Yes," I said. "We met not long before all of this started with Hope."

Expecting him to judge me, to give me a stern talking-to for dating when I was meant to be parenting the barely-alive teenager lying nearby, I was genuinely surprised when he smiled gingerly. "Sounds like it's a good thing too. From what I've been told, Officer, if you hadn't been there, things could have been a lot worse. And technically, you didn't need to be?" The timbre of his voice made it clear this last sentence had been a question, not a statement.

Hope's fragile form once again commanded my attention. I studied the uneasy rise and fall of her chest. Listened to the rasping sound of her inhalations. Breathed in the iron-rich scent of dried blood.

Worse than *this*? She needed what sounded like major surgery and was at the beginning of a difficult recovery. I couldn't entertain thoughts of situations where this had turned out worse.

"Not technically, no," Sole replied. "My shift was over. We'd been over at the casino and were driving back to the station to check the car and weapons. A call came in about an adolescent being dragged along and sworn at by a much older man outside of an Arby's a few blocks from the precinct; the description reminded me of Hope. Desi had told me she was missing, so I radioed in and said we would respond. If it wasn't us though, someone else would have helped her."

I tipped my head back to rest against Soledad's stomach, thanking her without words. Of course, other officers would have done their best for Hope, but there was no one else I'd trust more with her safety than Soledad.

What a fool I'd been to think Soledad's presence, that the space she occupied in my life, could ever be a danger to Hope. As the warmth of her body soothed me, and the gentle caress of her fingers on my neck slowed the beat of my heart, I knew she could be nothing but good. For both of us.

"Thank you, Officer..." Grant Barry trailed off as he glanced at his clipboard. "Reyes. Officer Reyes. They told me at the desk that one of the medical staff will be back in a moment to explain what happens next."

As if on cue, a middle-aged woman with a short haircut similar to my own strode into the room, her dark-brown eyes fixed on an electronic tablet in her hand. Petite and confident, she spoke whilst still examining the tablet. "Grant Barry?" She lifted her head and scanned the room. She held her hand out to Mr. Barry. "I'm guessing that would be you?"

He pushed at his glasses again before accepting the

offered handshake. "It would."

"All right. So, we have the case worker. We have the attending officer. And..."

Soledad chimed in. "Hope's carer. This is Desiree Adler; she's been Hope's foster carer nearly two years."

The doctor acknowledged me, sympathy framing her tired eyes. "Good. I'm Dr. Yamamoto. Let's go over what's happening.

"First of all, Hope is not currently in much danger of losing her life. I want to allay that fear first. There are always risks with surgery, and there are never any guarantees, but I feel confident, based on the scans we've had so far, that she has a strong chance of recovering nicely."

Soledad squeezed my shoulder, and I took hold of her hand, squeezing back. Relief swept through me, only to come to an abrupt halt when the doctor added, "But."

"But?" Mr. Barry said.

"There's some real work to do," she continued, slipping a hand into the pocket of her white coat, as though settling in. "The CT scan shows multiple bullet fragments located at the femoral neck and dispersed within the articular space of the right hip. The bulk of the bullet, however, looks like it has lodged in the transcervical region." The doctor withdrew her hand from her pocket and held it over her hip, near the socket, then moved it higher as she spoke.

"I thought...I thought she was shot in the leg?" I blinked against the harsh brightness of the lights framing Doctor Yamamoto's head.

"She was shot in the femur," the doctor clarified. "But the femur runs all the way up the length of the thigh and into the hip. The shooter was also on the ground, aiming upward, which has created an unusual angle of entry."

Confused, I twisted in the seat and gazed up at Sole. "Soon. I'll explain it all soon," she murmured. Frustrated but resigned at having to wait, I returned my attention to the doctor.

"We'll need to get in there to debride and irrigate. That will hopefully remove any debris, like fabric from her clothes or tiny particles of metal."

Made sense. They'd need to clear out all of that stuff. Infection was always such a big concern with any kind of wound or surgery. Infection. *Please, whatever gods might be out there, please don't let her get an infection.*

Dr. Yamamoto looked at each of us, pausing to make sure were paying careful attention before she continued. Her touch of the dramatic did nothing to settle the buzzing of my nerve endings. "But Hope will also need to have the fractures repaired, and given the location, that will likely require three screws."

"Screws. In her hip. At fifteen years old?" The indignation in Soledad's voice reflected my own emotions perfectly. I was glad one of us still retained the ability to speak.

"I'm afraid so," the doctor replied. "We will decide on a definite plan of action once we can see what's happened in there for ourselves. But, for now, that's my best estimate as to the surgical plan. There aren't any signs of severe trauma to surrounding tissues, and hopefully it stays that way once we open. She's lucky the gun he used was not high velocity. Otherwise, we'd be having a different discussion."

The blood drained from my face, and I could only assume the doctor noticed the nausea rising inside me because she lightened her tone and changed the topic. "In regard to the long-term outlook...after the initial swelling subsides, we'll start her on physical therapy as soon as possible. With the right approach and solid postsurgical care, Hope's mobility shouldn't be drastically affected."

I had no idea what to say. Hope was, unless something went terribly wrong, going to be okay. But she would have to endure months of frustration and pain. Maybe this would even cause her physical and emotional grief for the rest of her life.

"If there are no other questions right now, I'll check on the ETA for an OR so we can get started."

Grant Barry silently checked in with both Soledad and me. We shook our heads. "No. Thank you for coming in to give us that update."

"Certainly." With a well-practiced kind of mechanical pirouette, she left.

"This is so horrible," I said after a few seconds had passed. "My poor girl." Leaning forward, I wrapped the fingers of both my hands around Hope's forearm, dropped my head between my elbows, and settled against the mattress.

"Yes," Mr. Barry sighed. "What's worse is that this isn't even the first adolescent runaway we've had turn up in this hospital this week."

"Really?" Soledad said, a degree of annoyance in her tone. "Not the best time to share that sort of information."

I kept my forehead against the bed, next to Hope, as they talked around me.

I wanted it to be quiet. I wanted the lights to stop being so damned bright and for the spinning in my head to slow.

Reality had skewed into strange, unrecognizable splinters. I couldn't grip any of them. Couldn't understand why something like this would happen.

"You're right. I'm sorry," Mr. Barry said.

Soledad moved away, her boots squeaking against the floor as she approached him. "Listen. She's going to need to know. Desi, that is. Are you planning to terminate the placement?"

Mr. Barry scoffed. "What? Move Hope to another foster home? Is that what you mean?"

"That's exactly what I mean."

Unable to ignore their interaction any longer, I rose from the chair, turned to face them, and crossed my arms over my chest. It did not contain the chaotic beating of my heart. "Please." I rubbed at the floor with the toe of my shoe, avoiding eye contact. "Please answer her."

"No. Absolutely not. This would be a terrible time to relocate Hope. At her age and in her condition, we'd be unlikely to even be able to find someone willing to take her on, to be frank."

My knees shook, and I would have collapsed if I hadn't been able to grab the railing on the edge of the hospital bed. Soledad rushed to my side, looping an arm around my shoulders as I returned to the seat.

"To be clear," Sole said, holding her spare hand in the air as though she were trying to calm an animal, "Desi, who you can see is trying to process a lot right now, doesn't need to worry about your agency taking Hope away?"

Mr. Barry, mild-mannered Superman lookalike, took a few steps and knelt nearby, but not close enough to encroach on my personal space. "Obviously we need to have a discussion with Hope when she wakes up. But, assuming that there was nothing inappropriate happening in your household that forced her to run—and gauging from what we've found out so far, that is not the case—then there's no good reason to move Hope to another foster home. Are you willing to work with her through the recovery?"

"Mr. Barry," I said, my tone firm. "I'd work with her through anything. She's my family."

CHAPTER THIRTY-THREE

THERE WAS NOTHING to do but wait. Soledad and I made our way to the first floor, my feet dragging the entire way. God. I was so damned tired. Not only from the lack of sleep, but from the emotional drain. Eyes sore and puffy, throat scratchy and thick, I felt as though someone had connected a drip to my arm but, instead of delivering fluids, it had been steadily sucking the energy right out of me.

My entire sense of time was messed up. It had been dark, late at night when I'd arrived. Now, on the other side of the glass windows that acted as the front wall to the building, streaks of orange, red, and soft hints of purple announced the arrival of the sun. A new day had started and, as exhausted as I was, it felt as though only half an hour had passed since I'd run up those stairs, desperate for news.

Soledad eased me into a hard, plastic chair as though it had been me who was injured, bending down to press a gentle kiss to my temple. "Tea?"

Grimly I replied, "Coffee."

"Wow. You *are* tired." She fanned her thumb across my cheek, her eyes large with worry. "Coffee it is. Did you want me to call anyone for you?"

Heck. I hadn't even thought of that. Brenna, Clara, Mom...they'd all need to know what had happened. My hands were clammy even thinking about those conversations. I decided to call Mom first. Hopefully she could relay the key details to my sisters, and I'd only need to have the conversation once. "No. No, it's all right. I can do it. Thank you, though."

As Soledad made her way to the counter, I fumbled through my satchel in search of my cell phone. The battery had 10 percent left and there were no messages. Though, why I'd expected anyone to message me in the middle of the night, I wasn't sure. Mom picked up on the first ring, her words clear yet panicked. "Has she come home yet?"

"Mom..." Damn these tears. How could one person produce so many? I choked back my swelling emotions, my need to have my mother's arms around me, as best as I could. "We're at the hospital."

I relayed as much as I could, recounting the doctor's explanations as well as our interactions with Grant Barry. She interjected with questions, but I didn't have answers.

"I'll talk to your sisters," she said. She sounded worn out. The fact she hadn't slept either brought a strange sense of comfort.

"That would be good. Thank you. I don't think I could

say all of this again. Not yet."

She'd go to my house to feed and walk the dog, find some clean clothes, and meet me at the hospital in a couple of hours with my phone charger. By the time the call ended, Soledad returned and set two large coffees and a grilled cheese sandwich, cut down the middle, on the table. If you'd asked me an hour or two ago if I wanted to eat, I would have thrown up. Suddenly, however, with the smell of melted cheese and doughy bread wafting directly in front of me, I was ravenous.

"Hungry?" She sat opposite, nudging the sandwich my way.

"Apparently, yes. Thank you so much for this." Taking a bite, I closed my eyes and sank into the warmth and taste. It wasn't the freshest bread I'd ever had, but it brought an immediate and profound boost to my energy stores. After I'd eaten a few more bites and sipped some coffee, I dropped the sandwich to the plate. "And thank you for everything else. You didn't have to go looking for her when you heard that call on your scanner. But you did."

Soledad shrugged. "Of course, I had to." She lifted her coffee to her lips, then paused. I noticed the subtle shaking of her hands.

Reaching across, I grabbed her free hand, wrapping it up within my own, trying to warm her. "Hey. Sole...are you okay?" I'd been so selfish not to have asked her earlier. She'd been awake much longer than I had and, whatever unfolded last night, she'd been right in the thick of it. She sniffed, pressed her mouth to the rim of the coffee, and took a brief sip. She put it back on the table, then brought her free hand toward mine so I held them both.

"You can tell me." I smoothed my thumbs across the backs of her hands. "Letting it out doesn't make you weak, Sole. You're one of the strongest people I've ever met. It's okay to feel whatever you're feeling."

She nodded a few times, fast, as though convincing herself to believe what I'd said. She gave my fingers a gentle squeeze. "I was scared, Desi." Her eyes glazed over as she seemed to delve into her memories of last night. "I'm always scared when a weapon goes off, whether it's mine or someone else's. But when shots are fired around a minor? Let alone one I know personally…I've never felt fear like that. It was like a bolt of electricity. Like my heart stopped and it's only just started beating again, but my blood doesn't know what paths to follow anymore."

I frowned and dipped my face, touching my forehead to hers. She did the same and we both closed our eyes.

It wasn't only Hope who could have been lost to me, nor would it be the last time Soledad came under threat. This was what it meant to be in a relationship with a police officer. "I can't imagine what that must be like. You're an incredible person to risk everything, usually for strangers who might not ever appreciate what you do."

A small drop of fluid appeared on the table between us. Soledad was crying. Her shoulders heaved, though her tears came quietly. As best as I could across the table, I wrapped one arm around her. She nuzzled her forehead into the crook of my neck. We stayed like that for a while, until her breathing settled and her shoulders were once again still. Straightening, she pulled back, using a napkin to wipe at her now pinkened face.

Having collected herself, Sole reached for the other half

of the sandwich I'd been eating earlier. She cocked her head, surprised, and swallowed. "Better than I expected, for hospital food."

I gave a muted laugh. "I agree. Though it's hard to get a grilled cheese wrong."

"Hmm. I've seen it happen."

I smiled, but my lips were tight, fixed together in a thin, concerned line, and I realized my jaw ached from grinding my teeth.

The moment of levity faded, dissolving one heartbeat at a time. "What happened last night? Do you want to talk about it?"

Soledad sank a little in her seat, and her knees brushed against mine beneath the table. Freeing the top button of her crisp shirt, she prepared herself to tell me everything.

"I can stay for a while, but I'll need to get back to the station and fill in a lot of paperwork." She paused and I silently acknowledged her words. "Well, you already know about the call that came in."

"There was a man? Yelling at her and dragging her along?" I had no idea who he could be, but bile rose in my throat as I imagined him treating Hope like some sort of nuisance animal. However he came to be in Hope's life, I prayed that some ruffian would put him in his place in whatever cell he'd be rotting in. Cell. Prison. Shit, I thought. There'd be a trial eventually. Someday, Hope would be asked to tell people what had happened to her. How long would this nightmare drag on for her?

"Yeah. I think he might have been the boyfriend of Hope's mother. She was there too, but she was as high as a kite. I don't think she even realized what was going on until the sound of bullets firing shocked her back into the real world. Then she started screaming. That sort of terror-fueled, high-pitched ringing that only people who had completely forgotten they were even awake can have...you know, when they suddenly snap back into reality."

"Do you know why Hope was with them? She has contact visits with her mother about six times a year, but Hope must have been in touch with her on top of those." Soledad lifted a few fingers of one hand, a gesture to indicate she didn't know the answer. Perhaps Hope could tell us when she recovered.

"I'm guessing he didn't react very well when your patrol car arrived?"

She scoffed. "You could say that. Hope's mother, was her name Amber...something?"

"Yeah. Amber Murphy." I tried not to think about how much Amber had hurt Hope over the years. The neglect. The physical abuse. I needed to be a stone if I were to get through Soledad's story. It was always a struggle to remember that, often, people like Amber had themselves been through horrible ordeals, situations that meant they'd never learned how to be a parent, or even how to care for themselves. It was important never to say anything unnecessarily negative about a foster child's birth parents in front of them, but that could be difficult when the lingering consequences of their failings surrounded a person living under your roof, affecting them each and every day.

"Murphy. Yes, she was trailing behind them a few feet, but the guy had a vice grip of Hope's bicep. She looked like she wanted to get away, to run toward her mother, but he wouldn't let her. When he saw us, he shoved Hope's body in front of himself."

"Like…like a human shield?" I dragged one of my hands from the table and wrapped it around my knee in a white-knuckled grip.

Soledad set her mouth set like a barbed fissure.

"Then what?"

"He had his arm across her chest. She kept crying and he held her so damned tight. I'm not sure she even recognized me. Her eyes were clenched shut most of the time. The guy reached behind his back, and that's when Washington told him to freeze." Soledad's eyes became glassy again as she melted into her thoughts. Yet, she continued, unflinching. "He kept reaching and so I unclipped my holster, my hand on my Glock. When he whipped his arm back around, and there was a gun in it, I drew, but I couldn't aim, there wasn't a safe shot, so I directed the barrel at the ground."

Her pace increased, her tone starting to reveal the fear that must have pulsed through her last night. "Hope opened her eyes. She saw me and her whole face changed. Like she was angry. Really angry. I'll never forget that look. Or what she did next."

Soledad licked her lips and shifted her weight, her posture strong as she moved to the edge of her seat. "Desi, you would have been so proud of her. It was so damned dangerous, though. It could have gone so wrong, but the courage it took… She's got so much inner strength."

"What? What did she do?" I bit my lip, my stomach a magnetized vortex of suspense, alarm, and admiration.

"She elbowed the bastard. Hard. So hard that he lost his grip and doubled over before he could steady his aim."

"Holy shit."

"Yeah. Exactly. I know this sounds cliché, but it all happened so fast after that. Hope stumbled and he was cursing and yelling. Washington yelled too; he had his weapon drawn. I called to Hope. I wanted to get to her, for her to get to me. But the perp recovered faster than I expected. He looked like he was going to jump her, so I put a bullet in his leg. That was when Murphy came out of her daze. She started ripping out her own hair, screeching like it was her who had been shot. Everyone was yelling and her voice made it all so much harder to understand. She was so *shrill*, almost demonic."

The mist in Soledad's eyes as she looked right through me made it clear she had a lot to sort through. It was as though she needed to follow a thread to its concluding point, then backtrack and follow another until the connections asserted themselves and the bigger picture came into focus.

Under the table, I slid a hand from my own knee onto hers. "And yet you did what had to be done. You got her out of there. Yourself too."

Soledad drew in such a sharp breath that her entire torso lifted. Her lower lids glistened as tears threatened to return. As she spoke, her eyes remained open, unblinking, as though propped by invisible matchsticks. "When her mother screamed out like that, Hope got distracted. She turned. She turned away from me. The guy was on the ground, blood pouring out of his leg, but he saw her. Saw her come back. I think she wanted to comfort her mom, you know?"

I remained silent, allowing Sole to continue uninterrupted.

"I knew what he was going to do. I could see the hate all

over him; his entire face was distorted, gnarled. The gun had fallen away when I shot him, but it wasn't far. He only had to scramble a few inches to wrap his hand around it. Washington and I...we both screamed at Hope to get down, but she couldn't hear us properly. Murphy made that impossible, and all Hope was focused on was getting to her mom. I...I was too slow, Des. I hesitated too long."

Soledad dropped her face into her hands. Her body shuddered as she wept, louder and harder than before. In a second, I was out of my seat and by her side, one arm embracing her around the stomach, my other hand pressed against the back of her neck. "It's not your fault. I know I wasn't there, that I can't understand the intensity of the moment, but I know one thing. You have never given me any indication that you are anything other than an entirely selfless person. You're a cop because you genuinely want to help people. It's what makes you so amazing, Sole."

Turning, she rested the side of her head against my shoulder. I smoothed her hair as she cried, her sniffles gradually slowing. She lifted her head and made eye contact. Her lips quivered, then she forced a muted smile. She reached for another napkin and wiped her face again, the tip of her nose and the whites of her ears having turned a soft red. "Well, my fault or not, he got his finger on the trigger and he squeezed. When she fell, it was like the entire world crashed into the ground with her.

"I barely remember doing it, but when he made to shoot again, I fired. This time, I hit the side of his abdomen and he couldn't stand up anymore. Washington secured him, somehow wrangled Murphy into the back of the patrol car, and called for two ambulances while I got pressure on Hope's wound. The blood pumped through that hole so much faster than I expected. It poured between my fingers."

Cupping Soledad's jaw in my hand, I held her in place with the tone of my voice. "You saved Hope's life, Sole. This man, whoever he was, might have killed her if you hadn't acted. I'm..." Now it was my turn to cry again. "I'm...so grateful. You saved my family."

Placing her hands on either side of my head, Soledad smoothed away the fresh tears from my cheeks with her thumbs. "I'm grateful too. I've never been so scared in all my life, Desi."

I couldn't help but laugh. "Why would you be grateful for that? You always manage to surprise me."

"Because." She kissed me chastely before continuing. It didn't even matter we were both tear-stained messes. "I've never wanted, so badly, to *live*. I've never wanted, so badly, to build a new family. One with you. And if, when she and I get to know each better, she'll have me...with Hope too."

"I don't think I deserve you. You're so...so good, Sole."

"Deserve? Desi, you're worth a lot more than you seem to think."

As childish as I felt, given the circumstances, I asked the question circling in my head anyway. "What is it you like about me? Clara told me you kept our scheduled date even after I'd been rude to you. And I kept pushing you away, but you're still here."

Cradling my face in her hands, she gifted me a kiss that was as gentle as a whisper. "Everything about you is honest," she said, her forehead dropping against mine once more. "I love your vulnerability and your strength. Your honesty and your trepidation. Fire and ice, remember?"

Was it possible for a heart to explode? If such a thing had been possible, it would have been right at that moment when it wanted to shatter for Hope, and reach for Soledad. "I hate that you have to leave."

"I know." She drew back and I knew the moment was over. She needed to go and be a police officer. I needed to go and be a parent. "Me too. But I'll be back. You're not alone. Neither of you are alone. She's so strong. I can see it. And both of you will be okay. Probably not today, but eventually...we'll all be okay."

IF THE MOVEMENT of time had been confusing before, after Soledad left it became complete and utter chaos. I wore a track in the floor between the cafeteria and the bathroom as I tried to distract myself from imagining the minute details of Hope's surgery. I bit my nails until there was nothing left to bite. I started on my cuticles, only stopping when I made the skin around the top of my pinky finger bleed.

Eventually, I collapsed into an uncomfortable seat in one of the waiting areas on the bottom floor, gazing out into the space before me. Grief cleaved my sight. I knew the odds were in Hope's favor, but it overcame me all the same. A grief not only founded in Hope's reality, but in the possibility of what *could* have happened. What had *almost* happened. What *did* happen to people every single day.

The insistent prickling beneath my skin grew stronger as my mind raced through the scenarios. If Soledad hadn't shot the perpetrator and sent him to the ground. If Hope had been two steps closer to him when the gun was fired. If he'd managed to drag her away before the police even got there.

I jammed my elbows into my thighs as I leaned forward. My breathing was ragged, hot, and abnormally loud. A furious, ear-shattering note sounded in my head, an auricular exclamation point.

God. I was so fucking angry! Angry at everything. Everyone. Angry at assholes like Amber Murphy's drug dealer who'd probably gotten his weapon with nothing more than a wad of cash. Angry at lawyers and journalists and teachers who wouldn't discuss controversial topics.

If I was angry at all those people, I was fucking furious with the governments whose corruption and apathy had made it so damned easy for weapons to breed faster than people. Who'd failed to create a law enforcement culture that arbitrated behaviors, not colors, yet at the same time were technically responsible for the fact Hope was still alive, that she'd had protection. These were the same governments who'd made health care a privilege rather than a right.

But most of all, I was angry at myself.

I didn't protect her.

I couldn't see straight, and I couldn't wrangle my thoughts. They raced in a hundred different directions.

Hope had become a target because of an unfolding situation, a series of events instigated by the adults in her world, and that made my blood boil. But I couldn't imagine what it must be like to be a parent of a Black child. Or a transgender child. A Black, transgender child. To experience a paradox—cultivating pride in your identity while also fearing what it could mean for your baby, out there in the world, more of a target for no other reason than they dared to exist. They dared to exist in a culture blinded by centuries of colonial bias and structurally reinforced racism.

If Hope had been Black and different cops had responded to the call, how would they have interpreted the situation? What would they have seen in her face? In the dealer's face?

I had no idea what to do about any of it. My disdain for violence, for violent people—whether they be cops or criminals, though sometimes it was hard to know the difference—achieved nothing but frustration.

Similarly, my empathy for victims, whether they be victims of racial profiling, gang activity, or something else entirely like Hope had been, also achieved nothing.

What had I ever done that was useful to anybody?

We had been so lucky that Hope's wound was not fatal. So fortunate to access health care. To be surrounded by support and privilege. I didn't earn any of it. I wasn't my grandmother. I wasn't Soledad.

Soledad. God. If she hadn't been there!

It had been a gunshot that hurt Hope, that could have taken her life. Yet it had also been a gunshot, Soledad's gunshot, that had saved her.

I let out a pained groan as a sharp spike drove through my pelvis. I loosed a manic laugh as I wiped at my nose with the back of my hand because of course, *of course* my damned endo would flare up now. I couldn't focus my eyes enough and so relied on feel to dig for painkillers in my bag. There weren't any. I couldn't feel sorry for myself though.

Right now, my fifteen-year-old lay sedated in an operating theatre, surrounded by a team of medical professionals cutting, cleaning, and sewing. If I lingered on that image for too long, bile rose in my throat and my stomach shrank to the size of a pea. But, as my thoughts ticked over, I registered something endlessly more insidious, and a ghostly, cold sensation draped over me, like I'd stepped into a flowing river. I realized Hope was being *treated*. A fact I'd taken for granted. She'd get the help she needed. And yet, so many vulnerable people in a similar situation would have faced life-shattering hospital bills, or worse, no treatment at all. The thought made my limbs feel hollow and boneless.

Confusion made my skin shrink. Everything became tight. How could I possibly reconcile all the thoughts, questions, and assertions cascading through my head? And more importantly, what could I do, going forward, to contribute something—anything—to the realization of a world even just a little better, a little safer, than this one?

No parent, brother, sister, mother, father...no one should have to experience the horror of their loved one being the victim of violence they'd done absolutely nothing to deserve.

I dropped my face into my hands and, having no answers, sobbed until my ribs ached and there were no more tears left to cry.

CHAPTER THIRTY-FOUR

AS FAR AS surgeries went, Hope's was about as successful as anyone could want. Dr. Yamamoto's appraisal of the injury had been accurate, and they inserted three screws to repair the fractures caused by the bullet. On an X-ray, the screws looked horrific, invasive and painful, but they assured us that as time went on and Hope's body healed, she'd come to feel mostly normal. Physically, anyway. I had no idea how long it would take for any of us, Hope especially, to feel normal in any other way.

During the three weeks Hope remained in the hospital, my mom, my sisters, and, of course, Soledad were frequent visitors. As were Hope's two closest friends, Ava and Immy, who turned out to be the most supportive friends Hope had ever had, along with Carla and Tomas, who also came to see her every few days. That was one good thing to come out of the entire situation: Hope finally started to trust that the connections she'd made since changing schools were genuine, that her friends did care for her.

Brenna taught Hope how to play chess, a game that she came to thoroughly dislike after it caused at least three arguments with my sister. Clara on the other hand taught her how to play *God of War*, and unlike chess, Hope became kind of addicted. People responded to life-changing and life-threatening events in their own way. You never did know how it might affect someone, and I counted myself beyond lucky that my family was right there, with Hope, and with me, every step.

It was Sole, though, that Hope came to enjoy spending time with the most. My mom had been concerned that seeing Sole would send Hope spiraling, that it might trigger some kind of trauma-related reaction, but it did the opposite. Soledad had been there, she understood better than anyone else what went down, and she had protected her. Hope felt safer with no one else.

Over a week after the surgery, the day before her sadly uneventful sixteenth birthday, the doctors introduced Hope to a physical therapist who worked with her each day for about two weeks, focusing on movement that would not require direct weight being applied on the femur or hip. Soledad insisted on being there, with me, for the first few sessions. They were difficult to watch, causing Hope a lot of pain and frustration. Dr. Yamamoto had been right though; improvements to her mobility were swift, measurable, and at all turns, celebrated. Through the entire ordeal, Hope's positivity and resilience never ceased to astound us all.

I tried my best not to push her too hard, physically or emotionally. I didn't ask questions, but I knew we'd need to clear up some things soon. I hoped she would come to me, that I wouldn't need to ask.

As part of her recovery, we also spoke to a specialist about ways to proactively manage or treat any potential psychological impacts of what Hope had gone through. The doctor said, given Hope did not seem to be withdrawn, nor was she denying the fact she'd been shot, that there was a good chance she could be supported through an effective counselling program. He also gave us a referral to a wellness clinic for adolescents that specialized in teaching techniques for self-regulation and healing, such as meditation and mindfulness. Techniques that empowered young people to tap into their own intrinsic strength.

The main concern going forward, we were told, would be the damage that had been done to Hope's sense of safety. Someone had hurt her and hurt her badly. She'd come face-to-face with a vicious reality that most people observed only from a safe distance, secondary consumers of current affairs through news outlets and film. Connection, the doctor said, was key. Connection to her body through exercise, connection to her friends through social engagements, and of course, connection to family.

I didn't know exactly how the next few months, or even years, would unfold. But I knew I'd be there for her. As long as she would accept me in her life, I'd be there. I may not have done much else in my life that could be considered important, but I'd do this, I'd see it through.

After three weeks, I could take her home. At last.

"I am so glad to be out of that place," Hope said as we

exited the hospital parking lot. She pressed the button to lower the window and, positioning her face as close as she could to the opening without actually hanging her head out of the car, shut her eyes against the breeze that flew by.

"I'm glad too."

"Des?" She closed the window a few inches, leaving an opening at the top to allow for fresh air, then settled back in her seat.

"Mm-hmm?"

"I'm sorry."

"Are you sure you want to do this now? I know you're out of the hospital, but only just. We can wait to talk if you like?"

"I want to, though. I owe you this apology. If I'd told you what was happening, none of this would have happened."

I reached across the center console and gave her hand a brief squeeze before resting it back on the steering wheel. Relief swept through my body, lightening my limbs. She had come to me. For the first time, she'd come to me. "That means a lot. I want to be your carer, your parent, in whatever capacity I can be, and I can't do that if I don't know about the big stuff."

I checked the blind spot and my mirrors before changing lanes, then stole a quick glance at Hope. Her hair had grown so much and now tickled the tops of her ears and fanned across her forehead. "Did you want to tell me how you ended up out there? On the street with the two of them?"

She scratched at the back of her head, then jammed her hands into her hoodie. It was too warm for a sweatshirt, but it seemed to bring her comfort and so I didn't comment. "Yeah," she said. "I should. I should tell you. That shrink said it would be good for me to tell you, when I felt ready." She rubbed at her knees. "Yeah. I'm ready to explain."

In the ten minutes that followed, Hope talked, and I listened. The words spilled from her like water bursting its way free of a dam. She told me how her mother had turned up at her school one day, about four months ago, begging for help. Bony, yellow-toothed, and stinking of urine, Amber had been the epitome of desperation. She'd said she owed her boyfriend a lot of money and that, if Hope didn't help her get it, Amber would be killed. She'd also told Hope that if she told anyone, especially the police, they might both end up dead.

When Hope gave Amber all the money she had, about two hundred dollars in all, Amber had lapsed into a demented kind of laughter. She'd needed more. A lot more. As Hope did just about everything she could to get the cash, short of stealing from me, her mother had turned up more and more often. She'd started calling and texting, telling Hope how much she loved her, how desperately she wanted their family back together. She'd promised that, when her now ex-boyfriend had been paid off, they could run away together and start again. My heart ached when I heard that. How could Hope *not* have gone? No matter what happened, Amber was her blood, her mother. No matter what kind of distance, physical or otherwise, existed between them, of course Hope would want to do what she could to reclaim a parent she'd lost. To reclaim the promise of a life she'd never had a chance to properly experience, one where her parents knew how to do right by her, where they loved her in the ways other parents loved their kids.

"I believed all of it," Hope admitted, disbelief in her

tone. "I thought she could change. But when I met up with her, she was on something. She barely even knew who I was. Her boyfriend...*dealer* more like, said she owed a lot more than what I'd brought and that neither of us could leave his side until we'd coughed it up. I tried to get away, but he was a lot stronger than he looked and kept trying to drag me to his car. The whole time he yelled at me. Said that I could sell for him to work off her debt. I guess that's when someone called the police."

"Soledad said you were really brave. And that you kicked a bit of ass, too!"

"Yeah. I guess I did."

We could have kept talking, I suppose. I could have told her how much I loved her, and she could have told me how glad she was to be home. But we didn't need to say any of those things. We both understood, as I slowed into the driveway of my humble house, that we'd stick together. After all those weeks in the hospital, words weren't necessary anymore. She knew I was her parent. I knew she'd let me be her parent.

As we strode from the car to my front door, my core warmed. We were home.

"Surprise!" The collective cheer of Clara, Brenna, my mom, Soledad, and a few of Hope's closest friends had her clutching at her chest for a moment as we opened the front door. Knowing it was coming, I had my arm behind her, ready to offer support if she lost balance on her crutches, but she seemed fine on her own.

"Holy crap," she said loudly as she made her way inside, noticing the decorations and the enormous, albeit poorly constructed *Happy Birthday* sign hanging above the television. "For me? Seriously?" She grinned.

"Of course, my dear! You didn't think that get-together in the hospital was enough for your birthday, did you?" Mom planted an embarrassingly sloppy kiss on Hope's forehead before disappearing into the kitchen. Her voice trailed behind her. "I hope you're hungry!"

"Good work, Hope," Clara said as she leaned in for a gentle hug. "You've given your foster grandma an excuse to throw a dinner party using someone else's kitchen. This could be interesting."

Hope gave a small smirk. "I love when she cooks."

"Oh, so do we," Brenna said, also hugging Hope. "But Desi might not be impressed by the mess she leaves in her wake."

"I heard that!" We chuckled as Mom called out from the other room. "And let's not forget, we are celebrating two things this afternoon." She waggled her eyebrows at Soledad and I laughed.

"No no no." Sole held her hands in front of her body as though defending herself. "This is all about Hope."

"Nah-uh!" Hope grinned. "Aren't you officially becoming a police corporal?"

Sole bumped me with her hip. "You told them?"

"Of course I did," I replied, pride no doubt written all over my face. I kissed her on the cheek and she bit her lip, an uncharacteristic shyness in her eyes.

Sole gave me kiss in return, this time a soft and brief touching of lips. "Thanks. All of you. But really, Hope, happy birthday!"

The entire group echoed her words with a cheerful, loud "Happy birthday!"

For the next hour or so, my mother was truly in her element, bringing out tray after tray of delicious, homemade appetizers for the assembled party. Ranging from salmon and cucumber twists to mini–New York cheesecakes, we were all stuffed full of amazing food by the time she'd finished.

"Wow, Ms. Adler. These are absolutely the best polenta chips I've ever tasted." Soledad sat cross-legged on the couch, a glass of sparkling water in one hand, an empty napkin in the other.

My mom bent over from where she stood near to the couch and gripped Soledad's chin like she was a child. "You're a good one, Officer Reyes." Soledad blushed. "But stop calling me that. It's Abbey!"

"Right." Sole held her glass up in a mock-toast. "Abbey. Thank you."

The sight of all these people in one house, chatting, bantering, and even arguing a in the case of Clara and Brenna, brought a profound warmth to my core. I didn't think we'd ever all been in the same place at the same time. Certainly not with Sole there too. That was the interesting thing about events that challenged or hurt: they had a way of bringing people together. Of showing you how deep a family's love went. Of helping you trust your own feelings.

With Hope deep in conversation—a fact shocking in and of itself—in the living room, I took the opportunity to seek my mother out in the kitchen.

"Hey, Mom? Got a moment?"

"One sec," she said around a mouthful of food. She rinsed her hands, dried them off, then sidled up beside me, leaning back against the kitchen bench with her arms folded across her stomach. "What is it?"

"I had an idea and I thought maybe you and Grams might...or could, that you could help me with it?"

The corners of her mouth drooped into a concerned frown. "You know we'd help with anything we can. But what is it? You look so serious."

I scrubbed one hand down my face, rubbed at my jaw for a second. "It's not a bad thing. But I don't want to muck it up."

Her eyebrows rose. "Come on, out with it; the suspense is unbearable, my dear."

I held both of my hands up in surrender. "Okay, okay. So, I've been thinking a lot—"

"How unusual for you," she teased.

"Right. Exactly. But I want to do more than thinking. It might not make a huge difference, but I thought we could run a fundraiser. I'm not sure what type exactly yet. But we could use some of Brenna's contacts with the youth workers to get teens involved in the discussion. Nudge some Grams' colleagues. I could even ask Gina if we can publicize it through the agency."

Mom nodded, though her forehead remained creased. "Sure. We could help spread the word and get people to spend their money. Maybe even start with a trivia night or something? Approach businesses to donate prizes?"

"Yeah. That could work."

"What are we raising money for, exactly?"

I pinched the skin at the base of my throat. I didn't know why I was nervous. Maybe because I wanted, so badly, to step up, to contribute. "I was thinking we could sponsor racial justice workshops for local schools. Help provide more education to their teachers and students and support the interruption of prejudice at an institutional level. Stuff that might make a difference to how people treat one another down the line."

"Oh, baby." She had me in her arms before I'd fully registered her movements, engulfing me in an affectionate embrace. "Of course. That sounds perfect. Let's make it happen. Let's keep the conversations alive. Though, knowing you, I doubt you'll stop at a one-off fundraiser."

I buried my face in her shoulder, my entire soul awash with relief. "Thank you," I said, my voice muffled. "Thank you so much."

She tightened her arms, giving me one last squeeze before stepping back. "Hey," she said, remembering something. "Have you heard anything about that contest you entered? The one Gina told you about?"

I grabbed a tissue from a nearby box and wiped at my nose. "Not yet. I don't expect much to come of it, but they said entrants wouldn't hear for at least two months, and since it only closed last week..."

"Last week? Is that all? Time moves at a weird pace sometimes."

"Yeah, it does." I tossed the tissue into the waste basket.

"However it goes, I'm glad you sent in that picture. I know it was scary to let people see your work."

"Yeah," I agreed. "I'm glad too."

We chatted for a few more minutes, making cursory plans about how we could get started on our modest community project. Eventually Clara whisked Mom away to settle a dispute with Soledad regarding crowd etiquette at baseball games.

Gradually, the group dissipated. Hope's friends were the first to go, having felt awkward around so many unfamiliar adults, especially after the food stopped coming. Next, Clara and Brenna headed home because they had to be up for work the next day, though Brenna was also worried about tiring Hope out on her first night back. As my sisters had predicted, Mom left in a flourish of frizzy hair and exaggerated gestures, leaving the kitchen for me to clean in the morning.

As I clicked the door shut, Sole asked, "Should I go too?"

"You?" I pulled her to me, hooking my fingers into the waistband of her jeans. "It's finally quiet. Stay?"

Tilting her head, she brushed her lips against mine, soft at first, then more insistent, her tongue flicking between my lips to caress mine. My cheeks flamed as her breasts pushed against me.

"Ahh. Do you two need to get a room?"

I laughed as I disconnected from Soledad, stretching onto my toes to see Hope over Sole's shoulder. "Smart-ass."

"Hey. I'm not the one getting busy in the hallway."

Soledad raised an eyebrow at me as if to say, *She's not wrong.* "Actually," Sole said as she turned, looping her arm around my waist. "Why don't we watch a movie? It's too early for bed, but I bet you're both tired."

"A movie? I guess. But only if there's popcorn."

"Popcorn!" I blurted. "How can you still be hungry?"

Hope lifted a crutch off the ground and pointed it at me for a second before setting it down. "Teenager, remember?"

"Right. Popcorn it is."

A few minutes later, I found Hope settled into the recliner, surrounded by cushions. Soledad had coiled up against the arm of the couch, leaving me plenty of space to curl up next to her.

"One popcorn delivery." I moved a small side table to ensure easy access for Hope, and placed a large bowl of popcorn on top.

"Thank you." She elongated the vowels so the words sounded almost like a song. I gave her a *you're-kind-of-a-weirdo-sometimes* grin and settled in next to Sole.

I watched as Hope scooped up a handful of popcorn and started, one kernel at a time, dropping them into her mouth. There was no way that, especially at her age, I could have coped with all of this the way she had. The injury. The upcoming trial of her attacker. Her final break with her mother. It would be entirely normal, expected even, to crumble under that sort of weight. It had definitely affected her, and Mr. Barry had found us a counseling service to help her moving forward but, on the whole, she'd come out the other side with her resilience, and her optimism, intact. What an amazing, amazing human being Hope Murphy truly was.

"What are we watching?" I asked.

"Well." Soledad stretched forward to retrieve the remote from the coffee table. "I thought long and hard about this."

I looked at her with suspicion, my eyes narrow, questioning.

"And, I decided..." She clicked on the television, a familiar image filling the screen.

"No way!" I squealed.

"Yes. The time has come. Let's watch *Mean Girls*."

Throwing one leg over her, I climbed onto her lap and

kissed her repeatedly, fitting one word in between each kiss. "You. Are. Adorable."

"Umm, hello? I'm still here." Hope threw a handful of popcorn at us.

"Hey!" I rebuked, reclaiming my spot on the couch and dusting the popcorn away. "You're sixteen now. Don't pretend you've never seen two people kissing. Besides, this is a momentous occasion. Soledad is about to be inspired by the genius that is Rachel McAdams. She will be wowed by the comedic prowess of Lindsay Lohan and Lacey Chabert, and her expectations of weather reports will never be the same again."

"Don't get too excited," Sole warned. "I might not even like this movie."

"No pressure, Sole," I said, my tone serious. "But if you don't like this movie, we *will* need to break up."

"Let me get this straight. You've come to accept the fact I'm a cop and carry around a gun. You've managed to talk me into voting at the next election, and even talked my mother into voting too. But if I don't like this one movie, it's all over?"

"Exactly."

"Okay. Fair enough. Let's watch it."

I kissed the tip of Soledad's nose, excited, then sank into her, my legs curled beneath me and my cheek resting against her chest. Everything felt perfect. Truly, and unequivocally perfect.

"Hey, Hope?" I said, putting my hand on Sole's forearm, urging her to wait a moment before pressing play.

"Yeah?" she replied around a mouthful of popcorn.

"How are you feeling? Now you're back?"

She chewed a few times and swallowed. Her gaze wandered to the ceiling as she considered her answer. "How am I feeling?"

"Yeah. I just want to check."

"I'm..." She twisted slightly, cringing at the discomfort. "You know, it's kind of weird. I know something horrible happened. And I know life is, in a lot of ways, kind of shit. But..."

"But?"

She cocked her head pensively. "I'm happy." She locked her gaze onto me. "I'm happy and hopeful."

My throat tightened as a wave of gratitude washed over me. I looked to Sole. She squeezed my hand, a subtle but knowing smile tugging at the side of her mouth.

"Me too," I said.

BIBLIOGRAPHY

ARTICLES

Allende, I., September 2012. *Life Under Pinochet: The Day We Buried our Freedom*, Amnesty International.

Bradford Burns, E., April 2009. *The True Verdict on Allende: Nixon and Kissinger fiddle and Chile Burns,* The Nation.

Faundez, J., June 1980. *The Defeat of Politics: Chile under Allende*, Centrum voor Studie en Documentatie van Latijns Amerika.

Kandell, J., December 2006. *Augusto Pinochet, Dictator Who Ruled by Terror in Chile, Dies at 91,* New York Times.

Posner, P.W., November 2019. *Chile's Political Crisis Is Another Brutal Legacy of Long-Dead Dictator Pinochet*, The Conversation.

Read, P., September 2018. *World Politics Explainer: Pinochet's Chile*, The Conversation.

Trovall, E., April 2017. *A Complete Guide to Chile's Most Important Holiday: Fiestas Patrias*, Culture Trip.

Zaninovic, P.R., January 2019. *The Dance of the Chilean: What is the Cueca?*, Chile Today.

BOOKS

Alexander, M., 2010. The New Jim Crow, Mass Incarceration in the Age of Colorblindness. Penguin Books.

DiAngelo, Robin J., 2019. White Fragility: Why It's So Hard for White People to Talk About Racism. London: Allen Lane, an imprint of Penguin Books.

Oluo, I., 2018. So You Want to Talk About Race. Seal Press.

Saad, L.F., 2020. Me and White Supremacy: Combat Racism, Change the World, and Become a Good Ancestor. Source Books.

Slater, D., 2017. The 57 Bus. Farrar, Straus and Giroux.

Williams, J., 2013. Eyes on the Prize: America's Civil Rights Years - 30th Anniversary Edition. Penguin Books.

DOCUMENTARIES AND VIDEOS

ABC Australia., 1999. Fighting the Past - Chile Divided: Pinochet's Social Legacy, Journeyman Films.

DuVernay, A., 2016. 13th, Kandoo Films.

Furst, J., 2017. Time – The Kalief Browder Story, Paramount Network.

Lindsay, D. and Martin, T.J., 2017. L.A. 92, National Geographic.

Morris, M., August 2019. Augusto Pinochet: The Great Betrayal, Biographics.

Peck, R., 2016. I Am Not Your Negro, Independent Lens.

Vecchione, J. et al, 2006. Eyes on the Prize, Episodes 1-14, PBS.

PODCASTS

Saad, L., March 2020. *Stepping Out of Privilege*, The Goop Podcast.

Unknown., 2017. *The Dictators Podcast, Episodes 1–3: Pinochet.*

ACKNOWLEDGEMENTS

I can never give enough thanks to Claudia V., the colleague who became a friend who became an ally and a supporter. Claudia's enthusiasm for my writing, and her willingness to share the wounds of her family's experiences in Chile, as well as her personal insights regarding Soledad's life as the child of trauma survivors, were integral to this book. I can never thank Claudia enough for all her cultural insights, her encouragement, and her friendship. You give so much to your students, and not all those students are in your classroom, Claudia.

Another big thank you goes to Christina F. She was one of the first beta readers of my very first book, and to this day is the only person to read everything I've written since then. She's stuck by me since we first 'met' on Scribophile several years ago, and though we may never meet in person, she's been a great (writing) mentor and friend.

Support and well wishes are hugely important when you're trying to write a novel as a full-time teacher and parent, especially one that is totally different to anything you've written before. No doubt I'll forget some key people (to these, please accept my thanks and remind me to buy you a drink), but these people always help keep me motivated with their interest and encouragement: Shan and Anke D'B, Nicole B., Matthew T., Linda F., Liz T., Bryan G., and the lovely folks from the NSWTF Council and Restricted Committees.

Salt and Sage Books, thank you for your excellent service. Finding your company and being able to employ suitable sensitivity readers and editors for this story before I submitted to my publisher not only improved the book but led me to an array of amazing material suggested by your editors, much of which has become integral to my understanding of myself and of others.

To the folks at the Rainbow Literary Society: Rachel, Sarah, Kevin, KJ and so on, you're all beautiful, and I've loved being part of this burgeoning literary group in Australia. Sharing stories in the pub has been more inspiring and enjoyable than I can say.

Finally, thank you to the team at NineStar Press for taking a chance on another of my stories. I'd like to believe that my work gets better with each book, and your guidance has certainly played a part in that progression.

About Kara Ripley

Kara Ripley is the romance-writing alter ego of Australian sci-fi and fantasy author, Rebecca Langham. Even though she's named after two iconic sci-fi characters, Kara reflects Rebecca's inner romantic, that part of her secretly wanting to leave the aliens, magic, and spaceships behind every now and then.

Email
info@rebeccalangham.com.au

Facebook
www.facebook.com/RLanghamAuthor

Twitter
@rlangham85

Website
www.rebeccalangham.com.au

Other NineStar books by this author

Riding the Track

CONNECT WITH NINESTAR PRESS

WWW.NINESTARPRESS.COM

WWW.FACEBOOK.COM/NINESTARPRESS

WWW.FACEBOOK.COM/GROUPS/NINESTARNICHE

WWW.TWITTER.COM/NINESTARPRESS

WWW.INSTAGRAM.COM/NINESTARPRESS

www.ingramcontent.com/pod-product-compliance
Lightning Source LLC
Chambersburg PA
CBHW060618100726
47907CB00006B/1670